4,284 miles

A novel
based on the
1916 bicycle journey of
Joe Bruce and Lester Atkinson

R.L. Greene

DIVERGENT MIND, LLC
La Veta, Colorado

Divergent Mind LLC
P.O. Box 1053
La Veta, CO 81055

Jacket content and design by R.L. Greene
Cover Images Shutterstock License

Hardcover ISBN 978-1-947803-17-6

Paperback ISBN 978-1-947803-13-8
Copyright © 2021 Roger L. Greene
All rights reserved.

Greene, Roger L.
R.L. Greene. First edition.
Revised, 2024
267 pages

You can learn about the author and find other novels by R.L. Greene at: **RogerLGreene.com**

Summary: Over the summer of 1916, two young men, Joe Bruce aged 16 and Lester Atkinson, 20, rode their bicycles from Colorado Springs, CO to New York City and back. Random encounters gradually transform an innocuous cross country bicycle trip into a soul-searching realignment of rights and responsibilities of America and Americans under the stark light of the nation's founding principles.

[1. United States History – Fiction. 2. Friendship – Fiction. 3. Liberty – Fiction. 4. Discovery – Fiction. 5. Statue of Liberty – Fiction   6. War – Fiction. 7. Bicycle – Fiction   8. Coming of age – Fiction. 9. Metaphor – Fiction.   10. Understanding – Fiction.]

CONTENTS

for Lester

for Joe

Chapter 1

The Hellion

According to the station master, the train would be on time. Lester had already chewed his fingernails to the quick so I feared that any substantial delay could result in him taking them down to bone. In fact, they were beginning to bleed as I stood with him on the platform looking down the tracks, waiting to hear a whistle or see a heralding plume of black smoke coming from the north.

The call had been made. Even though it was a Sunday, the mortician would come shortly. It was the second time Guy had ever been on a train. At only twenty years of age, it would be his last. We were here for his bicycle and packs of belongings as they and the pine box that held his body, were all that remained of Guy.

Lester had recently turned eighteen. I was fourteen, a month away from turning fifteen. Guy's grave had already been dug beside his mother's and that of an infant brother, both of whom had died a dozen years ago. Lester's family was getting ready for tomorrow's graveside service and burial. Lester had volunteered me to join him in fetching Guy's bicycle and making sure his body was properly claimed. It seemed but an errand and that bewildered me. It had taken almost two weeks to recover Guy's body and another week to ship it. Maybe after all the waiting and vain hoping against hope that some mistake had been made, Guy's belongings amounted to little more than an errand by now – as did his body.

Lester knew grief well. I didn't know it at all. My family got by. His family did better. It was summertime 1914. America was on the edge of greatness. The world was on the edge of war.

Lester's dark brown hair was greasy that particular Sunday, sticking out in random hunks from beneath his newsboy cap on an afternoon far too warm for wearing a cap. His eyes were deep blue, too wet, fixed ahead, sparkling in the sun. I'd never really studied my friend's face until that moment, but then, why would I have? We were always busy. Busy working. Busy adventuring. Busy about the town we lived in.

Colorado Springs was a new creation, planned, not happenstance. Magnificent buildings of stone and the downtown they were creating was springing up from windswept prairie. Homes were being built by the score on gently sloping hills that had only known wind, cattle, horses and sheep until Colorado Springs' arrival. This *Little London* was the brainchild of a former Civil War General name of William Palmer who had also built the railroad on which tracks we waited for a whistle, an appearance of smoke, and a brother who had gone off on adventure to Canada. There, in spring's rushing waters, God had turned his face, a boat had capsized, cold water had engulfed Guy and a young man's days upon this earth had come to an end.

"Papa said he's gonna stink," Lester finally said, his eyes never leaving the tracks, his fingers never leaving his mouth, his jaw muscles never ceasing their work.

"He'll be embalmed."

"Papa said he was too decomposed to embalm."

"He'll be packed in ice," I offered. "I don't think he's going to smell."

Lester shrugged, pulled his fingers from his mouth, spit a bit of nail and skin he had gnawed off and shook his head. Wetness in his eyes welled deeper, threatening to spill. Then he looked down and they spilled. I didn't know what to do. I didn't know what to say. I didn't know whether or not to put my hand on his back. His shoulder was bone. His back was bone. No sooner than my hand had come to rest on bone, I saw smoke rising in the distance. I opened my mouth to tell Lester of the engine's plume when its whistle caused him to look up. His blue eyes were suddenly straightforward and as piercing as they were fearful.

Telegrams are real, but not as real as a train bearing the earthly remains of a brother as it is pulling into a station. I saw in Lester's face the reality of his past few weeks' struggle and the depth at which this occasion struck his heart. It was not the sacred moment it should have rightfully been. When the train came to a halt with a great rush of steam, a bustle of activity proceeded all around us. There was freight to offload. Freight to load. Baggage to haul. Passengers to greet. Passengers to board. We stood unnoticed and engulfed by it as if we were both lost and invisible.

My friend began to sniffle as the crude pine box that contained his brother was set leaking onto a cart and wheeled aside on the platform where a puddle began to form beneath it. Lester's feet seemed glued to the wooden planks we stood upon. I stepped forward to meet the conductor and wheeled Guy's bicycle and its complement of canvas packs from the mail car, over to Lester. He didn't acknowledge me, he only stared at his brother's pine casket and as much as he tried not to, wept.

My name is Joe Wheeler Bruce. When I first met Lester Edward Atkinson, he and I lived ten blocks from each other on the working-class side of town. Dryhurst and Son was the neighborhood market where from age eleven I'd stocked shelves and Lester, from age fourteen had run deliveries. It was directly across the street from the very compact two-story house my family rented. I knew all the Atkinson boys well, but Lester had become my friend. Guy, at five years my senior, had remained a much older and far more worldly acquaintance. Still, this day was hard for me as well.

I was methodical. Lester was exuberant. My father frequently called him a hellion, and Guy – may he rest in peace – Father had always said, was a hellion as well. That their names showed up in the Gazette newspaper at all was often enough that my father knew the Atkinson name and had, at Lester's employment at such near proximity to our abode, cautioned me and my brothers of any close acquaintance with said hellion.

Due to his employment as a deliverer of goods, Lester was familiar with every man, woman and child in our part of town and they knew him as well. Lester's pedaling upon the Dryhurst and Son bicycle with its accompaniment of baskets, was routinely conducted at breakneck speeds and with a degree of madness that made Lester antipathy to horses or anything horse drawn. Lester also presented a danger to pedestrians at least equal to that of the motorcar. Of course, Lester's mad need for speed did in no way interfere with his friendly shouts of greeting, frantic waving or near misses with trolleys, dogs, horses, pedestrians, and motorcars foolhardy enough to cross his path.

It was a rare meal at our board that did not include some tale of Lester's antics and father's glance of consternation in my direction that generally followed. Even if Lester was a hellion, his enthusiasm for life was as infectious as his smile, frantic waving, and shouted greetings. His gusto intrigued me. I don't know that parents ever fully know their children. If my father was to have truly known me, he'd have understood the yearnings of my soul did not match my appearance.

I was a thin, sorrowful looking, plain boy with brown eyes, sandy brown hair, a perpetually furrowed brow, and ears that stuck out way too far. To look upon me may have inspired a degree of curiosity, but not much by way of impression. However, if one were to have taken the effort to come to know me, they would have discovered a scrappy will, a degree of determination akin to that of Robert Peary, and a quality of inventiveness and perseverance similar to that of Orville and Wilbur Wright. I was a fighter in that the one way to make me succeed was to mention the unlikeliness of my success. I was intelligent, delighted in reason, and was resolved that the man that dwelt inside would one day become the man I presented to others.

My friend Lester, while not a man of much forethought or study, was a man of iron will and fortitude. He was wiry, far too lean for his height and his height was not remarkable. As noted by my father, a hearty gust of wind could blow him away. Lester was frequently ragged, perpetually moving, tenacious if not stubborn, but friendly in the kind of way that made others glad to meet him. I couldn't help but like him. He was the kind of man that inspired the budding man inside of me. Lester, it was said – and I don't necessarily disagree – possessed one speed: *hell bent for leather*, was capable of only one direction: *straight ahead*, and listened to only one mind: *his*.

4

Lester and I were more alike than my father ever suspected.

There are things that fortify a man. There are things that prompt a man to action. There are things that plunge us into despair. There are things that change us. Guy's death changed Lester. While Lester had been scattered in thought and action before his brother's death, the tragedy seemed to temper his exuberance and buffer his thinking. From this great sorrow and third profound loss in his young life, he gained a sense of reflection and a capacity for focus of which he'd never before been capable.

What I was coming to understand about Lester is that he possessed a brand of courage of which I was unfamiliar. As the greatest president of our new century – who was of course Theodore Roosevelt – had once said, *"Courage is not having the strength to go on; it is going on when you don't have the strength."* Lester found a way to go on, and where he found his strength, I may never know. He never said a word about his struggles. He just did what he needed to do and went about living his life day-by-day.

Guy was buried on the twenty-ninth of July 1914. I don't understand how it can be said of someone so young – *laid to rest*. Guy did not long for rest. Guy longed for adventure and thought the world should be his. Privately I wondered whether God had indeed turned his face that fateful day or had instead opened his arms. I wondered if somehow all worlds beyond this world now awaited Guy's adventures. But those were things that a brother's grief was not ready to hear and that I could not bring myself to mention, so I kept my wonderings to myself.

And even if it seemed so far distant from my day-to-day reality that it warranted no concern, the day of Guy's internment was the very day Austria declared war on Serbia. Russia, headlines predicted, would enter the conflict shortly. Europe was no longer on the edge of war, but at war.

Aside from international events, I realized that day, life is just as unforgiving of those who seize it and lunge headfirst into peril as it is of those who stand at its sidelines clinging to safety. Both will perish. One will perish in satisfaction of having given life his all, the other will perish in regret of having expended his lifeforce on nothing more than a monotony of days.

As I've come to think back on it, something changed in me that day as well. Until Guy's death, my early years had been a carefree romp and life had been something I owned all rights to. That thought ended the day I watched the casket that held Guy's earthy remains lowered into the ground. My carefree childhood died that day. I realized that life was something to be seized and cherished, that I owned nothing but the moment that lie in my hand and the single breath in my lungs.

And not one thing more.

Chapter 2

Opportunity Presented

Lester, being the way he was, came careening over to my house bright-and-early one August morning that same summer of 1914 with big news. "He passed on, Joe," Lester explained through the catching of his wind and with full expectation that I should know exactly of whom he was speaking even though he had given me no hint.

My blank expression and dullness of my recently awakened eyes were sufficient to prod him into detail.

"Yesterday. The hypochondriac Bartholomew Grainger," Lester exclaimed happily and threw both arms outward as if this had been the subject of our conversation only moments ago.

I squinted and wiped a crust of sleep from my eye.

"Word is that it was a heart-attack while he was soaking in Epsom Salts and wailing about his scoliosis. His family needs money for a casket and that nearly-new bicycle of his is for sale – barely ridden because of his condition. You can get it for a song."

I gave my head one long, slow nod that was accompanied by a sound meant to pass as my response. I fished in my mind's groggy waters for a conversation that may have at one time or another alluded to the nearly-new bicycle that belonged until as recently as yesterday noon to the now deceased hypochondriac Bartholomew Grainger – who in hindsight – was possibly not as much of a hypochondriac as he was reputed to be.

"A song, Joe! A song!"

While I was not inclined to sing to the tune of owning a dead hypochondriac's used bicycle, the brightness in Lester's eyes was telling me this was an opportunity I would regret passing up.

If anyone was to know firsthand about a passing or about a bargain for the worldly possessions of the recently deceased, it was

Lester. The sick and old would phone the market and Lester would mount the company bicycle and deliver, in addition to lard, chicken and flour – a variety of pills, potions and elixirs to comfort the sick and dying, and this he did all over town. Hence, this was breaking news and hordes of villagers, it seemed, would soon converge upon the bargain if I should be laggard enough to let it pass by.

Bartholomew Grainger had gone to meet his Maker at the ripe old age of twenty-five. Lester swore that his bicycle – save for a few cobwebs and layer of dust – was as pristine as any that belonged to a long-skirt girl who might have ridden downhill to the soda fountain exclusively on sunny Saturday afternoons and then turned right around and ridden downhill all the way back home with nary a turn of its crank.

I had been born the last of five children to a household prudently ordered by a very conservative and cautious man. My three brothers, one sister, and I, had shared in our possession, two bicycles that even in their best days came no where near the quality and durability of a proper, new machine. And, I might add, with three energetic older brothers, the best days of our two bicycles had long since passed. I'd counted my savings just the night before and my dreams of purchasing a brand-new Sears Master from the Sears and Roebuck catalog was two years away – at best.

Lester and I daily sketched plans of adventure dependent upon properly durable bicycles – of which we were not in possession – and therefore had found our plans thwarted almost as quickly as we made them. It wasn't that Lester and I didn't ride all over town, along country roads or up into the Rocky Mountains that embraced our town like a hug. It was that repairs to spokes, chains, tires, rims and axles of our decrepit bicycles invariably interrupted and delayed our pleasure of flying down summer lanes and repeatedly proved our need for new equipment.

It was a red Carter and my heart beat faster just to look at it. With my jar of coins in hand, the tearful father of the recently deceased standing at one side and Lester at my other, I raised my free hand to wipe a layer of dust from its chromium handlebars. The sun's reflection dazzled my eyes and I was smitten. Our transaction was complete less than four minutes later. Lester was holding my empty mason jar with a picture I'd clipped from the Sears and Roebuck catalog pasted to its front when I raised my leg over the bicycle's bar and rested my rear end on its saddle. I placed my foot on its pedal and I was off.

Lester wasn't far behind. He caught up with me in the wink of an eye, riding Dryhurst and Son's delivery bicycle at my side. He looked as exhilarated as I felt.

There wasn't anything I loved more than a bicycle. Forget the stink of horses, stepping over their mess in the streets and all the hitching and unhitching of wagons, carts and buggies. Forget the motorcar's noise, smoke, infernal honking, and its drivers yelling for others to get out of their way. A bicycle was silent as the breeze and just as swift. It was flight without a need for wings or threat of imminent demise. A bicycle was a gift straight out of Heaven above – a wonderment even to the Almighty himself.

It was on my first ride on the former bicycle of recently deceased Bartholomew Grainger that I realized from Lester's broad and toothy smile as he rode at my side, that I had, in this leap of faith and opportunity of commerce, bought onto something more than a new bicycle. For you see, Lester's mind was always working on creating an opportunity and I had not yet failed to seize upon one when presented – or more accurately – pressed onto me.

When Lester came riding over to my house later that day on Guy's bicycle with that same toothy smile on his face I had earlier observed, I sensed a plan was in the making. It seemed likely the former bicycle of one recently deceased hypochondriac and I would soon play a role in that plan.

I did not attempt to conceal my suspicion, not that I could, as it showed quite clearly in the crease of my brow. I looked between Lester and Guy's reappropriated bicycle. "Um, why are you using Guy's bicycle?"

"I've been thinking he would have wanted me to have it."

I nodded slowly. *"Aaaaand…"*

"Father said it best not end up like mine and that I was to learn proper methods of repair and maintenance and shelter it from the elements if I was to use it."

I squinted, again nodding. So far his story seemed likely enough. To Lester, a bicycle was nothing more than a frame of steel, nuts, bolts, axles, wheels and bearings – a means of transportation rather than a treasured possession. Lester had not been much for the care and maintenance of his previous bicycle which had become a forlorn affair of patches, crude repairs, and rust.

I looked between Guy's well-maintained machine and Lester (who was somewhat less than a genius as a mechanic) and calculated a mere two months before Lester's idea of maintenance and the elements would render it a beleaguered eyesore.

But he still hadn't answered my question. "So why are you using it?"

"Well, because, you know how my bicycle tends to break down. Now that you have a new machine and I have this one, I thought we might go for some longer rides – you know – longer rides than just around town. Maybe this evening we could head up to the bluffs – you know to test it out."

I squinted. Lester's smile was both broad and toothy. A ride to the bluffs seemed innocent enough. My nod of doubt became a nod of cautious agreement.

Moments later we were away from town on the maiden voyage of bicycles whose previous owners were no longer of this earth. We rode into the Templeton Gap – a break in a series of bluffs northeast of town that were as rife with rattlesnakes, coyotes and cougars as any place on God's green earth. This is where Lester finally stopped pedaling, dismounted, and leaned his bicycle against a tree. He pulled a pistol from a rear pack, stuck it in his belt, then produced a canteen of cool water of which we both had desperate need. It may have been wise for Lester to be armed and prepared for danger because even more hazardous than wildlife, were bandits and Indians who might – *and very possibly were* – lying in wait for innocent travelers in craggy hills on the outskirts of towns. Such places were – *as everyone knew* – the preferred abode – or rather – lair, of both.

Still, there was a distinct possibility that I may be safer with cougars, poisonous snakes, outlaws and savages than under Lester's armed protection. Nevertheless, we began to hike around on eroded sandstone rock formations as we loved to do on summer evenings as the day began to cool.

Bit-by-bit, Lester began to relate his plan, not forthrightly, but in installments that I would be more likely to agree to. For you see, Lester was an apprentice of the door-to-door sales techniques of gypsies, possessed the hawking genius of snake oil vendors, and had the disposition and sly grit of a carnival midway huckster – all of which were concealed by the likeability of an innocent farm boy.

I, on the other hand, was apparently a dullard in that my realization of Lester's schemes invariably came too late. Usually, by the time I recognized his intention, I had already become ensnared.

We breathlessly topped a pinnacle of stone. As we marveled at our view of plains and our distant town below, Lester passed me his canteen. As I drank the last of it, he set about his proposal with an airy tone. "What would you think of packing Guy's bicycle packs with provisions and coming up here, setting up camp for an overnight?"

I swallowed hard, capped his canteen and passed it back, trying not to let a sudden episode of terror show in my eyes.

"I'll bring a rifle and a pistol. There won't be nothing to be worried about."

Then before I could answer – not that I had formulated an answer – he continued because I had not yet refused, and that, in gypsy etiquette and snake oil salesmanship, constitutes agreement. "Then the next day we'll head up to Palmer Lake and camp there."

"Palmer Lake? Where exactly is Palmer Lake?"

"About thirty miles north, up Monument Hill and then back into the Rampart Range a bit. It's another of General Palmer's gems, beautiful, peaceful, a place I know we'd like. Guy told me about it."

I think I may have whined a very little bit. Then Lester drew another breath. I braced myself.

"Naw. I don't want to set up camp twice. How about we ride straight to Palmer Lake in one day? What do you think?"

"I hear that's quite a climb. Father has told me about motorcars overheating and breaking down going up, then running clean off the road with no brakes going down."

"I'll have all the weight of our provisions in my packs so you'll just have to ride. It's no worse a hill than some around town – you know – maybe a bit longer – but we can rest when we need to."

"So thirty miles?"

"Absolutely. And you'll only have to pedal getting there. The whole way back will be coasting downhill. Forth and back, I promise you, will be no more than a hundred miles."

I grimaced because by far, the largest proportion of my legs happened to be my knees.

"You'll be amazed at how easy it will be. We rode up here, didn't we? I'm fine. You're fine, right?"

"That's not it at all. I mean, if it's spread over a couple days, I can probably do that easy." I considered the plethora of hazards we might encounter on such a ride: Indians, outlaws, snakes, and cougars among them. "Isn't it forested up in those parts?"

"Good point. We'll have to be prepared for bear – not that they're dangerous – but we could come upon one by surprise. I'll bring a shotgun just in case." Lester's striking blue eyes blinked a couple times as he waited my response.

"Ummmm." Blood-splattered visuals flickered through my mind of pitch-black nights pierced by wild thrashings of claws and fangs. Of course there would be screams and shotgun blasts illuminating scenes of pure carnage.

"Um, why do you want to go so far? I don't know that my parents will agree to me going that far *and* having an overnight."

"I got an itch, Joe. I feel all closed in. I gotta go places and see things."

"Like Guy?"

"It's in our blood. And now we have the means."

It would be an interesting trip. I was, after all, fourteen and quite able to look out for myself. I too, wanted to go places and see things. Thinking, *damn the consequences*, I swallowed both caution and common sense in a single gulp. "When can we both take off work?"

Lester slapped my back hard enough to make my teeth clunk together and nearly enough to knock me from the rock we stood upon. "I'll ask old man Dryhurst for a couple days off next week."

I blew out a breath with greatest relief that we weren't talking about this same night, for with Lester, you never quite knew. Whatever else was stirring in his mind, and there was *always* something else stirring, I was pretty sure, it would be related beside a campfire one fair evening next week somewhere along the Palmer Divide, hopefully someplace near Palmer Lake, preferably without blood loss – mine specifically.

Opportunity – from Lester's perspective – was everywhere. Now it would fall to me to sell that same sense of optimism and confidence to the powers that controlled my life.

My father was a man who dealt in real estate and sold insurance and was, as I have mentioned, a cautious and well-ordered man. Add to those innate traits, his words of prudence regarding the Atkinson boys, my seemingly unhealthy attraction to Lester's boldness, the over three years difference in our ages, and the fact that one hellion had already perished as a result of far-flung adventure.

Our proposed exploration to Palmer Lake was met with more derision than fruition. The concept never cleared committee, much less made it to the floor or saw a vote. In layman's terms, Lester's grand plan got the kibosh and, to tell the truth, I was not completely disappointed nor was I entirely relieved.

Chapter 3

The Chicken Lady

Downtown Colorado Springs was shiny and new – as were the motorcars that traveled its wide boulevards. It is fair to assume – at least according to my father – that I had seen more millionaires in one jaunt through town than most would ever see in a lifetime. They drove Steamers, Rios, Packards, and Cadillacs as if they owned the town – which they did – and fine buildings that had been erected from prairie dust bore their names to prove said ownership.

Hidden veins of gold laced throughout high, bleak mountains had called a gaggle of hardscrabble men westward. A handful of those adventuresome men had found their fortune. They shed poverty to become benevolent men who – although not opposed to displays of wealth and prestige – shared a common vision for this brainchild metropolis dubbed Little London. Their town was to be the finest city west of the Mississippi – if not this entire great, united, budding nation of states in these modern times upon this American continent.

There were, however, exceptions to the refinement and sparkle of this burgeoning metropolis.

It was considered good fortune by Lester and me to be downwind of her. Even if it should cause a gag to convulse at the back of our tongues, this position afforded an opportunity for us to change course before it was too late. Free speech was a cornerstone principal of our great nation. It did, however, seem this right of speech was routinely entered into more by those who had lunatic leanings than by those who were well-reasoned and sane. The local character known (at least to Lester and me) as the Chicken Lady, cared not one whit about rights, nor reason, nor sanity – for her ravings and mumblings were carried on regardless of audience –

14

which would have been difficult to amass given the stench that prevailed around her. Not that this prevented her attempts to be heard by any and all – and this she did with great waves of her arms and heightened pleas of passion – the words of which could not be discerned – and that was due as much to her lack of teeth as to her lunacy.

Rumor was that she had come west along with her husband at the height of the gold rush sometime in the late 1800's. It seemed that they had found gold but that she had been widowed at an early age, supposedly by rockslide, although I would not rule out murder most foul – or given her husband's choice of mates – suicide most blessed. No one had memory of her man, but on her occasional trips into town for supplies, her first visit was always to the assay office in the Mining Exchange Building whereupon it was said that she routinely bartered gold for legal tender. Therefore, it appeared they must have found some degree of success in their mine.

Another report was that she had bags of gold dust strapped to her bosom. Some said gold nuggets were concealed in her boots. No place or places on God's green earth could have been safer – for the woman had no use for soap or water – and the odor that emitted from her was such that it could remove wallpaper and singe the hairs in your nose. Her arrival into the assayer's office was comical in that her entry was followed by an exodus that would have made Moses envious. I know this close to firsthand for my father's insurance office is located in the Independence building near the Exchange Building and I trust his account.

Anyway, on this particular day of summer leisure, Lester and I had ventured downtown to the Boys Club for a game of basketball. Whereas Lester had been blessed with the kind of tenacity, boldness, and exuberance that I desired – if not envied, I was not totally bereft of God's gifts. For although I did not look like an athlete, I could catch, throw, or bounce any kind of ball as I ducked and weaved with the best of them. I excelled at the new game called basketball so much so that Lester, although he could keep up, could never win, and my ability on the court balanced both the age and respect deficit of our friendship.

From the club, it was our routine to visit Robbin's on the Corner for a sweet and to peruse whatever other form of sweets in skirt and bonnet that had attraction to such places. Our minds were filled with visions of frills, giggles and feminine loveliness when we found ourselves critically distracted in an upwind position. This is when we had the misfortune of encountering the dreaded Chicken Lady. Further complicating our predicament was our temporary dumbness and shock to find ourselves so. We were drawn into her spell and became quite powerless to escape the magic we were now under.

She stood four-foot, ten-inches tall and weighed not one ounce more than a house cat. Her skin was tough as saddle leather and had a bronze sheen. Deep tanning melded seamlessly with grime that filled the recesses of her features and creases of her hide and ran like an outline along her hairline. A mad frizz of gray hair shot off one side of her head like flames in a windstorm whilst on the other, formed a mat of such thickness that it could likely stop a bullet.

"What is you starin' at?" came quite clearly from her toothless gums and puckered lips when we stopped our bicycles at the corner we'd just come around. It didn't matter that a dozen other sets of eyes were upon her as well – for we were the only ones within range of her clouded, fierce, pale blue eyes and it seemed unlikely much else was. Pupils that ought to be black, glistened gray and white in the midday sun. "You never seen a lady before?"

While we had seen more than our share of fair womanhood, we'd never seen one in such a state of grizzle that had just disembarked from a wagon filled with chickens that was piloted by a swayback horse as old, gray, filthy, boney and blind as the woman whose eyes at present, held us prisoner. "You thinkin' you want to rob me?" The hag reached for a six-shooter wedged in a rope belt cinched just beneath her armpits and around her tiny chest of ribs – that if it held a bosom – it was not in any way apparent.

The goat that had shared the wooden seat of the buckboard with her moments before, jumped down onto the sidewalk and bleated what must have been a word of caution. Its owner withdrew her hand from our certain death and that of at least a dozen innocent bystanders as I was confident that the lead that would have flown from her six-shooter would have done so quite randomly. Citing two reasons: the gun would have produced enough kickback to dislocate her shoulder. Due to her blindness, proper aim or discernment were never going to enter into the calamity of death and mortal wounding she would have inflicted about the entire intersection.

"*Ohhh*. I'm gettin' a feeling," she said as a complete change of demeanor came over her. Cloudy eyes that had raged a second ago now took on an appearance of concern. "*Ohhh*, boys. You is not alone."

I looked at Lester.

Lester looked at me.

We both looked behind us.

"We isn't?" I asked dumbly and then caught my breath for the slight breeze that had been carrying her odor away, shifted and now Lester – whose breath also caught – and I found ourselves in a predicament.

"Who is that with you?" The woman squinted at nothing beside us. A passing motorcar's sputter and hoof falls of a late returning Sinton's Dairy wagon did not cause her gaze to shift from the nothingness she so intently stared at. She stepped toward us. A half dozen chickens flapped down from her wagon to commence scratching and pecking at the planked walkway and dirt street.

You cannot see a person's humanity when avoiding them from a distance, but Lester and I were now face to face with the Chicken Lady's humanity and coming closer to that humanity with each step she took toward us.

She raised her tiny hand of sinew, veins and bone. As if divining for water, she let it be guided by forces unseen until it landed on Lester's handlebars. The filth between her fingers was nothing compared to the crust caked in, under, around and over her nails. We both took a breath and fought back a gag. "Passed on," she asked or stated and then waited with her pale eyes locked on Lester's fearful blues.

"This was my brother's bicycle," Lester answered what he imagined to be her question.

"Passed on?" she asked more clearly.

17

"Drowned."

"Ohhh."

Then the hand that had divined the deceased raised from his handlebar, came to mine and landed gently upon it. "Passed on?"

"Yes."

"Ohhh."

The goat nudged her wrapping of rags. "Both is here with you," she stated with certainty. "Both is yearning. Both has unfinished business." Then she listened to voices that we could not hear and answered them as she had answered us, *"Ohhh."*

Conversations were being had all around us and I was not exempt from them. Her story entered into me like fresh air through an open window. I saw not only her past, but her present. Even if it was small and vile and filled with pain, I heard laughter and I felt love. I saw her youth and understood that she had once upon a time believed in promise. At one time. In one place. Not here. Not now. Not anymore.

My pity, although strong, was short-lived for a breeze picked up and with it, took her odor and apparently the spirits of the dead away with it. My window was closed and her conversations with the unseen hushed. Now Lester and I were boys stopped on a street corner with an aberration of humanity peering back at us through clouded eyes that saw more than anyone knew.

"You know what you need to do," she stated firmly to Lester and then as if an electrical switch had been flicked, lifted her hand from my handlebar and began to scratch the goat that had just nudged her again. Several chickens made a ruckus as they traded places between wagon bed and sidewalk. She walked back, turned, then she and her goat entered the dry goods – from which several patrons and a few less hardy employees promptly evacuated.

Lester and I kicked off and continued around the corner. Having totally forgotten about sweets at Robbin's on the Corner, we'd ridden a couple blocks eastward toward home in silence when, after slowing for a trolley to cross our path, Lester pulled over and stopped. I pulled up alongside. Not only was I still stunned by our face-to-face encounter with the Chicken Lady, but it was not in Lester's constitution to slow for a trolley. He routinely chanced certain death under their wheels as Lester waited for nothing, *especially trolleys*. Lester's pride simply could not bear a lumbering wooden conveyance upping his God given preeminence of all roadways everywhere – or so he believed.

"She's clairvoyant," Lester commented, his eyes looking nowhere. "She's an authentic clairvoyant."

"What is it you need to do?" I lifted my cap and wiped a ring of sweat off my forehead. "She said you needed to do something." I replaced my cap.

Lester ignored my question as he gnawed his lip and stared ahead at nothing in particular with his intense blue eyes. He brought a hand up to his mouth and chewed back a nail that had had the audacity and misfortune to grow. I idly watched his flexing jaw, not realizing his thought's direction was about to bring about an epic collision of wills – not least of which would be mine and his.

When Lester turned toward me, my stomach dropped, for I could see in his eyes that *a fight was a comin'*. "I apologize," he began and my stomach dropped a second time. If Lester was apologizing, this was going to be big. "I'm about to bust open, Joe. There's been things on my mind for a while and now I know what I need to do about it – I apologize – but you're my best friend and I need you at my side for this."

I squinted. Lester was making less sense than the Chicken Lady.

"You don't have to come if you don't want to."

Then Lester kicked off and wobbled a bit as he turned his bicycle around and headed back toward town. I watched him through squinted eyes until he was about a half block away – and then it hit me. *"NO! Lester! No!"* I kicked off and pedaled like mad to catch up. It was no use, for Lester was a determined, headstrong sort that slowed for no one and no thing, especially caution – as caution – more so than trolleys – was his *absolute* antithesis.

He pulled up at the Independence Building mere seconds ahead of me but had flung his bike to the sidewalk and entered before I had yet come to the hitching posts. Oh, sweet Mary and Joseph – please let my father be out on a call.

19

But he was not.

On this particular day my father was hunched over a ledger as it was month end. Lester's opening volley had already been launched by the time I, breathless, had run down the marble hallway and slid into Father's open doorway. Lester's posture left no doubt. He had plainly squared off against my father, whose lower jaw was hanging dumbly. Father turned to me, his face growing redder by the second.

"There ain't nothing to worry about. Joe is safe with me and I won't let anything happen to him." Then Lester added, "Sir."

My father looked from Lester, to me, back to Lester.

"What did you say to him?" My eyes burned into the side of Lester's face. Both of my hands somehow found their way up to my head – possibly to contain my brain's explosion – which was forthcoming if Lester had done what I thought he had done.

Father's slack jaw pulled up to rejoin the rest of his face. He looked again at me, then turned squarely to Lester – who at this moment looked as formidable and fierce as a wolverine.

"We're riding to Palmer Lake," Lester stated with no room for dissent. "And camping there overnight."

"Jesus," I shouted.

Both looked at me only long enough for my father's eyebrow to rise and me to die. Then they looked back at each other.

"When?" my father asked.

"Next week."

Father looked at me. He looked back at Lester, raised both eyebrows, then nodded with a caveat, "If your father agrees." Then his eyes went back to his ledger and straight edge he was using to keep his rows and figures straight. He jotted a number, then his eyes raised up under the Bruce brow that my brothers and I had inherited – but with the exception of the despot (my brother Irvin) – had not learned to use nearly as effectively. A chill ran up my sweat-drenched spine.

I had not received a paddling since the unfortunate flour sack incident of 1909 and I had determined that thrashing would be my last. I had been well on my way to success until this very moment. The look that came out from under my father's brow left little doubt that my posterior was going to be heated to the temperature of hell later that evening. Taking of the Lord's name in vain was not something any child named Bruce was going to do but once – and I had just used my once.

Effective or not – when Lester turned to me with a victorious lift of his chin – I looked out under *my* inherited sharp brow and gave him the hardest look I could. The fire in my eyes communicated my displeasure with Lester to Lester in a way that not even Lester could misunderstand. Then I directed him out of my father's office with a sweep of my arm and stern point of my finger. I had to cash in every bit of self control I owned not to stick my foot up his...

Chapter 4

Pancho Villa Rides Again

"Now I know you're mad," Lester began before we had cleared the front doors of the Independence Building. That's when I shoved past him viciously enough to knock him off balance and hopefully hard enough to have dislocated his shoulder on the doorframe I'd slammed him into. I was picking up my bicycle when he rushed to stand in front of me with his arms spread wide.

My three older brothers had already taught me the laws of physics with regard to my inclination to punch Lester squarely in his mouth. I strongly suspected a refresher course in said physics would be provided if I attempted to dispatch a few of Lester's teeth to the great beyond. I stopped long enough for Lester to put his arms down and draw a breath – at which point I hopped on my bicycle and took off.

Not only was I never going to speak to him again, but I was also already working on a plan for how I could avoid him and still work at, and live across the street from, Dryhurst and Son. Then, accompanied by shouts of "Joe! Joe! Joe!" he caught up with me and cut me off. Since I am no fan of having gravel embedded into the palms of my hands, I gave up my inclination to ram his bicycle with mine and stopped. We both panted for a moment, but then Lester, with his hands held up as if I were holding him at gunpoint, begged, "Humor me Joe. This is bigger than this moment. You have every right to be mad but let me show you one thing. One thing, Joe. Just one thing."

Then he put his foot on his pedal and he was off. I watched him a moment, then as usual, followed.

He and I had traveled these streets before, so when I realized where we were headed, I had no need to ask. Mrs. Grainger, a worn looking woman of middle years, was taking in laundry when, having gotten no answer at the front door, Lester and I invited ourselves onto the property and walked around the back. Her surprise was temporary but not as much surprise as easy familiarity. "Lester. What are you... I didn't phone in an order."

"I know. I wonder, have you done anything with Bartholomew's room?"

Apparently Lester's trademark directness and perpetual lack of explanation was something the woman was accustomed to as she answered without hesitation. "We have not."

"May we look at it?"

The woman's eyes shifted toward my cringe, but again unflustered, she acquiesced by dropping a handful of wooden clothes pins into a bag, stepped around the wood slat bushel of blazing white sheets at her feet, and led us into her home.

Curtains had not been opened yet that day – or week – and the air was stale. Bartholomew's bedpan, crutches, canes and braces lay atop his bed, cleaned and I assumed, ready to be gifted to whomever or whatever charity may have need of them. Mrs. Grainger entered ahead of us, then turned toward Lester, the only young man audacious enough to barge into her home and grief unannounced.

Even if I had no idea what he was looking for, Lester went straight to a series of newspaper pictures tacked to a corkboard, pointed at them, and looked at me as if I should know exactly what they meant.

Photographs of buildings of great height and steamships and the lady of New York's harbor, Liberty, adorned the wall.

Then Lester abruptly thanked the mother of the recently deceased for her hospitality and pulled me from the room.

Tears were beginning to well in his eyes when we got back to our bicycles. He bent and opened one of the canvas packs. From it he pulled a battered cardboard photograph frame, then removed a couple very fragile newspaper clippings kept safe inside. With hands I'd never seen shake before, he extended them to me. "Joe, I never put it together until the Chicken Lady said it." I looked at the worn clippings in his hand – of tall buildings and steamships and Lady

Liberty.

Lester's eyes began to turn pink and glossy. "They both had yearnings, Joe. Guy carried these with him to Canada. I watched him pack them. I remember him telling me about wanting to see the Green Lady just as our father had when he came to America. He said he wanted to go there one day. He *planned* to go there one day. I've kept these clippings in his bag as a tribute to him. Joe, we're still here and we have their bicycles. This is why I've been restless since we buried Guy. *This* is the thing I *have* to do."

I looked at Lester dumbly.

"This is what *we* have to do," he clarified.

And then I understood. Somehow in life's fates we'd been handed a baton by those who could no longer carry it. Somehow a fallen adventurer and a cripple whose world went no further than the walls of his room had shared a vision. It seemed unlikely that vision was of seeing buildings or ships. Their unfulfilled quest pointed us to the Green Lady, Liberty, a lady whose passive lips cry *Freedom!* A lady who holds the date that shook the world's foundations on her tablet.

But why would they have wanted to see her? Why should we, a cautious and prudent boy and a hellion, be handed their batons? It seemed to me the voices of the dead, if one could hear them, would be a cacophony of things left undone. Everyone leaves something unfinished.

I looked at our bicycles, the only way we had to get from one place to another. For a moment I thought I could feel souls of both brother and cripple – hear their voices without hearing their words. However, what Lester had proposed without actually saying as much was impossible – totally and utterly impossible.

Lester wiped his eyes, sniffed, and sniffed again. "We gotta prove we can do it."

I nodded – even if it was impossible – totally and utterly impossible. At the end of the day, Lester was my friend and at some level, I believed everything he said. More than that, I believed everything he believed. If Lester believed we needed to fulfil Guy and Bartholomew's quest, I believed we needed to fulfil Guy and Bartholomew's quest – although I had no idea how we possibly could.

Lester's home was many times the size of our humble abode and breathtakingly beautiful – at least in my assessment. His father was an Englishman who had immigrated to America in search of opportunity. Englishmen, I was coming to discover, were generational tradesmen to whom craft and excellence were revered qualities that defined their family name. As a result, Lester's father had become quite well known among the elite and well-to-do who sought to build mansions in our Little London that reflected proper English craftsmanship, style and grace. Lester's father possessed such expertise and was preeminent in the field as he was employed by E.G. Pastor – Colorado Springs' foremost homebuilder.

As was apparently custom in Lester's lineage, names were not an original quantity. They seemed to be randomly dispersed and reassigned within the family without regard to the ensuing confusion for those of us outside the family. Therefore, Lester – whose proper name was Leicester, and his father Lester – whose proper name was Leicester, presented a dilemma to my well-ordered way of thinking – because they could not have been more different – or more accurately – diametrically opposed.

A hard life had tempered Leicester the senior and left him with a demeanor that was quite judicial, if not detached. That, combined with his proper English accent and stern manner, caused me to be somewhat fearful in his presence.

Although I did not think it wise, Lester, who had been quite incited since our encounter with the Chicken Lady, had devised a plan. My protest fell on deaf ears, therefore Lester took no heed of my caution – not that he ever had.

And so, we waited the afternoon on a porch that wrapped around his family's Costilla Street home. This was strategic in that it happened to have a fortress view. We lingered there for first sight of his father's deep green truck and rack of ladders. Then as it chugged and sputtered up Costilla, my friend dragged me inside so as not to appear we had been lying in wait – which of course we had been.

Lester and I assumed uncomfortable positions at the kitchen

table and tried to appear natural. Leicester at long last, entered his home via its back door carrying his lunch tin and water jug, quite unaware of our scheme. When he looked at us, suspicion came instinctively to his eyes. He set his vessels down, kept hold of his suspicion, and turned toward us as if he already supposed the worst.

Leicester's forearms and hands were a mass of rock-hard muscle. Even if his frame was slender, I had no doubt his strength was significant. Lester invited him to sit and once his father was at our level and not hovering over us, Lester immediately began to state his case with flailing arms and impassioned pleas. He reminded me of a street corner preacher alternately promising Heaven to the righteous and warning sinners of damnation. Throughout, I held my breath lest one of Leicester's rock-hard arms shoot suddenly forward, grab Lester by his throat and give it the wringing it likely deserved.

But the man's powerful arms with bits of sawdust and wood shavings held in their hairs remained atop the kitchen table. Leicester heard him out while idly drumming fingers that could crush anything they wanted. Leicester drew a breath through nostrils quite flared and coated with wood dust from his day's work. "Palmer Lake," he repeated when a pause in Lester's impassioned pleas provided him opportunity.

"Yes sir."

"Why must you and Guy…" he trailed off.

"I don't know, Papa."

"Why can't you…"

"I don't know, Papa."

"Palmer Lake?"

"Yes Papa."

At that, Lester's father shook his head, rose from the chair he had landed on at our ambush, and walked away. Lester stood as well and was about to give pursuit when I stood with a mad shaking of my head and spread my arms to stop him.

Lester's Aunt Adelaide had stood nearby, barely concealed by the kitchen doorframe as Lester had stated his case and made his plea. She entered his father's vacuum with Lester's youngest brother Leslie in tow. Leslie was quite attached to Adelaide, and always in tow for I cannot recall a single memory of him ever not at her side.

Allow me to explain another complication of Lester's household. Way back in 1902, Aunt Adelaide had come from Canada at her sister's passing. Mary had given life to the clan of hellions named Atkinson. Her death had been sudden on a random afternoon with newborn infant, Leslie suckling at her breast. According to her doctor, cause of death was due to a complication from her fifth birthing which had gone undetected until it had claimed her life.

Aunt Adelaide came from Toronto at the news, battling her own grief – as she and her sister had been close. She'd planned to help with Leslie's care for a time, but she inherited a lost and bereaved brother-in-law for whom her heart broke. Not only had Leicester already lost a child born a year prior to Leslie's birth, but he had now also been widowed. She could not leave him to be the sole provider and caregiver for an infant as well as his three other sons: Guy, Lester, and Miles Henry – who, throughout their childhood, had all been hellions.

Not many women would have left their homeland to take on their sister's life, but Adelaide had done so willingly. Eventually she came to love Leicester and took him to be her husband three years later. Even if Adelaide had taken on full role as their mother, Guy, Lester and Miles Henry continued to call her Auntie. Even Leslie who was always in tow – although he called her mother – knew the distinction.

Mary Langford Bullen had given the Atkinson boys life and would forever be revered – or blamed as the case may be – as their mother. Aunt Adelaide humbly and wordlessly honored her sister's motherhood even if she did all the work and gave all the love of a mother.

So, Adelaide, who never had a child of her own, but cooked and washed clothes and bandaged wounds, came and sat beside her now oldest and most impetuous nephew/son who plopped carelessly onto a chair in dire disappointment at his father's response that I had not discerned as affirmative, contrary, or even issued.

"He's afraid, Lester," she explained kindly, then tenderly touched his arm. "For you."

"I'm not going to drown. Nothing's going to happen to me." Lester's arms flailed again – disregarding Adelaide's touch meant to comfort him.

"It's raw right now. It's only been a month since we buried Guy. You have to give it time."

"There isn't time, Aunt Adie. Guy's spirit is restless and he isn't yet at rest. The clairvoyant saw his ghost with us today and said so."

Now, Methodist women are among the most practical of creatures the good Lord has ever put upon this earth. Although clairvoyants were regularly advertised in the newspaper, it was not a claim to be used in Aunt Adie's presence. Ditto for ghosts. The subsequent puckering of Aunt Adie's lips explained that all quite succinctly. Their conversation continued only moments longer in fits and starts until Lester was instructed to go to his room and I was told to go home. It seemed to me that a proper clairvoyant might have added a word of caution and advised use of tact along with her instructions to Lester of what Lester needed to do.

This whole encounter was followed by a great deal of discontent about the Atkinson home that went on for a week or more. Lester continued to assert his manhood and independence while Leicester expressed his frustration concerning a household of boys who not only lacked any inclination to continue his craft, but who seemed as hell bent on pointless adventure as they were self-destruction.

Besides hellion, tenacious is the second-best word to describe Lester. I was kneeling, stocking an inventory of cornmeal on a lower shelf at Dryhurst and Son when Lester, who it seemed was always breathless, came up from behind and kicked my shoe. "He agreed Joe!"

I looked up at him dumbly.

"My father. He finally agreed. We can ride to Palmer Lake and camp overnight! I already asked old man Dryhurst and he said he can let us off next week! I have to take a delivery right now, but we can formulate a plan at lunchtime."

I stood and swatted dust off the knees of my knickers. Then, still attempting to formulate my response, I faced Lester. Apparently the look in my eyes spoke words I couldn't bring myself to say.

"You don't want to go," Lester asked or blamed with such profound disappointment that I immediately felt ashamed. The blushing of my face communicated that quite well.

Lester threw his arms outward, span around, and stomped away.

I closed my eyes. My bed's warmth and safety, as well as a hot breakfast, were comforts I'd grown accustomed to. And I was not entirely immune to inherited tendencies for prudence and caution.

Nor was I immune to guilt. "I'll do it," I called after him. By now Lester was in a tizzy. Although he did not turn around, a slight hesitation in his gait let me know he had heard me.

My brother Irvin, affectionately referred to (by me) as the family despot was a master of our father's beneath-the-brow-stare-of-consternation. He was also a master of wit, sarcasm, and could speak in a tone that could make his younger brother – *me specifically* – wish to crawl into a hole and disappear. At the crack of dawn on the morn of Lester's and my departure for Palmer Lake on the great Palmer Divide, Irvin had answered the door, most likely given Lester his Bruce under the brow stare, then turned and dryly called up the staircase, "Pancho Villa is here for you."

Since I had heard Lester's mad rapping at our door, I was already three steps down the stairs when my brother had announced Lester's arrival. Therefore, I had to endure Irvin's look of disapproval for the remainder of my descent. Irvin's left eyebrow had a habit of rising to a peak at any mention of Lester's name or presence of his person. I snarled at his peaked eyebrow that would have appeared even without my friend standing on our porch with a shotgun strung over his right shoulder, a pistol strapped to his left hip, and a knife sheathed to his belt – all of which immediately drew my attention as they had Irvin's.

"All he needs is a band of revolutionaries, a sombrero, and a motion picture crew following him around," Irvin added just before he stepped away shaking his head. I opened the screened door for Pancho – I mean Lester – to enter.

My mother had already peered out from the kitchen doorway where she was busy preparing our breakfast and so, had seen the revolutionary. That meant Father's appearance was moments away. With a hushed and somewhat strained tone, I gestured at Lester's armament. "Do you think you could make this appear any more dangerous?"

"I couldn't get them to stay on the…"

"Take them off before my father sees them," I urged, then changed my mind about Lester's entry into our home and pushed him back onto the porch. A fumble of the shotgun – that was most likely loaded – could well blow a hole through the ceiling, seriously wound whatever sibling was still asleep upstairs and doom our friendship forever. When I pushed him out on the porch, my heart sank a second time. His bicycle was loaded so that it had the general appearance of a pack mule.

As Lester was disarming, Irvin stuck his head out the door, beheld the contraption and its burden, shook his head again and raised his eyebrow at me before he retreated back into our abode.

Modifications would be in order – as I had suspected the previous day when Lester assured me that he had the situation handled.

After breakfast, a rearranging, and a fretful mother's goodbye, Lester and I were pedaling around horse droppings left behind by the morning's dairy deliveries. We traveled up Pikes Peak Avenue trying to outdo motorcars as we pedaled toward downtown. We turned north onto Nevada Avenue and passed by the new Colorado Springs High School that had been erected just the previous year. Lester already attended the turreted, magnificent red limestone school. I would attend one year hence. Its monstrous clock chimed eight as we passed – which Lester apparently took as the starting bell of a race – because upon hearing it, he was off.

For as tense as the morning and preceding week had been, I readily caught his enthusiasm and threw myself into the race.

We cleared The Colorado College campus within minutes, sped through a smattering of grand homes that lie north of it, tore through Roswell like a tornado, and shot past the dairy's grazing lands like two bullets shot from a gun.

It was then, in the sudden absence of man, in nature's silence

30

and stillness, with our tires rolling over a madly rutted road that I became aware of birds singing, butterflies fluttering, and bees buzzing all around us. A sensation of freedom entered my soul. Freedom is an experience as superior to comfort and safety as a fresh breeze is to a slog of mud. Ahead of Lester and me lay the kind of adventure that presents challenge and self-reliance, both of which a budding man such as myself yearns to experience.

Had my heart not been racing from exertion, it would have been from the thrill.

The great unknown stretched out before us as we began the long ascent north through the rolling foothills of the Rampart Range. Our race from town had already sapped our muscles of their strength and our lungs of breath. If Lester was panting and grunting with each rotation of his pedal, I could not have heard him over my own. We were soon to discover the sparsely traveled dirt roads that twisted ahead of us held far more challenge *and mud* than we had considered.

But now with muscles burning, air stinging my lungs and passion ignited in my soul, I had discovered not only my independence, but my freedom. And once freedom and self-reliance get into a man's heart, Liberty seemed not that impossible.

A yearning to see the Lady of the Harbor began to burn in my soul, possibly as it had the hearts of Guy and Bartholomew – who had imagined, if not claimed – the same adventure. No doubt their very spirits traveled with us that day through quiet foothills as we made our way north to the Palmer Divide.

Chapter 5

Decision

I dragged an eighty-pound sack of flour from the back of the dreaded mill delivery wagon and heaved it up onto my shoulder. Lester pulled and flopped another one up on his shoulder. I turned toward him, puckered my lips and narrowed my eyes hatefully as I attempted to bounce the sack into a position where its weight might not cripple me for life. Lester returned my hostile stare with equal anger. We walked, or more accurately, he walked, I staggered, across the grocery's back room where he flopped his sack onto the heap. It landed with a great whoosh of choking white powder. Not to be outdone with his display of temper, I did the same.

Mill delivery day was by far my least favorite day at Dryhurst and Son. Lester was already sore as hell about having to help me with such dirty work in the back room's dingy recesses. He'd much rather be riding pell-mell about town in bright sunshine, breathing clean air. But that wasn't the reason for his anger. He'd been at me all morning. We were having a tiff, and to be fair, I had been giving whatever he gave me right back. Mutual annoyance stuck to our faces much like the white dust swirling around that had turned Lester and me into ghosts.

"Why can't you let anything just be?" I snapped.

"Why can't you just agree to things?" he countered. "Have I ever steered you wrong?"

I couldn't think of any blatant examples so I said nothing and we headed back to the wagon squinting hatefully at each other. I had been slow to realize that my father's likening of the Atkinson name to hellion, had been more gospel truth than parental opinion. It wasn't so much that Lester was the Devil himself. Lester was more like the Tempter – who as we all know – is at the very least, a henchman of the Devil and probably a blood relative.

It had only been one day since we'd returned from our trip to Palmer Lake. It had been a great experience but my legs still hurt and my rear end hadn't yet quit complaining. While freedom may have entered my soul and a spirit of adventure may have excited my budding manhood, a different spirit had entered Lester. Precisely, the spirit of pestering. His proposal for us to undertake a second trip had started with the first words out of his mouth this morning.

"I'm getting a little tired of daily asking my father for permission to go places with you." I drug another sack across the wagon bed. "Couldn't we let him recover for a week or two?"

"I'm getting a little tired of you dragging your feet on everything I propose. If I can't even get you to ride eighty miles without you raising a fuss, maybe I should be planning the trip to New York with Miles Henry." Lester pulled a sack as well.

The impatiently snorting and stomping draft horse at the wagon's other end seemed as annoyed with us as we were with each other. We both heaved heavy sacks upon our shoulders. While I knew there would be no way in hell that Leicester the senior would allow two of his remaining three sons to undertake such an adventure, I also knew that Lester would not let this go. I also knew that I would ultimately not prevail regardless of the silent, stubborn glower that I gave in response.

And Lester – knowing that my wordless scowl was generally my last stand – simply smiled in victory. "Oh yeah," he added as I stumbled across the back room, "ask for a couple nights this time. I want to do some exploring." Lester's annoying habit of inching, prying, negotiating, and nagging until he got his way had once again eroded my rock-solid will into fine sand that flowed through his fingers. To top it off, a dozen more sacks of flour, cornmeal and barley awaited us. Gosh I hated mill delivery day.

I had been naive enough to fully believe Lester's intention was to bicycle once again to the Palmer Divide where we would spend a couple nights beneath the stars. I'd assumed his intent was to explore the forested hills around Palmer Lake, shoot a rabbit or two, and chat beside a campfire as we roasted our dinner. The *entire* truth was to be revealed the following week under the rising sun's glow, as after only one night of camping, Lester had inexplicably decided to break camp.

"Why are we packing up?" I asked again over my shoulder although I was certain Lester had heard me the first three times.

Lester kept his eyes on his bedroll he had bundled and was strapping to his bicycle. My stomach sank as it did when I was about to find out that I had been duped. "L-e-s-t-e-r..." I repeated, now with accusation in my tone.

"Well, we're packing up, you know, in case we find a better place to stay tonight. I mean, we are exploring, right?" Lester continued to keep his eyes on task. Then he chanced a curious and somewhat sly glance back at me.

"Goddamn it, Lester!"

"I said that we would go exploring today and that's what we're gonna do." Lester prepared himself for attack – that if I had been stronger would likely have occurred at this moment. I think I may well have looked like a skinny, snorting bull at this point. I looked around for something to kick and if not kick, then throw, but found nothing handy. Since I could think of nothing to say beyond the taking of the Lord's name in vain a second time which might guarantee some time in purgatory, that as a nebulous Episcopal, I was not entirely sure did not exist, I remained speechless.

"I thought we'd ride into Denver this morning and locate the Colorado loop of the Lincoln Highway – you know – so we have a better idea of our future route." Lester's slight smile at my entrapment enraged me further.

"You lied to me."

"I didn't lie. I said we would ride to the Palmer Divide and go exploring."

"But we told my father..."

"...exactly that," Lester finished, then smirked smartly.

"Jesus," I shouted – hoping that if I referred to Jesus as his fully human incarnation and not his fully divine incarnation, I could argue my way out of purgatory on a technicality.

That is when a look I'd never seen before came to Lester's face – a look so unfamiliar that I didn't even know what it meant. Any trace of the smirk that had infuriated me left his face. With flaccid cheeks and his jaw nearly loose, he drew a breath, turned and looked across rolling hills toward the eastern horizon's brightening sky. Then he raised a hand to his mouth and began to chew a fingernail. His back was now to me, so I stepped alongside and studied eyes that remained on the horizon. Disappointment was the look I'd not seen before, and not just disappointment with a thing, disappointment with *me*.

He withdrew his finger from his mouth and spit the bit of nail he'd removed from it. "Maybe I need to do this on my own – or just find someone else to do it with."

My heart fell to my knees. The thought of not being *allowed* to join Lester on the greatest adventure of our lives had never occurred to me – but then again – he'd said it before and I had chosen not to hear him. His previous mention of Miles Henry as his traveling companion had been a warning shot across my bow. This time he was serious and I was about to feel a torpedo in my midsection.

I tried not to let the pain of being left behind show on my face. Somehow – and at some depth – New York City and Lady Liberty had become my dream as well. I didn't know what to say.

"Yeah, I lied to you," Lester explained. "I had to. Every time I suggest something, I have to convince you and then you have to convince your father. You dig your heels in on everything I propose and your father is a brick wall to contend with and it ain't worth it."

I wanted to defend myself, deny what he'd said, but it was true. I had inherited not only my father's sharp brow, but his cautious and prudent nature – neither of which I longed to possess.

In that instant I realized that maybe it was not I who endured Lester, but possibly Lester who endured me. And to him, the name of Bruce was by now more likened to a stick in the mud than a partner for adventure. I said nothing.

"We'll just forget it Joe. The whole thing – New York, Denver, the whole thing. Either you're in it or you aren't and from what I can tell, you aren't in. It's been my idea all along and I've pulled you kickin' and screamin' into it and maybe that wasn't fair. We'll just go back home."

"Lester, I want to go."

He turned to face me. "No. You don't."

"Yeah. I do. I want to go to New York."

He snorted, shook his head, looked back at the brightening sky. "You may want to go, but you don't want to do what it's going to take to get there."

There are things that change a man. Sometimes it is a profound loss. Other times it is a mirror. I did not like the reflection I'd seen in Lester's eyes. That was not me. Cautious, prudent, reserved, safe, comfortable, was someone I'd let myself become. I'd taken to heart the raised eyebrows, critical looks of consternation, and thoughtless scoffing of others toward ideas out of the ordinary.

Lester's jaw flexed a few more times. His eyes remained on the horizon. "It's a long ways Joe – to New York City – to the Lady of the Harbor. If you don't have that kind of resolve, now is the time. Today is the day. You decide, in or out. And I'm not arguing or coercing or trying to convince you anymore. You're in it as much as I am or you aren't in it at all. You're my partner in this or you aren't."

Lester's eyes stayed where they were as I blinked. A few seconds of silence passed as I thought about what I would say. I became aware of the morning's breeze and its gentle hum through the pines. I listened to a distant song of birds. All of nature is still and quiet. It exists in time that has no meaning – just days and seasons – nothing more.

Time for man is precious, fleeting, crucial, critical. What we intend doesn't wait – can't wait – will disappear if we don't seize it. I could argue nothing Lester had said of me.

I drew a breath. *"I'm* going. *We're* going."

Since words without action are meaningless, I turned away and resumed packing up camp. If we were going to Denver, we had miles to ride and we needed to get started.

I packed alone for a minute or two, seeing out of the corner of my eye, Lester now turned – doubtful – hoping to trust – not sure if he could. My iron will had just received its first tempering blow. If I had to, I would pack camp and ride to Denver by myself. Doubt who I am? I will show you who I am.

Saying nothing, Lester came to my side and added his hands to my effort. Camp was packed, stuffed, cinched, and strapped to our bicycles a few moments later. Still wordless, we rode a badly rutted, lurching trail along a ridgeline until it intersected the North and South Road. We paused for a drink of water amidst bird song, buzzing of bees, and the sound of gentle winds in the trees. As we overlooked the great expanse of rolling hills, springtime's verdant green now faded from them, we said nothing. Our thirst satiated, we began to chat idly about the day ahead and the prospect for good weather as we stretched our recently awakened but already warmed muscles.

Then Lester fell quiet, long enough that I looked over at him and found him looking back at me. "Sorry about this morning."

I nodded, swallowed the water I'd just taken in my mouth, capped my canteen, slung it over my shoulder, and put foot to pedal. "Understood," seemed enough of an answer. In the glorious orange glow of the rising sun, Lester and I began our descent from the Palmer Divide – not a timid boy and his bold, older friend – but two men of similar mind and resolve making destiny's necessary foray. As my hero Teddy had once said, *"Believe you can and you're halfway there."*

We were sole travelers on the North and South Road for the next hour or so but then as the day warmed, commerce began. Trucks and motorcars would appear as infrequent dots upon intersecting auto trails north of us before they enjoined the highway. Some headed our direction in what became a steady stream of maybe ten or so an hour. Of course, horse-drawn wagons were still the mainstay of farms and ranches bisected by the highway. They shared the ruts, ridges and mud bogs along with us and motorcars. We delighted in guessing, should we observe any vehicle's approach from a knoll, the point of our intersection given their speed and distance as well as our own.

But those motor conveyances that came from behind presented dilemma more than delight. Motorcars and even trucks frequently and suddenly appeared behind us without a sound. We had no warning before an impatient beep of a horn that usually preceded our likely crushing by mere seconds and scant yards.

But in lapses of traffic, we sailed principally downhill toward Colorado's capital city. Our anticipation became more enthusiastic with each passing mile. As we weaved along ruts, around chuckholes, dodging traffic, Lester raised his hand to point out the traverse of a steam locomotive and boxcars west of us.

I smiled and nodded, thinking the bustle enjoined around us to be nothing less than a symphony of progress and a herald of changing times. As we crested the last knoll above the confluence of streams and rivers that flowed down from snowcapped mountains, Denver at long last stood before us. Distant plumes of smoke rose from its stacks and hovered above the growth of trees endemic to the arrival of man on the previously barren plains.

To capture the moment, we stopped, again not feeling a need for words. Then with his eyes locked ahead, Lester said something I'll never forget.

"This is how freedom is won, Joe. You don't wait for it to be bestowed. You take it and don't give it back."

Chapter 6

Unsinkable

Colorado's capital city, Denver, had gleamed white as heaven in our imaginations: tall buildings with Roman columns, intricately carved cornices, and gargoyles to keep demons at bay. Its wide, pristine boulevards would be graced with elegant carriages, fine motorcars, and mannered drivers. Its women would be perpetually dressed in hoop skirts, lace shawls, and flower-adorned bonnets. Its men would be attired in black suit coats, if not tails and top hats. Of course, they invariably sported either parasols or ivory canes as the distinguished are apt to do. As dignified citizens strolled along the city's wide avenues they would greet one another with happy comments about the day.

But as we entered the gleaming city we found shacks and settlements scattered along waterways and people living in conditions we had never imagined. The nicer shacks were of tar paper tacked with strips of wood to crates or planks of wood. The poorer shacks were scraps of fabric hung on rickety stick frames. Bits of rusted tin scavenged from garbage heaps, driven through with nails and wire, held them together. Water was fetid. Sewage was raw. Children were dirty. Men were shiftless. Women were haggard. They stared at us as we rode past. We stared back at them as if they were a moving picture newsreel and not real people – for how could real people live in such conditions?

Then came tenements situated downwind of smokestacks and rail lines – black and grimy with soot. Electrical lines hung like handfuls of spaghetti flung between poles and buildings that were crammed together so that people lived atop people. Men and women sat on stairways and curbs or hung from windows. Their children – just as filthy as the ones in the shacks – played stickball in the streets that were heaped with garbage encrusted with flies, lousy with maggots, and crawling with ants. Mangy dogs ran loose and feral cats hid beneath stoops. Lester and I rode through, mouths agape, holding our breaths, dumbfounded.

You hear of the poor. You see hobos riding trains. You pass by an occasional beggar. And you think they are anomalies. Until you see them by the score and living generation upon generation. I could tell by just looking at these people that they knew no other reality. They had not the vaguest understanding of enough to eat, a home that keeps out the cold, a bed – much less a bed with clean sheets, or water that runs from a spigot. We rode in silence past that which we did not understand, our expressions communicating our shock.

Tenements gradually gave way to small businesses, diners, factories, cottages and boarding houses. Busy around them, in streets and on walkways were people more like ourselves, a world the same shade as the one we knew: working people clad in denim, moving purposefully, faces stern but friendly. All about us buzzed motorcars, trolleys and people who lived as Lester and I had imagined all people everywhere always lived.

Then in the space of a few blocks, this world gave way to fine buildings of commerce, the city we'd imagined: concrete sidewalks, clothiers, markets, dry goods and fashionable eateries where men and women dressed in finery, dined.

We disembarked and stood on a corner, still wordless amidst sputtering motorcars and clanging trolleys, chatter of the carefree, and monologues of the opinionated – which were in abundance – for we had come within sight of Colorado's gold domed capital.

This was the Denver of our imaginations, not in shades of gray depicted in photographs, nor in Heaven's shining white, but in full color and alive – more alive in fact, than we had considered.

Not to distract from our amazement, but worthy of note: urban terrain is far more hazardous to life and limb than any amount of windswept plain, wilderness, or threat of ambush by scoundrels and highwaymen. For in the big city, bicyclists such as ourselves were guaranteed near misses with the ever-present progress of trolleys. They seemed to come from all directions at any time and tended to be as silent as the death they brought to hapless individuals who had ventured forth unaware. A fate Lester and I hoped not to endure.

Not quite as deadly – for sometimes a pedestrian or cyclist did survive – was the automobile's pell-mell traverse. This was utterly random, habitually careless, and usually accomplished at breakneck speed. Curiously, motorized conveyances were as likely to be operated by a child of ten with a lollipop in his mouth as a mature adult smoking a cigar as an enfeebled old man whose curses and gray whiskers buffeted about on the breeze of his progress.

Equally prevalent but not quite as dangerous, usually resulting in skinned palms and bloodied knees – fates that had not yet befallen us – were frequent encounters with stray dogs and children playing. Worse were adults *who ought to know better,* who would suddenly and without warning, simply decide to cross the street. This they seemed to do whenever they so pleased and seemingly preferred to do so only if concealed from view until they appeared directly in front of a moving conveyance. Then, as if a conveyance had no business on the road, they greeted their near collision with a quick turn of their head, eyes wide open, and mouth agape.

Hopefully they were spry and possessed enough agility to either twist aside or jump away before impact. These encounters were invariably followed by their indignant shouts at whatever form of traffic had dared impede their random impulse. As a citizen of the land of the free, did they *not* have the inalienable right to random changes of direction and arbitrary street crossings? Never mind the physics of size and speed that would assure them the short end of the stick in any given collision.

In general, the morass of hazards presented in the big city seemed to incite a fearless competition for both devil-may-care survival and personal victory. Lester and I had thus far strangely enjoyed the challenge and enjoined it gleefully as if it were a game rather than a life-or-death situation – as it most assuredly was.

But as we surveyed the strangeness around us, our stomachs growled. We set about locating a lunch counter to assuage our hunger – feeling a little guilty that we could, at will, do as we wish. Given our youth, we thought it remarkable that we had the means to purchase a meal within our pockets – provided whatever lunch counter we chose was within the means of said pockets.

Thus far in our day of exploration, the stations, fates, and inequities of the human experience could not have been more clearly stated. They were impressed upon us more so than any classroom or textbook could ever have hoped to communicate.

Since we had arrived in town before the sounding of lunch hour whistles, we had been ahead of activity that now gently and gradually enveloped us. We sat on stools at a long counter, of which occupancies gradually began to outnumber vacancies. Conversation which before could be spoken, now had to be shouted. We gobbled roast beef sandwiches and slurped lemonade as if both starved and parched. We were unfortunately, unaware of the savageness of our gobbling and slurping until we were satiated – whereupon we had pause to consider the somewhat aghast expressions of those nearby.

Our embarrassment, however, was short-lived.

He stood four foot nothing, weighed sixty pounds at best, was of an innocent age somewhere between eight and ten but looked a hard living thirty-five. He oozed sweat, reeked of the same, and came dashing in breathless. *"Water,"* he gasped and then flung half of himself atop one of the few remaining counter stools and the other half upon the counter – that had previously been suitable for dining. The waitress, without a word, filled a glass and no sooner set it before him than he downed it, slammed it down and once again gasped, *"Water!"*

I looked at Lester.

Lester looked at me.

We shared a bemused smile, then both turned full about to observe the urchin as he gulped a second glass of water. Rivulets of sweat ran from his newsboy cap, down the sides of his face, leaving tracks in layers of roadway grime on his moist skin. Freckles adorned his nose and most of his cheeks. A threadbare plaid vest attempted to cover his naked arms and shoulders. It was complemented by a striped silk tie looped haphazardly around his neck. Both were as filthy as the day is long. Ratty knickers and tattered leggings covered his other half. His shoes, that seemed to serve no purpose other than garnishment, were of worn leather. Their soles flopped loose, revealing bare toes and shreds of blackened stockings. *"Water!"* he demanded a third time and slammed his glass upon the counter. Then as if he had felt our eyes upon him, he turned directly toward Lester and me and scowled like – well – like a constipated elf.

Lester laughed aloud. I brought a hand to my face, turned away, and kicked Lester. He laughed louder. I snickered, afraid that I too would begin to laugh and then neither of us would be able to control ourselves. We simultaneously leaned to the side to dig in our pockets for coins to pay for our meal. Twenty cents later, we stood, turned, and came chest to face with the urchin. He wasn't very big, but then neither is a bobcat, and you wouldn't want to unnecessarily provoke one of those either. I cleared my throat and amidst the din, stated rather firmly, "Excuse us."

The urchin remained, defiantly blocking our path.

Then the kindly waitress that had served him *Water!* leaned forward over the counter, winked, and extended a sandwich wrapped in waxed paper. When he stepped aside and reached to take it, Lester and I made our escape – laughing again – although our laughter could not be heard amidst lunch hour chatter.

We had no sooner cleared the door and approached our bicycles that we'd leaned against the diner's storefront, than the urchin scrambled out and again cornered us. "What's so funny?"

"Nothing. I'm sorry." Lester extended his hand to confirm his apology's sincerity.

The boy's face contorted doubtfully: lip up to nose, nose over to one side, one eye squinted, the other narrowed suspiciously – elfin constipation. A firm bite on my lower lip prevented an all-out guffaw, but could not subdue my smile. Saying nothing, the urchin folded back waxed paper, ripped a bite of sandwich and chewed while seemingly never closing his mouth even once. Lester withdrew his hand. I put mine on my handlebars. "You ain't from around here," the boy asked, noticed, or stated.

"No," I answered.

"Is you tourists?"

"Explorers," Lester replied.

The boy looked at our packs and bedrolls. "Show you the sights. Two cents each. Fabulous sights. Things you ain't never seen before. Up close. Personal. An' I revel to you the secrets that nobody else knows."

"Reveal?" Lester questioned.

"Huh?"

"You said revel. You meant reveal."

"That's what I said."

I laughed, then choked it back.

The child glared, ripped another bite of sandwich, then while chewing, his eyes riveted on mine, continued unabated. "You heard a the Titanic disaster?"

Lester rolled his eyes. "I think everyone has."

The boy continued to look only at me. "What about the worl' famous Unsinkable Molly Brown?"

Lester shrugged.

I shrugged, uncertain where this line of questioning might lead. I had not yet been blamed for the Titanic's sinking and if I could avoid that and the ensuing publicity it might bring to the Bruce family name, I'd be eternally grateful.

"Show you her manson. It's a fabulous manson."

I fought back a snicker and cleared my throat. "You know we'd love to see that but today we're looking for the Lincoln Highway."

"I'll show you that too. It's on the way."

Thinking this boy wants only to relieve us of two cents each, I demurred. "We can find it ourselves." Then as soon as my words had cleared my mouth and his face had fallen, my heart did the same. This child was poor but trying – from his tattered vest and silk tie down to mileage worn shoes that barely contained his feet. Because of a stranger's kindness, he paid not a penny for an eight-cent sandwich but because of my stinginess, he may be hungry again tonight. I added, "But then again, we might get lost." When I nudged Lester and began to dig in my pocket, light returned to the boy's eyes. I could easily afford to part with two cents. He could not afford the lack of two cents.

Newsboys were loudly hawking the morning's leftover papers

from street corners and doorways of office buildings as we rode past – the bobcat mounted atop Lester's handlebars. The lad alternately pointed the way, shouted at pedestrians, cursed at motorists, waved at other newsboys (who all seemed to know him), and shouted greetings to anyone and everyone he recognized. It was as if he was the miniature, stinky, grimy, grand marshal of his own vagabond parade. Given our contrast to the current environment, Lester and I looked every bit to be of his direct lineage – the family crest of which – I smiled to imagine, would likely be of a sad hobo sitting fireside roasting a pigeon.

Lester and I thrilled to view the prominent red and blue bars and distinguished "L" of the Lincoln Highway road sign and discover its route to be directly through downtown Denver. It was spitting distance from the grand state capital building and its gleaming dome painted in real gold. Our guide cared not one whit about our exuberance to see the great highway and not a lot more about the Capital dome.

The mansion, my mistake, *manson*, of one Margaret Brown was the highlight and seemingly only stop on his two-cent tour of fabulous sites. He had, in fact, *"Done onect met the famous lady,"* and as it turns out, sold her a newspaper. According to the lad perched upon Lester's handlebars, he was an enterprising sort of businessman that began his workday before the crack of dawn running newspapers. On the occasion of his having met the famous shipwreck survivor, her photograph had graced the front page – he wasn't sure for what as he could not read – but possibly as a candidate for the Senate – if not the Presidency.

My sister Nell had mentioned the famous Molly Brown on occasion at mealtime and so the famous woman's politics were familiar to me. Also familiar was the disquiet any mention of Molly Brown's politics brought to my father's face. Vaguely, it seemed to men who held the reins of power, Molly Brown was a rabble rouser with political ambitions that seemed unlikely – given that women had yet the ability to vote. To women, Mrs. Brown was a savior, a champion, who had continued to throw women in a figurative lifeboat long after the unfortunate ocean liner's sinking. Regardless, our urchin had become infatuated with and by the unusual lady whose home we now, stopped in the roadway, beheld.

Her fortune had come from silver – or possibly gold – maybe both – likely both – our guide was unclear. Given the standard and scale of mansions erected in Colorado Springs by men that dripped gold and didn't bother to pick up silver, the structure was unimpressive. Lester and I beheld it with more disappointment than enthusiasm.

Our guide failed to notice.

"Isn't it loverly?" he swooned, then jumped down from Lester's handlebars. We watched him pull at his trousers which had crept northward and into a rather uncomfortable bind – or so it seemed by the apparent relief their readjustment provided. "Can you 'magine? Living in such spendor? Everyday. Spendor like that?"

I brought a hand to cover my mouth. Lester sucked in his lips. The assassination of the English language had commenced – not with a direct shot to the heart – but with a scattergun wound more likely to bring death by infection than grievous injury.

"Do you mean splendor?" Lester asked.

"That's what I said. Splendor. Can't you hear so good?"

Lester pulled down the corners of his mouth.

"She was on the madent voyage of the Titanic jus' two years ago, all by herself, when on that clamatous night it striked a iceberg whereupon she looked death right in the eye an' spit." The little man's arms rose and waved majestically unlike the flowered words that stumbled and fell from his lips. "Not contend to save jus' herself, she threwed other womens onto the lifeboats to save them until some man came along and threwed her into the boat for fear she would purish helpin' others but not herself." Our guide paused to catch his breath for as his explanation continued, his passion had heightened to a point where he had apparently failed to breathe. Once restored, he shook his head in disbelief. "Can you believe such a truistic woman, what with her being rich an' all? It's 'cause she knowed hard times an' hard livin' that she cared. An' you know what?"

We shrugged.

"She ain't home. She's in 'urope suffering right now."

"What's she suffering from?"

"Gettin' womens the vote."

"You mean suffrage and probably Europe."

"That's what I said." The boy stuck his head forward and pointed at both of his ears. "Maybe you should clean out your ears." Then he muttered something about our "ignance" before he resumed the tour. "Come on, I'll take you up the alley."

And so continued our tour of Molly Brown's home: standing on an incinerator and garbage cans to look over its rear wall. We beheld absolutely nothing beyond drawn lace curtains that obscured the windows of rooms of which we could scarcely determine purpose, much less discern a wealthy inhabitant within. "In there is likely a Vanderbilt, or a Rockefeller, or possible even an Astor," our guide insisted. "She rents the place out whenever she ain't home. The maid tol' me."

I glanced at Lester who glanced at me. "So does this complete our tour?" Lester asked.

"Sure does."

I again bit my lip to keep from laughing.

"Well, thank you very much. It was quite informative."

"Yer welcome. Spread the word."

As we mounted our bicycles, the urchin ran down the alley, four cents jingling in his pocket. Nevertheless, he was proud and important and *"victorous"* to have not only added four cents to his fortune, but that his voice had been heard and his fondest story told.

I looked after him for a moment. For whatever condition he had been born into, he saw himself not. From the silk tie he wore to the difficult words he massacred, he saw himself higher and he saw himself better. He cared not for great architecture or domes of gold. He delighted in a gutsy woman's sacrifice and service. Perhaps he would be – amidst the swarm of anonymous humanity born and cast into desperation – as unsinkable as the woman he admired. I'd like to think he would be. I have to think he was.

We began to ride. I looked to my side, at my friend Lester. He too was unsinkable in many ways and always on his way to be

47

somewhere other than where he was.

As we rode to find the red, white, and blue Lincoln Highway signs and explore the great road, I was now truly embarked upon a journey to take me somewhere other than where I was, to a place I imagined myself already to be.

And I knew without doubt that I would make this journey with Lester, not in spite of the road and its distance nor its trials nor its unknowns, but *because* of the road and its distance and its trials and its unknowns. Not because I was fearless or immune to doubt – but because as of today, I saw myself so.

Chapter 7

Anything Drawn to Scale

"The Lincoln Highway," I repeated with the same hoarse whisper that my nervously constricted throat had produced a moment earlier. My brother Irvin's eyebrow raised to that know-it-all point that I'd come to hate. Father squinted his eyes. Lester sighed wearily, rolled his eyes, leaned over the table we were all seated at, and gave my attempt at the official presentation of our grand plan a more assertive enunciation.

"The Lincoln Highway, Sir," he said so clearly and distinctly that it could not be misunderstood again.

It had been three weeks since Lester and I had tasted true freedom in our expedition to Denver – or more accurately – had committed the kind of disobedient act where freedom is taken and not given back. The budding man inside of me had come to life on the road to Denver. Ever since, I had been consumed with the kind of confidence I had always admired in my friend Lester. From that day to this, Lester and I had devoted every free moment to the study of any and all maps and guidebooks of this great country. We had become as familiar with the coast-to-coast highway as we could.

We had also consulted with anyone and everyone who had any experience with over-the-road travel. Then we had drafted a comprehensive map of our proposed journey's route. The brown butcher paper we had appropriated from Dryhurst and Son that contained our anticipated route, lay rolled on my lap, hidden beneath the table for its unveiling at the moment now at hand.

My father's eyes remained squinted as he drew a long breath and released it through slightly flared nostrils. He looked from his timid, nearly quaking but nonetheless determined and confident son – yours truly – over to Lester, whose face was flushed pink with excitement. Although Father said nothing his belabored sigh did. I clearly divined my father's single thought as if he'd spoken it aloud: *hellion*.

Fearing that Lester was moments away from standing up to my father *again* and perhaps ruining any possibility of consent, I pulled the scroll from my lap, set it on the table and began to unroll it. By now Irvin was pursing his lips and shaking his head. Irvin's presence at the unveiling of our plan had not been part of our strategy. Irvin's firm opinion was that he was second in command of the Bruce household and also held a position as my personal advisor – for what could knobby-kneed, floppy-eared little brother Joe possibly know?

Nevertheless, it was his hands that helped my shaking fingers unroll and flatten the somewhat distressed and ink smudged paper to its full 36 inches. The dots and lines we'd drawn across an outline of the United States represented the cities, towns, rivers and byways that Lester and I would have to traverse in order to get from Colorado Springs to New York City. My father's previously squinted eyes widened with what I had to assume was pleasant surprise – for he was a well-ordered sort of man that appreciated thorough planning and anything drawn to scale – which we had been careful to replicate.

"The Lincoln Highway." Father's tone was as flat as our map, and understandably so. For you see, in 1914, the great road was more a grand idea of the Good Roads Movement than actual reality. Its inception had been barely one year prior to our present conversation. Its completion was far more speculation than fact. It didn't help that its surface was reputed to be not much more than tire tracks through prairie grass. Rumored, was that it consisted more of chuckholes, ruts, mud pits, and quicksand than traversable road surface.

"We aren't planning our trip until two years from now, in nineteen-sixteen, Father," I pleaded more than asserted, then glanced at Lester who shot me a look of disapproval. As we'd discussed, or more accurately, *as I had been told* – my mealy mouth – as well as begging and pleading – were *not* going to win the day. I checked my tone, lowered my voice, and called on the brand of enthusiasm that Lester said we would need in order to prevail against doubters and naysayers, two of whom sat opposite us.

"It's going to be the new thing for the entire U.S.A. – roads and highways – and it already is. The government has committed twenty-five million dollars in matching funds to the states to make it a reality. *Twenty-five million dollars!* Lester remembers back in oh three when the second cross country motorist ever drove through Colorado Springs in a Packard."

As per our rehearsal, Lester added his testimony. "I was only seven but I remember it as clear as day and standing with Guy and Papa and everyone was cheering..."

"There are already dozens of people going cross country on motorcycles and..."

"Trains," Irvin interjected. "Trains are for traveling cross country. If you want to go to New York, save up your money and purchase a ticket like any sensible person would do."

"That isn't the point of our trip and Mister Ford is planning to produce millions of Model Ts over the next couple years. Millions! There are already nearly a million on the road. It isn't like we are going to be pedaling through the wilderness. People are going to be driving all across this land by sixteen and Lester and I will be part of the..."

This is when Irvin decided to pull out all the stops and be patently ridiculous. "Why don't you and Lester just fabricate one of those areoplanes and fly yourselves to New York City? Maybe you and Orville here," he shot a thumb Lester's direction, "can attach some wings and a propeller to your bicycles and..."

At this point, Father looked over at Irvin with eyes hanging under his sharp brow. This – as all Bruce boys know – is a first warning. And as all Bruce boys also know – there will be no second warning. I secretly delighted in watching Irvin actually shut his mouth for once in his life and then squirm for the full ten seconds Father's eyes held him captive.

After a clearing of his throat, Father began anew. "Now," he began to trace a bit of our route with his finger, "wasn't this pretty much the Pony Express route?"

"Yes Father, all the way from Saint Louis to Cheyenne. There's towns every fifteen miles or so. We won't ever be very far from help if we need it and there will be travelers on the..."

"The Pony Express ran for less than two years when *trains* took over and now those towns are ghost towns, *Joe*." Irvin glared at me, then glanced at father who began to tap his finger in irritation but whose eyes remained focused on our map. Irvin resealed his mouth but I narrowed my eyes at him, nevertheless.

"Got family here in Missouri." Father positioned his finger on the roads I'd marked in Missouri.

"That's part of the plan, Father." I broke a smile for the first time in the last very tense five minutes. "We figured we'd swing up to the Great Lakes and spend some time with Lester's family in Detroit and Toronto on the way out. Then I've marked our course here through Missouri on the way back so we could visit our family."

Lester leaned and reached over my father's arm to point our route – you know – in case my father, *dullard that he was*, wasn't keeping up. As Lester traced our proposed loop forth and back across the country he explained, *"Ouuuuut and baaaaack."*

Father squinted at him, cleared his throat and drew a breath. "You know when I was making my plans to come out west, everyone told me I had to be crazy to leave civilization to go to the frontier." That's when I saw my father smile nostalgically and look up at me with what I had to assume was as much pride as astonishment. "Do you think you can actually do this?"

Irvin slapped his hands down on the table, stood and stomped away. I was beaming ear-to-ear when mother, who had been listening to every word from the kitchen, entered the room and curiously took Irvin's place at the table. Now we were not only cooking with gas but developing a full head of steam as well – if not enough to power a train, enough to ticket Irvin out of the conversation and that was a start.

Lester's victory on his home front was not as victorious as we had hoped or frankly, expected. Leicester the senior had refused to even so much as listen to Lester's "nonsense." Lester's proposal came to an ill fate shortly after his mention of New York City – which – as luck would have it – was referenced in the first sentence of Lester's proposal. But having expected initial failure, we remained undeterred. Lester and I decided on a *wait him out* strategy this time around instead of the *pout and pester him to death* strategy Lester had previously employed.

So, with my parents' tentative support and the addresses and subsequent correspondence with every aunt, uncle, grandparent, cousin, and Y.M.C.A. along our proposed route, Lester and I proceeded to fill in the details of our plan as if it was more certainty than folly.

We amassed stacks of correspondence assuring us of safe lodging, proper meals, and trusted guidance along the way. Then two months later we ambushed the quiet man with rock hard forearms. After he had run aground on protest and arguments, we obtained a disgruntled sigh of resignation – which we took as his blessing – even if it most certainly was not.

Chapter 8

Destiny and Destinations

The rumblings of our nation's entry into war grew louder as the years changed from 1914 into 1915. They grew louder again as 1915 passed into 1916. Although President Wilson was campaigning for reelection in '16 with the slogan, *He kept us out of the war*, the language used was notably past tense rather than future promise. That detail was not lost on men nearing, or of the age of conscription. The scale of this war was already unlike anything ever seen in the history of man. Plans for conscription were rumbling not only through our chambers of Congress, but governments around the world as men on the fronts were being killed by the thousands and willing replacements were in short supply.

Our long planned and saved for trip could be instantly scuttled by our nation's entry into war. My ever-growing concern about the war's effect on our trip wasn't entirely selfish. My concern was that if conscripted, Lester's very life could be scuttled.

And it wasn't just soldiers who comprised war's fodder. German zeppelins had been bombing French cities for some months and were now sailing the skies above London. Like fire breathing dragons, they were taking lives, destroying homes and ruining civilian livelihoods. Ferries, passenger, and merchant ships were being sunk by German submarines and ships of war. It seemed treachery was overtaking the world and *mankind* would soon become a word that could no longer be spoken in truth, present tense, or future promise.

Colorado Springs was as far from war in Europe and violence on the high seas as one could get. Yet in our modern world of telegraphs, newsreels, newspapers, and radio – *not that we or anyone we knew had one* – the other side of the world and events as recent as yesterday had entry into our homes. Unfortunately, that which had entry into the safety of our homes also disrupted the peace of our minds. Unbidden concern wove through and colored everyday life even in our safe haven of Little London.

Talk of bicycling across country for fun and adventure seemed by comparison to reports of war, starvation, dismemberment and death, a petty expenditure of life and energy. Especially troubling, even to me, when considering the weight of the times, was the immense preparation Lester and I had thus far invested solely toward that end. Yet we had pressed on, undeterred.

Lester was fully a man by the spring of 1916 – having just turned twenty on June 5th. At sixteen I was no longer a boy. I would be turning seventeen on September 6th, during our return trip, somewhere on the road between New York and Missouri. My freshman year of high school and varsity season of basketball were beneath my belt. Old man Dryhurst had been intrigued by our plan since its inception and therefore had given us every available workday for the past two years. As a result, our savings had grown along with our anticipation, determination, and strength.

As for provision, we had mailed supplies of jerky, raisins, biscuits, along with bicycle chains and tires we would likely wear through, ahead to general delivery at key post offices and relatives' homes along our route.

We were as ready and prepared as we could be.

I looked at a platter of fried chicken that was once again being passed to me – or more accurately – to Lester and me – the guests of honor. Already so full that I could barely breathe, I shook my head and handed it on to Lester. With his mouth full and his ever-moving jaw masticating whatever combination of potato, spring lettuce, pole bean, gravy, or chicken already in it, he gladly snatched another leg and thigh, then passed it on to Miles Henry.

Our families had come together on this Sunday to send off their oldest and youngest sons – whose bicycles were packed and ready for our 6 A.M. departure the following day, Monday, June 12th, 1916. My mother, sister Nellie, and Lester's Aunt Adelaide, had been busy cooking all afternoon in spite of such activity being in direct violation of the Sabbath commandment.

As we ate, Mother watched me as if to film my every movement on frames of a cellulose reel. This she did so intensely that I half expected to hear the clatter of a shutter and the whir of a spool come from behind her eyes. I looked across the table we had set up on the expansive hilltop lawn of the Atkinson home and smiled at my mother for probably the hundredth time. "Thank you," I offered, then added, "All this is so good."

My father and Leicester the senior sat at one another's side to the left of my mother who sat at the left of Adelaide – a veritable wall of parents that appeared to face down their wall of offspring across from them. Father's inherent distain of all things Atkinson had, over the past two years, evolved into a level of respect. He and Leicester had become, if not fast friends – at least allies in the cause of keeping Lester and I in check. The word *hellion* had not been used in reference to an Atkinson boy for quite some time. Then as I turned toward Lester, he pulled some sort of gristle from his mouth, and with all the finesse of a savage from some time-forgotten tribe in darkest Africa – flung it over his shoulder.

I raised my eyebrows as this was not acceptable etiquette for a Sunday dinner even if it was a picnic dinner on the lawn. I chanced a glance over at my father – who smiled knowingly. Irvin, who had become a detective with the Colorado Springs Police Department, sat at the end of the table. Instead of shaking his head and rolling his eyes, he smiled as well.

I returned his smile. Lester was Lester and thank the Lord he was. I needed that savage in my life more than anyone could ever know. Irvin apparently knew my thoughts and having come to the same mind, just nodded.

Something was changing between Irvin and me, or maybe more accurately, something had changed. No longer just his foolhardy, easily led, little brother Joe, I had proved myself to be a young man who had set his sights on a goal and never waivered. At school, I had become a scholar and athlete, already the captain of my school's basketball team. I diligently labored at everything I set my mind to and it had not gone unnoticed. I had at long last gained my older brother's tolerance and my classmates' attention.

Pike, had become my nickname at the Colorado Springs High School where, for some unknown reason, no student was ever actually called by their given Christian name. I had inherited the moniker of Pike after intrepid explorer, Zebulon Pike – whose mountain, so named, rose like a snow-capped sentinel some 8,000 feet above our town and some 14,000 feet above sea level. While neither Lester nor I intentionally set out to boast about our plans to cross the nation, our eastward expedition had been no secret from classmates or teachers. Miraculous as it seems, I was already being described as a star athlete and leader. That, in tandem with the journey before me, came my christening of *Pike*.

Pike was a nickname I cherished in that spring of 1916, for I was becoming who I saw myself to be by doing what I believed I could do.

These thoughts had no sooner swum through my mind than Irvin leaned to his side and dug in his trouser pocket. When he extended his downturned hand across the table and nodded his head, I extended my hand to meet his.

He dropped in my palm a compass of polished brass complete with a cover and chain like that of a pocket watch. The exclamations, curious comments and peering eyes of everyone at the table focused on the treasure my hand displayed. None of them noticed that I was dumbstruck.

I continued to stare at Irvin who in turn continued to gaze at me. "So you always go the right direction," he said amidst the comments, unheard by anyone except me. He winked and smiled again.

Two years ago, I suspect he would have explained the gift thusly: *So you don't get lost, knucklehead.*

Respect, rather than merely a compass, had been placed in my hand. I'll never forget its feel nor the coarse brush of my brother's fingers against my palm as he placed it there. This was the compass of a true explorer, the compass of a young man christened Pike. It was everything I could do not to weep.

The adverse effect of years-long preparation is that it removes thrill and novelty from adventure and renders that which ought to be stimulating into something more akin to checking an item off a list of things to do. It was on that early Monday morning, after handshakes from our fathers, hugs from our mothers and a hearty pat on my back from Irvin, that Lester and I at long last saddled up on our packed bicycles. We pedaled west to the Colorado Springs High School in silence, then turned north. There was no starting bell from the massive clock this day.

We began to ride up Nevada Avenue, weaving around ice wagons and milk carts stopped in the roadway, their drivers scurrying forth and back to porches with deliveries. Newsboys with emptied canvas sacks flopping from their handlebars stared at Lester and I curiously as we passed going opposite directions. Our clip was predetermined in order for us to roll into Denver's brand-new Y.M.C.A. by 5 P.M. that evening.

We'd planned every detail. Our first stop for water came after we had cleared both town and Sinton's dairy. With song and flitter of birds around us, we straddled our metal steeds loaded with identical canvas bags, bedrolls and tarpaulins. As we drank from canteens we looked ahead at rolling hills that glowed of spring's verdant green under the rising sun. The shadows they cast appeared as emerald waves. It was as beautiful a sight as I'd ever seen.

Yet somber described not only the state of my soul, but my entire countenance. Lester, as always, looked straight ahead unwaveringly. I observed a subtle flexing of his jaw between sips of water. No doubt he was already as far as Nebraska in his mind. I recapped my vessel and let the strap around my neck take its weight. Then while balancing with one hand braced on my handlebar, I bent my knee and pulled my foot up behind to stretch my thigh muscles. As I alternated one leg, then the other, I couldn't help but notice the way sunlight was striking Lester's sharp features. He didn't have to turn toward me to know there was sorrow in my eyes. He knew me well enough to expect my melancholy mood. "It'll be all right, Joe," he commented between flexes of his jaw, his eyes still on the horizon.

"I know."

As he nodded, I could see his mouth pull into a half smile. "I'm thinking about Guy," he admitted – which surprised me.

"Mother," I confessed.

He nodded again, smiled again, still not looking at me. He capped his canteen, lobbed it over his shoulder, and began to stretch his thighs as I had done. I re-opened my canteen and relished water's cool refreshment as it passed my lips, swirled in my mouth, and ran down my throat. I noticed for the first time that day, the freshness of the breeze and sweet smells of grass, dew and wildflower. Then – for a moment – just standing there – I felt as if I might cry.

Here I was, Joe Wheeler Bruce – *Pike* – standing on God's green earth in this enlightened age – upon the soil of our world's newest and most idealistic nation – embarked upon an epic adventure – another soul at my side with whom I shared this same vision. And in that moment I realized not only the many facets of human destiny, but that destiny always requires a destination. Today I was seizing both destiny and destination – not on some vague and unrealized tomorrow – not on a checklist of preparation – but on this very day.

Then Lester turned from the horizon and looked at me. When sunlight sparkled in his very blue eyes, I saw, for a moment, not Lester, but Guy. I heard maybe what the Chicken Lady had heard. I felt life's ironies. I felt time. I felt man's quest for adventure and need for freedom. Then as quickly as I'd seen Guy in Lester's eyes, those blue eyes sparkling in morning's sun once again belonged to my good friend Lester. I smiled, more to myself than at him, capped my jug, and slung it over my shoulder.

I drew a breath and let out a banshee's cry. Lester jerked back so abruptly that he nearly lost his balance. I laughed, drew another breath and whooped again. I put foot to pedal and lunged forward.

Cattle, horses, deer, antelope – maybe even the hills, must have thought we were crazy. Lester was right behind me screaming and shouting as loud as I was. We laughed and pedaled for all we were worth into destiny's rolling hills that lie before us. This was it. Every turn of our crank and spin of our wheels was bringing us closer to places we'd never been before, things we'd never seen.

Like horizons, destiny had always seemed before us. But now as we were embarked, I'd come to realize destiny is something that can never be realized if its significance isn't grasped in its attaining.

Here.

Right now.

This day.

This breath.

And destiny is something else. On this day it was the leaving behind of who I was, of childhood, of innocence – to purpose, to risk, to who I would come to be. Had I not felt so exhilarated, I may have wept at childhood's final molting. As we rode, I felt it fall in pieces behind me upon the gently curving, sometimes ascending, sometimes descending, always rutted road.

I never once turned to see it pass or watch it fade from view behind me.

Chapter 9

The Path More-or-Less Traveled

By spring of 1916, it appeared Mr. Ford had indeed made good on his promise to build a million more Model Ts. As our day warmed, the North and South Road began to fill with dozens of Model Ts, not to mention Reos, Packards, Cadillacs, Oldsmobiles, and Studebakers. They chugged past us on uphill pulls and careened past us on downhills, coasting along with backfires that discharged like gunshots from their tailpipes.

Lester and I had traveled this road many times to increase our stamina and strength. We'd learned that motorcar tires falling into ruts or tires climbing out of ruts would cause an automobile to suddenly lurch whatever direction said ruts happened to fling it. It seemed to Lester and me, such flinging tended to be in our general direction.

Agility and quick departures into grass and gullies alongside the road had been key to our survival when encountering – either from ahead or behind – as many as 20 automobiles an hour! Today was no different. It seemed as soon as one motorcar disappeared behind us, another appeared heading toward us. Travelers coming from behind passed us just as often.

When the road became too busy with motorcars nipping at our rear tires or bouncing happily toward us, Lester and I simply stopped and pulled our bicycles from the roadway. Mankind, it seemed, had developed great affection for a motorcar's speed, although not nearly so much for control of their machines. Consideration of other motorists seemed hardly a thought, and drivers cared nary a whit for bicyclists. It would be fair to say that the motorcar's proliferation had been as straightforward and purposeful as the motorists' use of it had been joyously haphazard. Lester and I had therefore decided it wise to wait out surges of traffic from the roadside, in fear of, or maybe more accurately, in anticipation of, head on collisions – of which we did not want to become entangled or entombed.

Motorists – if you will pardon my rant – fully believed the road was their exclusive domain – and by that, I mean *each motorist* believed it was his. Highways were essentially lawless domain and motorists oft as vilified as Jesse James, Billy the Kid, or any other variety of scoundrel. Popular assessment of motorists was that they were careless, soulless, and hell-bound – opinions I found not entirely without merit. Although I believed motorcars to be wonderful inventions, I understood the preceding generation's lament over lost days of horse, buggy, and more courteous times.

But without a modern-day Wyatt Earp to corral and tame such scoundrels, when outnumbered, roadside was the best place for a cyclist if he preferred to avoid imminent death.

Lester and I arrived in Denver, limbs intact, with our hardest day of pedaling now behind us. The relatively flat great plains were next, endless, monotonous, hot and dry. We chose not to think about it as we treated ourselves to a clean, soft bunk at Denver's new downtown Y.M.C.A.

Tuesday morning we awoke early from our comfortable night and quickly downed a bowl of oatmeal in the cafeteria. We were mounted up and rolling while the sun was yet a glorious orange glow forming on the eastern horizon.

There is nothing quite as sacred as a sleeping city: empty roadways and comforting sounds of humanity and commerce coming to life. Feeling as though I were in church more so than upon the road, I relished them all as last goodbyes to our known world. Our tires rolled over Denver's streets, mixtures of cobbles, brick, gravel and dirt – almost noiseless – and ourselves wordless – as all things sacred ought be beheld.

Rows of fine buildings and proper downtown boarding houses became neighborhoods of cramped homes and narrow lodging establishments squeezed together. As we neared city limits, those gave way to far less worthy structures scattered about. They in turn gave way to corrals, barns, and farmhouses. We traveled steadily northeastward along roadways sparsely marked with Colorado's version of the Lincoln Highway's official red, white and blue signs.

Signage for the great highway had become an issue by that spring of 1916. The Good Roads Movement and the great state of Colorado had come to an impasse over the movement's sanction. Colorado had reportedly failed to provide roadways that lived up to Good Roads standards. Their rift was compounded by the independent and somewhat unrepentant western pioneer spirit that permeated Colorado's capital.

Subsequently, relations between Good Roads and Colorado had become as rough and impassable as a mountain road mired in spring's thaw. Lincoln Highway signs emblazoned with blue and red bold bars with a giant L in the center had been removed from Colorado by Good Roads officials. Unfortunately, along with them disappeared helpful mileage indicators and arrows directing motorists to adjacent towns. Colorado, as the independent and unrepentant are apt to do, then erected their own signage bearing the same name and likeness as official signage – sans helpful footnotes.

Issues of adequate signage would be compounded, other travelers had warned us, across the nation, by a generally sign-less situation. Vandals, it seemed, routinely appropriated any sort of roadway signage for home construction and/or target practice. And if not for those purposes, then out of pure spite. Frontier lawlessness was not a quality entirely reserved for gunslingers, villains, or motorists. However odd it seemed, a handyman in search of quality steel was the primary nemesis of any and all Lincoln Highway signage.

Old guidebooks had provided Lester and me with enough knowledge that we felt confident navigating Colorado's unofficial loop of the Lincoln Highway as it headed northeast of Denver – whether with signage or not. We would eventually intersect the official great highway in Big Springs Nebraska. How lost could we get?

As we rode, structures of any kind eventually petered out to quiet country lanes that paralleled the South Platte. Loneliness, even with Lester at my side, began to find its way into my soul. There, it conversed with fears that had kept me awake for an hour or more amidst Lester's snoring the previous night.

Nature provides no finer sound than that of birdsong. Marshland and groves of cottonwoods along the high-running Platte River concealed many thousands of birds that while mostly invisible, were nonetheless greeting the day's morning sun and favorable blue skies with joyous celebration. As we rode, sensations of freedom chased loneliness from my soul. My burden grew light and youth's natural courage caused my fears to retreat back into darkness and lonely hours where fears ought to dwell.

As much as I would have liked our journey to be all birdsong and morning cool under a perpetually rising sun, the Colorado spur of the great highway soon became a monotonous, unattainable horizon. Waves of grassland and brush stretched for unknown miles ahead of us. In the day's stillness and building heat, our breaths, travel of tires, and rotation of chains became the only sounds.

Miles became meaningless as each mile we put behind us revealed one more ahead. There was nothing to mark our progress but waves of rolling grassland and sagebrush that looked like all previous waves of rolling grassland and sagebrush we'd left behind.

While Lester and I had gabbed quite profusely and excitedly on our first day of travel, the present stillness around us had caused us to fall silent. When we stopped to drink and relieve ourselves, it was with sparsest conversation. "How far have we ridden?" I asked as Lester righted himself from checking his cyclometer.

"Not far enough." Lester smiled, a spark of maturity flickered in his eye, telling me – *patience, Joe.*

I bent backwards, rolled my neck and listened to popping tendons. On this particular stretch of road, miles traveled did not equal progress and of this, we had both been fully aware. The road was comprised of mile-long section lines that ran either east-to-west or north-to-south, doubling miles a straight road would have provided. Add to that inconvenience, our invariable debates at section line intersections of where and when to turn. Lester's unspoken, *patience, Joe,* repeated itself in my mind many times.

Several miles of left/right turns later, we came upon an intersection so sparsely traveled that it actually lacked ruts. Its few scant tracks were windblown, their recentness indistinguishable. Lester began to thumb through his guidebook. I was trying my best to push fears of being hopelessly lost back into darkness. How far would we have to backtrack if we'd taken a wrong road? Did we have enough water? *This* is Colorado's version of the Great Lincoln Highway? I totally understood Good Roads' disappointment. This muddle of section lines was not by any means a respectable attempt at a highway.

When Lester looked up from his book, peered left, then right, forward, then backward, I realized the worst had befallen us. As prairie dogs watched curiously from their holes, I dug in my trousers, produced the compass Irvin had gifted me, popped its cover and oriented it north. North was the failsafe direction at this point in our travels as any route north would eventually intersect the nationwide east-west road.

Lester drew a breath, looked north, then again at the faint tracks on which we stood, released his breath and twisted his face. After this last survey of our situation, he pointed toward a distant patch of trees. "I'll bet there's a homestead over in that windbreak. If it's all the same to you, I think we ought to stop and ask directions."

Having feared Lester might be the sort whose pride would result in refusal to ask directions and whose determination might just as well take us to Oregon as New York, I exclaimed, *"Halleluiah!"*

Lester's response was a quite skilled imitation of Irvin's beneath-the-brow look of consternation complete with his annoying pointed eyebrow. This gave us both a hearty laugh. We began to pedal toward the distant windbreak where hopefully, we would come upon a homestead where we could glean some desperately needed direction.

Spittle flew from his mouth as he spoke, or more accurately harangued, shotgun in one hand, his other flailing about as if caught in a tempest. Nearly as much salt and pepper hair grew out his nose and ears as from his chin. He was foul of temperament, foul of smell, and foul of language. *"I have me the right to keep dadblamed infernal motorcars away from my horses and herds.*" His protest, while impassioned, failed to answer Lester's innocent inquiry of which road might lead us back to the Lincoln Highway – or if we might still be on it.

Since I had yet to observe a herd of anything but prairie dogs, I glanced around the rancher's junk and trash strewn barnyard. I observed one emaciated cow standing beneath a couple broken and diseased trees. Another chewed at a low sod home – or shed – I couldn't be sure. Perhaps on Colorado's eastern plains, a herd of cattle was defined differently than I'd come to understand it.

I listened aptly to the rancher's tirade concerning motorcars and their drivers with the kind of attention that speakers with shotguns in their hands tend to command. Above us, a crow taunted from a shack's rusted tin roof – its cawing similar to the scraggly old man's harangue – and its logic, comparable.

As the homesteader's tirade continued, he built up more steam, prompting our increased attention on his shotgun. Then, quite by chance, I happened to observe a collection of rusted official Lincoln Highway signs complete with their helpful arrows and distance annotations some thirty odd feet behind him. The nut had apparently stolen them and then to compensate him for his trouble, had used them as patches on a shed – or house – I couldn't be sure. I nudged Lester and inclined my head.

"*Country folk should rightly never have to encounter such machines upon our slice of turf,*" the lunatic huffed. "*My cattle and horses are scared witless by the goddamn infernal motorcar's backfires.*"

As Lester leaned to peer at the signs, I glanced at the lone horse in sight. Its ribs protruded so that they cast shadows upon its dusty brown mange. If it horse could hear – *which I doubted* – it didn't look to have enough gumption to be frightened.

"*...and as if backfires wasn't bad 'nough, the dadblamed fools honk fer no reason other than to honk. An' I didn't ask for them to wave. I don't know them an' don't want to.*"

Lester's head was now about sideways as he tried to determine an answer to his query from repurposed signs, none of which had been affixed right end up, which crossroads we might have come upon.

According to the rancher, drivers of motorcars, are invariably wretches of questionable lineage. In addition, they are evil and as far as he was concerned, deserving of eternal hellfire.

Then, quite inadvertently, he let slip the information we'd requested. *"I didn't ask for no dadblamed highway to come past my place an' I ain't gonna have it!"*

Bingo.

With one look between us as the rancher took to restoring breath he had forfeited during his tirade; Lester and I began to back away slowly. Lester thanked the man profusely – for what – I could not be certain. I suspect Lester's outpouring of gratitude had something to do with the shotgun. We mounted our bicycles and headed north as quickly as we possibly could.

Eventually there would be another sign, and if not, northward in one, two or three-mile increments of left/right turns would be our path as we were not likely inclined to ask directions of a prairie homesteader again.

Chapter 10

House Call

Beep, beep, beep, went the horn from such a distance behind us that it seemed ridiculous. The horn itself was barely audible and the Model T it emitted from, hardly visible.

As it neared, we found at the wheel of this particular motorcar, a lad that looked to be about eleven years of age. Bouncing about in the back seat was a fairly rotund man with a handlebar mustache. One hand was upon his bowler and the other, white-knuckled, clutching the seatback of his diminutive driver.

"Out of the way," the child shouted as he overtook us, his hand still working the horn's rubber bulb. This seemed redundant in that Lester and I had already vacated the single lane roadway.

Neither driver nor passenger so much as glanced our direction as they passed. The child was nearly standing in order to exert his entire strength upon the wheel. And if I may, no doubt to be able to reach the pedals as well.

The well-dressed man whose bouncing about in the back seat had been discernable even at a distance, was of a strangely unafraid countenance, as if such manner of transport was routine. But then again, he may well have been preoccupied and in deep conversation with the Lord above, as folks who might become airborne at any moment are apt to be. And if the rotund man should suddenly be propelled from his seat and meet his Maker halfway, I further suspect the large man's departure would not be noticed by his driver. Therefore, the soulless but well-dressed body would lie in the road until an unsuspecting traveler was to come upon it, look heavenward, and scratch his head.

"Never seen anything like that before," Lester commented as we watched the comical sight grow small in the distance.

"Nope. Me either."

"What do you suppose the emergency is?"

I considered the bouncing man's portliness. "Lunch time?"

"Could be."

We wheeled our bicycles from the grassy side of the road into the ruts that would allow us to ride side by side, put our feet upon the pedals, and continued on our way. Several miles later, we nearly failed to notice the Model T now parked in front of a tidy farmhouse and practically concealed by lilacs.

We were nearly past before Lester, his head turned sideways, stopped. I came to a stop a few lengths in front of him and turned full around. Lester was not one to stop without cause.

He inclined his head and raised his arm to point out the motorcar. "I gotta know, Joe."

I shrugged, grateful for any break in the monotony and my posterior, grateful for any break from its seat.

We lifted our steeds from the ruts and headed into the farmyard. Pecking chickens milling about and lazy dogs sleeping in the shade are standard accompaniments for barnyards. Also standard is the barking and rile of those same lazy dogs when strangers have the audacity to step foot in their domain. We were about to be eaten alive or at least torn limb-from-limb when the young driver of the T rose from the weeds, called out to the dogs and commanded, if not their calm, at least their retreat. The boy approached us through the agitated, circling, still vigilant dogs, his hands cupped around a squirming bright green grasshopper whose legs and head were at present attempting escape between the child's fingers. The boy looked at our packed bicycles, then warily at us.

Lester gestured toward the dogs. "Thanks for…"

A ghastly scream came from a screened window of the farmhouse, closely followed by a second ghastly scream and then a third.

Brown juice squirted out from between the boy's fingers, whereupon he cursed and flung the squirming grasshopper toward the chickens. They descended upon the snack with a great rustle of

69

feathers and commotion of clucking. The boy proceeded to wipe his hand on his trousers. "What do you want?"

Lester looked back at the farmhouse window as I edged my hand toward the pack that held our pistol. Clearly, the Model T's haste had been due to their lateness to the murder now in progress. To this fact, Lester seemed oblivious and I, determined not to become a victim.

Lester countered the lad's question with a gesture toward the house. "What's going on?"

"Baby comin'. What do you want?"

"Wanted to know what the hurry was."

"I tol' you. Baby comin'." The boy threw his arms out and rolled his eyes impatiently.

Lester ignored the lad's impertinence. "So, the man in the back seat was a doctor?"

"And coroner and mayor and sometimes the postmaster."

"You his son?"

"Chauffeur."

Lester raised his eyebrows and turned to find my eyebrows raised as well.

"You're in what, sixth grade? How in tarnation are you a chauffeur?"

"Will be in the sixth-grade next year. Doc can't drive a motorcar worth a darn an' can't start one neither."

A protracted moan of ever-increasing volume began to come from the home.

"Came across the doctor one day cursing an' spitting turnin' the crank and goin' back an' forth to the throttle an' choke an' about to blow a vessel when I showed him how to do it. He asked me if I knew how to drive 'cause he was none to fond a that aspect of motorcars neither. I said I thought I could figure it out. I might'a shaved a couple gears smooth, but I got him around the block. He hired me on the spot. Been his driver ever since." The boy raised his brown stained hand and rubbed his fingers together. "Got to have the touch and I got the touch."

Two more bloodcurdling screams turned our heads.

"Where are you two headed?" the boy asked as if nothing of concern was going on inside the home.

"New York City," Lester answered distractedly, still looking at the farmhouse.

The boy burst into laughter. "New York City! That's a hoot."

We blinked.

"Oh." The boy's head pulled back. "You're serious."

"Absolutely."

"Well, I'll be."

The gentle baying cry of a newborn carried from the open window — to my great relief — as I had not been entirely convinced that a murder had not been in progress.

"The doctor normally don't do birthing but this one was breaching an' the midwife was havin' trouble an' they had a telephone, so..." the boy trailed off. "I sure would like to see me New York City someday. Ain't that gonna be one hell of a ride?"

I smiled wryly.

It already was.

Chapter 11

The Laws of Physics

The Milky Way stretched from horizon to horizon, its countless stars sparkling across a pitch-black sky. Lester and I lay upon a patch of grass we'd tromped down to be our mattress. On this second day of travel, good and tired described my body. I could not find words to describe my mind's state. And truth be known, I didn't have enough energy to try.

We'd thought the hilly ride between Colorado Springs and Denver would have been our hardest day. After scaling Monument Hill's 7,300-foot elevation we'd imagined all roads to be downhill from there. Denver was a mile above sea level and it was to sea level that we were headed. That's downhill, right? Today was endless, equally exhausting, and if any part of our ride had indeed been downhill, it hadn't been noticeably downhill.

"We had a good day, one hundred, twelve more miles behind us," Lester commented as much to himself as to the good Lord above – whose presence surrounded us with countless worlds.

I said nothing, any ability to form a word temporarily elusive.

"Our encounter with that cantankerous rancher seems more like something that happened a week ago than a few hours ago."

I would have nodded agreement, but again, lacked adequate fortitude to move my head.

"You all right?"

"I'm afraid that if I close my eyes and fall asleep that I may never wake up again."

Lester laughed. "We're gonna sleep good tonight."

"Or die in our sleep."

Lester laughed again.

A gaggle or flock – who knows what it's called – of bats flopped overhead, silent, creepy, and looking more like crumpled paper caught in a wind than creatures graced by God with flight.

"We're doin' it, Joe."

I would have nodded, but... Hearing a rustle of Lester's bedroll at my side, I could feel Lester's eyes now upon me. I watched a shooting star pierce the night sky. Its trail shimmered a moment, then disappeared. My friend continued to look at the side of my head. "It's like a free fall," I admitted, "once begun, there's no going back."

"Would you want to?"

I smiled. "No." I turned to Lester, even in the dark, able to discern the ever-present sparkle in his eyes.

"I'm glad we're doin' this."

"Me too."

I turned onto my side, feeling the road's rhythms run phantom through my body. All around us stood prairie grass, tall enough to hide us from gunslingers, Indians, or outlaws who might very well travel lonely roads in search of campers asleep at its side. Our mattress this night was nearly soft, albeit a bit lumpy beneath our tarpaulin and bedrolls.

I pulled my blanket tight around my neck and hoped it would stay tight throughout the night. I could deal with a cricket or two, possibly a centipede, maybe even a spider, but the last thing I wanted to wake up next to tomorrow morning was a rattler coiled up in the crook of my legs sharing my body heat – as rattlers are apt to do. My concern was not unwarranted as we'd encountered three of the devils just today. The first two didn't seem to care about our presence but a third had struck repeatedly at us as we passed.

My bedroll was warm and the sun well above the horizon when I stirred, uncertain at first where I was. As my mind assembled pieces of the day before, I rolled from my side onto my back, arched up and raised my arms. I let out a groan adequate to relate the sheer displeasure of stiff muscles forced back to life. Then as my mind sharpened, I recalled my qualms about waking to a snake coiled inside my blanket. I flung my cover aside and scrambled to my feet.

Lester stood twenty paces away from me in the road, looking

blankly back at me. Thinking I'd rather not explain my rattlesnake fears, I wiped a crust of sleep from my eyes. I glanced again at the sun's position, then back at Lester. We should have been riding at dawn. "I let you oversleep," Lester explained. "You needed it." He grinned. "The way you were snoring last night, I dreamt I was sleepin' next to a goddamned lion."

I wobbled a bit, ran my fingers through my hair, decided I needed to pee sooner rather than later, and turned away to unbutton my trousers. I was as stiff and sore as someone who'd endured a beating. I called over my shoulder. "Did you kick me last night?"

"I wanted to."

I laughed. Even that hurt.

Although Lester laughed along with me, he did not deny he'd administered a thrashing, and I was halfway of the mind that he may have, for this morning I hurt in places I didn't know I had.

One hundred miles of progress per travel day had been Lester's plan. Our route and stops had been planned accordingly. Sunday would be our first day of rest. Roughly two hundred miles were already behind us. We had four hundred more before a day of rest. My weary bones grew faint just thinking about it. If we got a tail wind I could *possibly* make it twenty miles today. Then I'd have to see about tomorrow. Given Lester's allowance of an almost two-hour late start on day three, it appeared he may have already realized the folly of his one hundred mile a day plan and abandoned it.

Appearances can be deceiving.

As our day progressed, it seemed to me that I had to pedal in near desperation to keep up with Lester. Lester, in turn, seemed committed to keeping a healthy gap between us regardless of my effort. In jaunts in and about Colorado Springs, he had previously employed this same carrot/stick routine with me anytime he had come of opinion that I was dallying. I knew it well and would have cursed him but he was consistently too far away to hear it.

Salt pork, raisins, and melba toast had been my breakfast. The little bit of moisture I had not sweated out in my exertion to keep up with Lester was trying its best to reconstitute dry nourishment sitting

74

rock-hard in my stomach. It was a hot day and thus far, I was not enjoying it much. Nor did I appreciate the carrot riding ahead of me who turned about every few minutes to confirm that I, apparently its trained jackass, was still in pursuit.

As much as I appreciated the laws of physics, they were about to be rewritten and I, Joe Wheeler Bruce, was going to be their author. When I had had enough of Mister Carrot, I coasted to a stop, dismounted, leaned my bicycle against a fence post, uncapped my canteen and went about a leisurely and long overdue reconstitution of breakfast rations.

I casually looked between Lester's form growing distant, the sun above, and some small yellow birds cavorting about beside me. Lester continued to ride and had done so for at least a couple minutes at a fairly good clip before he turned about to check my progress. I chuckled a little to myself to observe a stunned wobble of his bicycle before he came to a stop. Even with a considerable distance between us, I could see Lester fling his arms out from his sides in dismay.

I waved, using my entire arm so that he could see me.

"Joe!" he yelled angrily.

I waved again.

"JOE! What are you doing?"

I took another leisurely drink and resumed looking at birds.

Lester turned his bike about and took to pedaling.

I waited.

"What do you think you're doing?" Lester demanded as he, nearly breathless, but still able to yell, came to a rather abrupt stop in front of me.

I raised my canteen – as if he could not readily see it – then swallowed. Oh my, was that refreshing.

"It doesn't take five minutes to take a drink, Joe. We have miles to go and I let you sleep in and now…"

"I'm not havin' this."

"What?"

"I'm not havin' this. We're on this trip *together* and we're going to ride *together.*"

Lester's head pulled back as he began to compute Joe Wheeler

75

Bruce's new laws of physics.

Then he rejected them.

"Oh really, *Pike*, captain of the basketball team, are you telling me the way it's going to be – how this trip is going to go?"

"Yep."

"We need to be in Brush by…"

"We don't need to be anywhere but where we are. We've allowed four months for this ride. You are not my boss and I am not going to suffer in order to make you happy."

"My relatives in Detroit are expecting us in nine days. We wrote ahead and gave them dates of our arrival and now…"

"A couple hours here and there isn't going to derail our plan. If we need to make up some miles on another day, we can make them up on another day. If we're late a day, so what? We'll get there. Meanwhile, you can ride *with* me, not ahead of me. I am not going to chase you across this country."

"See if I let you sleep in again."

I lifted both shoulders and tipped my hands out. "Don't recall asking you to."

Lester's eyebrows rose, nearly to his hairline. Then his eyes narrowed, he turned his head aside, and began to nod the kind of slow, measured nod that a new law of physics warrants. Without another word, he turned his bicycle about and waited – his back toward me. I recapped my canteen and slung it over my shoulder. I straddled my machine, put my foot on its pedal and *we* began to ride together in silence.

Due to diligent rehydration, I was out of water by the time we rolled into the next town which was, quite literally, a one-horse town. A lone horse tethered to a rail was the only sign of life in sight as we rode, still not speaking, abreast up Main Street. If there had been a breeze, I'd have expected a solitary tumbleweed to roll across the road in front of us as an eagle shrieked from above. As it was, last fall's tumble weeds were entangled in bunches anywhere a structure or post had provided a catch. The only sound was the creak of decay. An empty water trough, a few hitching posts, and a half-dozen boarded up shops were a silent eulogy for this prairie town. From the looks of it, it had expired well before the enlightened age.

Amazingly, the water pump adjacent to the trough still produced water – although it took a little elbow grease to get it primed. I took my time drinking and refilling my canteen, the horse and I eyeing each other suspiciously. Lester, still a bit aggravated with me, chewed his fingernails as he waited for me from a spot of shade cast by an abandoned building, his eyes looking anywhere but at me.

Motorists had been as rare upon this stretch of road as shade trees or cool breezes, none of which we'd happened upon yet today. So, when a tin lizzie of unknown vintage and brand – *if it had one* – sputtered into town, I was surprised. It rolled up to me, stopped, chugged, rattled, then either died or was shut off – I could not be sure. The town horse showed the whites of its eyes, whinnied, tugged free of the post it had been tied to and trotted away, its reins leaving traces in the road's fine sand as it went.

The conveyance now before me was lashed with luggage, packs, jugs and spare tires as high as it was wide. I might note, it was wider than it was supposed to be. A woman at the wheel and another woman riding shotgun removed their goggles which left an outline of at least a day's worth of grime. Both smiled and rose from their seats. I imagined them to be in their mid-twenties and not so much of an overly feminine or demure nature.

The driver looked around, then inquired, "You the mayor?"

My eyes shifted from the woman to my packed bicycle then, back to the woman. Both women giggled, got out of their motorcar and began to stretch out the cricks and crinks of the road.

Still laughing at her own joke, the first woman looked around while leaning backward, hands on her ample hips. "I'd pack up and leave too. Don't suppose there's any petrol here."

"Don't think they'd know what that was, you know, if you could find anyone to ask."

"How far to the next town with bang bang juice?"

I turned to Lester who had by now decided to mosey this way. As he was keeper of the Cyclometer, he bent, wiped its dial clean and did a calculation in his head. "Twenty miles, give or take."

"Well, we ain't gonna make that." Simultaneously stretching her limbs and arching her back as she walked, the woman went directly to what looked to me to be a pot hanging from the side of her motorcar. She unlashed it, uncapped it, sniffed it, took a moment, I imagine deciding whether or not it might be gasoline, then proceeded to pour its contents into the gas tank – well – mostly, as quite a bit of it ended up on the dirt. One would hope the liquid was indeed gasoline, but considering the vehicle's sorry condition, it might well have been cooking grease.

"That water good?" the other woman asked, pointing at the pump beside me.

I lifted one shoulder. "Fair."

She took to unlashing another vessel of some sort from the side of the vehicle and carried it to the pump.

I looked again at the motorcar that was by now emitting a solid hiss of steam. "Where are you headed?" I considered the state of their conveyance and thought likely not very far.

"Anywhere the wind takes us, hon," the woman splattering petrol on the road as much as pouring it in the tank replied. "Denver today. Maybe Estes Park tomorrow. We're on the right road, correct – or the correct road, right?"

"A few twists and turns and it'll take forever, but yes, correct, you're on the right road."

"They still runnin' them Steamers from Denver up to Rocky Mountain National Park?"

The second woman was working the water pump with her entire body as if she were operating a railroad pump car chimed in. "We saw it advertised in a magazine. It looked like quite the adventure."

I vaguely recalled from our expeditions to Denver, touring cars emblazoned with some sort of advertising that were filled with folks sporting wide brim hats and fancy bonnets as tourists were apt to wear. Remembering the vehicle's unusually quiet operation, I realized they may well have been Steamers. I nodded. "Think so."

"Don't think our gem here could make it up in the Rocky Mountains too far." The woman now smelling of gasoline looked momentarily at our bicycles and packs. "You headed toward the mountains or away from them?"

"Away. Home is in Colorado Springs."

She nodded thoughtfully. "How do you people breathe in that kind of altitude?"

I shrugged.

"Where are you boys headed?"

"New York City."

"I'll be damned." She then shouted at the woman working the pump. "These boys are headed to New York City!"

The woman looked Lester and I up and down, assessed the robustness of our physical stature, concluded our success to be doubtful, made a face, and continued to pump.

"Well best of luck to you, fellow vagabonds. Too bad we're blowing different directions. Well, you terrorize the east coast and we'll get the other." She threw her head back, laughed, then suddenly became serious. "Is Colorado wet or dry?"

I squinted as her inquiry was most likely not about the weather. "Went dry this year."

"Thank the good Lord we thought to bring hooch."

My squint remained as this was not the direction of conversation I expected from a woman. She interpreted my squint as a lack of comprehension.

"Moonshine, firewater, whiskey." She leaned forward and cupped her hand secretively to her mouth. "Don't tell no one but we just love, love, love our hooch."

I looked around. Revealing her secret didn't seem much of a possibility.

She tapped the last drops of gasoline from the pot into the tank. "This stuff is like gold," the woman commented. "And out west in the barrens it's just about as hard to find." She capped the vessel and the tank. "Hope that does it. If not, I suppose we'll be walkin' a ways."

I nodded. "Are you doing this all by yourselves?"

"You mean, where's our man?"

I shrugged.

"Don't need no man. We're armed to the teeth, ornery, and premenstrual. If the Kaiser himself saw us comin' he'd tell his armies

79

to turn tail and head back to the Rhineland."

As both women laughed heartily, the woman at the water pump hefted her vessel and began to lurch unevenly back to their vehicle. I grimaced, hoping we'd not stumbled upon alcoholic suffragettes with bad attitudes and were subsequently about to be shot dead on the street on account of our gender and sobriety.

"Made it this far from Georgia without a man. Hoping to get all the way to San Francisco."

I cleared my throat. "There are a few mountains between here and San Francisco."

"If this baby doesn't make it," the woman patted the motorcar that I wouldn't trust to take me across town, "then we'll go wherever the wind takes us or a horse can tow us."

I looked at their motorcar and noticed it was missing its right rear fender. A crease came to my brow. Having noticed my observation of the missing fender, the woman explained with a wave of her arm. "Not sure where we lost that."

Both women laughed as they stepped over the doors that were missing handles and had therefore been wired shut. They plopped into their seats. The driver handed me the crank. "Mind doin' the honors?"

I didn't have the touch, and Lester knowing that, had already extended his hand. He inserted the crank, took the pistons to maximum compression, backed it off, gave it a kick, and the engine fired up. As he handed the crank back to the lady, he inquired, "I take it you came in on the Lincoln Highway. How's the road?"

"Been on it since Misery..." then thinking we might not know what she was talking about, elaborated, "Missouri." She began to shake her head morosely. "Oh hon, you are in for some mud. We picked up five hundred pounds of the stuff going through Nebraska and it's been falling off in chunks ever since. When you come to a bog, we suggest going overland even if you have to take out a fence or two to do it – which come to think of it, might explain the fender. Anyways, Nebraska mud is axle deep and sticky as cookie dough.

"And if you find our fender along the way, send it parcel post to Vagabond, General Delivery, Windblow, California, or maybe Oops,

Oregon, or possibly, What the Hell?, Washington." The women laughed, put the rig into gear, nudged the throttle and sputtered away. The horse that had lingered at the edge of town, whinnied and trotted off ahead of them – surely never to be found again.

Lester and I had pedaled another five miles or so in silence when he slowed and came to a stop. When I stopped beside him, he was still not ready to look at me and therefore kept his eyes straight ahead. "I've been thinking about those ladies," he admitted more in the vein of thoughtfulness than recollection. "They sure were lighthearted."

"Laughed at just about everything," I confirmed.

"Didn't take anything seriously."

"Sure didn't. Not a thing."

Lester nodded. "Sorry."

I didn't know what to say.

Lester turned to me and smiled a little. "Come on Pike. We'll get as far as we get."

Lester never called me Joe again.

Chapter 12

Circle the Wagons

I saw them as I motored past. Judging by their turned heads, they saw me as well – but then a sight such as a woman like myself presented would have been hard to overlook. They appeared dirty, but more than dirty, tired, and more than tired, beleaguered, as they stood beside their packed bicycles looking forlornly up and down the main street of Julesburg. The day had long since ended and now that prohibition was in effect, every establishment on this side of the state line had closed except the grocery, and that was due to close shortly.

I was myself overdue but something about those two young men and their packed bicycles piqued my curiosity. I slowed, then at the next corner pulled the wheel of my Model T and braced my foot against the sidewall for leverage. As my husband would say – I was lucky to weigh one hundred pounds soaking wet – but the obstinate steering wheel of my trusty T had yet to best me.

Montgomery was used to my flights of fancy. Since this particular hound knew not only the way home, but that it was time to eat, he also knew I had just diverged from two things very important to him. He raised his head from the seat beside me and looked up. "Oh, you'll get your supper." He lowered his head onto his paws that hung over the seat edge and groaned his discontent. "Don't you give me any of your guff." His brows rose and fell rhythmically above his eyes to further express both his displeasure and resign.

By the time I'd come around the block the boys had mounted up and were riding north. Between working the wheel, gears, and throttle I couldn't get my hand on the horn in time to get their attention so I did what any respectable woman would do upon passing strange men in the street, I shouted. Too bad it hadn't been an actual word. My brain was as busy as my hands and just as befuddled, so "Hey" and "You" came out as "Heyouhoo!"

They stopped.

I tried to.

For you see I was towing a bright red stagecoach, the tongue of which was rather haphazardly chained to my rear bumper. I no sooner hit the brakes than I heard the chain rattle. I grimaced. The stagecoach rammed the bumper hard enough to jolt my head back and bring Montgomery up on his haunches. My foot was knocked off the brake and I coasted a bit before I could get the whole works completely stopped.

The boys turned a wide circle in the vacant street, then stopped and looked at me warily. "You all right?" asked the dark-haired young man with striking blue eyes and a week's worth of stubble darkening his jaw line.

"Oh, fine, you know, sudden stop." I waved my hand in the air. Montgomery was on all fours sniffing the air, trying, no doubt, to determine the character of the strangers his crazy mistress was speaking with.

The gangly boy on the other bicycle squinted as he looked repeatedly between me and the bright red stagecoach behind me. "Why are you towing a stagecoach?"

"Read the door."

"Circle the Wagons – camp and hotel?" The boy's eyebrow rose to a peak as his wariness turned into outright suspicion – most likely of my sanity.

"You have a place to stay tonight?" I asked.

The boys looked at one another.

"How about Circle the Wagons. On the house. It looks like you could use some rest and a good meal."

They looked at the stagecoach.

"Not in there. I am the proprietor of a right proper hotel." Then I added a disclaimer. "Albeit a very unusual establishment."

"You have running water, hot and cold?" The dark-haired boy inquired. "We're in terrible need of a bath."

"Showerbaths. Private. Comfortable mattresses. Clean sheets. No bugs. No mice. Lots of cats. One hound. Very few raccoons. An occasional skunk. Just me and my husband to contend with. And you'll be lulled to dreamland by a veritable symphony of crickets and frogs."

"How far?"

"Half mile. Double your money back if not satisfied."

"I thought you said it was on the house."

"Double it. Oh, what the heck, ten times back if not satisfied." I laughed. They smiled. "Follow me." I waved my arm, put her in gear. The boys faced each other and lifted their shoulders.

It had rained the night before so the boys weren't choking on my dust as they followed me into the farmyard paradise I'd created. I'd arranged one Conestoga, a single shepherd's wagon, three stagecoaches and two teepees along the slow-running stream that meandered through the windbreak of huge cottonwoods. These migratory dwellings were everything I could collect of those who'd crossed and lived upon this land before me.

"My husband humors me," I explained as I got out and Montgomery jumped down behind me, trotted over to the boys and began sniffing them. "I told my man before I married him that I'd be a farmer's wife only if I didn't have to act like one. Wasn't gonna do canning or have me a brood of children so he'd better marry for love and not labor and we agreed." A few dozen cats stared at us from anywhere a feral cat could hide but still see what was going on. "Take your pick. I think you'd like the Conestoga. Sleeps four end-to-end if you aren't too tall and don't mind playing footsie. It fits two easy and gives ya room to stretch out."

The gangly boy with ears like saucers and splotches of red/brown whiskers interspersed with a couple pimples continued to look around. I strode briskly past them toward the wagon. They propped their bicycles against one another rather than lay them on the ground.

I added over my shoulder as I walked, "Showerbaths are on the back porch of the farmhouse. We have a toilet but guests use the two-seaters, of which there are four on the other side of the stream, downwind." I waved my arms to indicate the entirety of my rustic campground. "Don't you just love this?"

I chanced a glance over my shoulder and caught a glimpse of their doubtful expressions. I'd seen this look on many a guest who'd later become entranced, so I ignored it. They too, would come to understand and appreciate the character of the unusual.

Upon reaching the Conestoga, I climbed a couple wooden steps and opened the plank door my husband had installed at the rear of the canvas hood. I entered, the fabric's white glow enveloping me. The boys followed, then stood with heads bent to the side beneath the swayback canopy. Narrow mattresses ran along both sides, each with a comfy feather pillow. The head of the wagon had the amenity of a screened window. The board arch above it was graced with a portrait of Abraham Lincoln.

Between bunks I'd inserted a nightstand complete with a Bible and kerosene lantern to see by.

"I'm Erstine." I thrust my hand out.

"Joe."

"Lester."

"Where you from, Joe and Lester?"

"Colorado Springs."

"Long ride. Where are you headed?

"New York City."

I blinked. "No kidding?"

"Nope."

I found I couldn't shut my mouth, nor could I quit staring at one, then the other. "That's absolutely remarkable."

When they shrugged and smiled, I couldn't help but fall in love with them. Humility is my favorite virtue, mainly, I suspect, since the good Lord above hadn't blessed me with much. Audacity and a knack for tasteful decoration had been my gifts. So far I'd like to think I'd made the good Lord proud every day of my life, and God willing, every day yet to come.

"I'd hoped the Lincoln Highway would have come through Julesburg and not through Big Springs since Julesburg had been a stage hub once upon a time. Alas, pride and politics got in the way and Colorado insisted the road go all the way to Denver if it entered the state. Unfortunately, a several hundred-mile detour isn't what folks expect on a transcontinental highway, so that didn't work out so well. Since I wasn't about to have done all this for nothing, I tow the old stage up to Big Springs and steal their borders every chance I get – not that I was doin' that today. Had to run an errand and didn't feel like unhitching the damn thing. So, what do you think?"

"About what?"

"You want to stay here tonight?"

Both boys shyly smiled.

I'd expected my boarders to be up and at my kitchen table shortly after dawn. The grandfather clock was striking its sixth chime as I pulled back the window's lace curtains. Their packed bicycles were still leaned against the side of the old wagon. My husband had long since gone out to work in the fields.

The boys had been awful tired after I'd fed and conversed with them an hour or so. With their eyelids hanging they'd pleaded for mercy and hobbled off to bed at last light. I smiled to myself to consider their likely weariness, pulled a box of waxed paper from the shelf and began to wrap the breakfast I'd prepared for them.

My first rapping at the door of the Conestoga was greeted with silence, the second with a series of creaks and groans, and the third with the hoarse and raspy speech of first awakening. "Pike, get the hell up! We overslept!"

When I heard feet land upon the floor, I stepped down a couple steps and stood back. A moment later the door flew open with Lester in its wake, his hair standing all directions, naked from the waist up, and as angry as he was groggy. "Oh, hello Ma'am. Sorry for the language."

I tipped my hand out – having expected nothing less.

He bobbed a moment. "I apologize, but I got to…" He pointed away, quickly descended the steps and disappeared around the far side of the wagon. As I stood forlornly listening to his relief, Joe took his place in the doorway – puffy-eyed, staggering, pillow wrinkles on his flushed face. He bobbed in the open doorway as he rubbed one eye and then the other.

"Mornin'."

"Good morning."

The young man listened a moment to Lester's relief, held up a finger, then staggered down the steps. He held onto the wheel of the wagon to steady his progress and disappeared the same direction as his friend.

I chuckled softly to myself and bent to scratch Montgomery's ears – as his curiosity had drawn him to make an inquiry. Then not to be out-scented – he lifted a leg for some relief of his own. I looked at the brightening sky, then a bird, then scratched Montgomery again before the water works finally went dry and the boys reappeared.

"Sorry," Lester apologized again. "I know that wasn't proper."

"But apparently very necessary."

"Oh yes Ma'am."

Joe rubbed both eyes again, wobbled, and smiled shyly.

"I packed your breakfast." I raised the wrapped meal I'd prepared.

"Oh, thank you, Ma'am. We've got to get on the road. We need to be in North Platte by tonight. We have a general delivery waiting for us at the post office there."

"Miles to go." I smiled the kind of comforting smile that middle years and its accumulated wisdom allows a woman to smile.

"Thank you for the night's sleep. It was real nice."

"You're welcome. Glad you slept well. Glad to be able to offer you help you along your journey."

"Well, I suppose we better get dressed." Lester motioned at his bare chest. "Sorry. I know this isn't proper."

I laughed and waved my hand at the boys. Then as Lester edged past me and put his foot on the step of the Conestoga, I blurted out the thought I had been reluctant to offer. "You know, crossing Nebraska is endless and depending on the rains, the road is every bit like a slog through wet concrete. Ain't nothing to see nor a town worth a dang in forever plus a day. I've been thinking that you two could stay here through Monday morning and get rested up for the week ahead before you took off."

The heads of both boys pulled back.

"You aren't gonna get anywhere by Sunday and then you'll be

87

taking the Lord's Day of rest in some farmer's field getting eaten by flies and mosquitoes and that just isn't something I'd look forward to, personally, that is."

"We can't afford…"

"I didn't say anything about money. It's called hospitality and I already talked it over with my man at breakfast this morning. As you may suspect, the poor man humors all my whims. We'd like to be part of what you're doing and getting you good and rested before you cross Nebraska is what we can do."

"We surely appreciate the offer," Lester began, "but we have miles to go and…"

"Can I show you something?"

Lester stopped mid-sentence, looked at Joe, then back at me and shrugged.

A vine had found its way up the massive front wheel of the Conestoga and had wound itself from there to the axle and then to the rough wood of the wagon bed. I pulled its tendrils loose and unwrapped the woody creepers enough for the boys to see the recessed panel just behind the axle. I stood aside as they leaned in. "Lenore, eighteen forty-two," Lester read aloud.

"Horatio, eighteen forty-three," Joe added. "Agnes, eighteen forty-four."

Lester brushed aside a spider's web and squinted. "Baby Hubbard, eighteen thirty-nine."

"There's eight names and dates there," I said softly. "We're not too far from what used to be the Oregon trail. People were born, lived and died on that trail. Whereas it might take us hours or days to get where we want to be, it took them seasons. If truth be known, the unmarked graves of settlers and explorers lie all along the road you're about to travel."

The boys looked only a little longer at the carving on the panel, then stood aright.

"Why did you show us that?" Lester asked.

I smiled. "Every Saturday afternoon, long about three in the afternoon, we put aside all the work we have to do. Our guests here in the circle as well as our friends from town gather together at the house. Some weeks it's quite a crowd. We usually end up with a square dance caller, a couple banjos, a six string or two, an accordion for sure, and sometimes a horn. The men pick up the piano and bring it out on the porch. I can play Ragtime like a fiend, but it's also a player and we have all kinds of cylinders. We dance and sing and stomp and clap and eat and laugh right on up to the middle of the night. At midnight we pack it all up. Then when the Lord's Day has begun, we lower our heads, and say a prayer of thanks for the week of work behind us and the joy of music, friendship and laughter."

Both boys said nothing.

"You're welcome to join us tomorrow if you'd like, you know, if you decide to stay." I winked, patted Lester on the back, then began to step through the growth of weeds and grass as I started back around the wagon.

Lester repeated himself. "You didn't answer my question. Why did you show us this on the wagon?"

I didn't look back, only replied over my shoulder. "Make of it what you will." I continued to the house.

Over the sound of my footfalls, I heard Joe read, "Marlin, eighteen-forty."

They'll do with it what they will.

We all do.

Chapter 13

Treachery

Nebraska – my God, what a mess. The motorcar we'd just pushed free of a bog of ankle-deep mud was happily sputtering away with its occupants' arms waving both goodbye and appreciation. We watched it roll down the road dripping black ooze and flinging dollops of mud high into the sky.

Although Lester and I waved in return, he glowered as the motorcar grew distant on the road, shook his head, and looked over at me. His clothing was as mud-splattered and soaked as mine. He began to lift his leg to step out of the bog when I heard a sucking sound. His shoe had stayed where it was as his foot pulled free of it. I braced myself for a tirade and turned aside lest the tirade involve a slinging of mud as tirades in ankle-deep mud were apt to do.

"Mud! Mud! Mud!" Lester shouted at no one in particular – except maybe at the good Lord above – as he'd been registering his unhappiness with the Lord's green earth and the rains that made it so, for nigh on three consecutive days.

His glower turned toward me. I may have *known* better than to laugh, but that didn't stop me.

It was then that a large sling of mud assaulted the only part of me not already covered in mud (which was technically only the whites of my eyes – so maybe I should be more specific) the only part of me not already *layered* in mud.

Motorcar fenders, it should be noted, are a little light on gratitude. They are not at all designed to provide protection to pushers kind enough to free them and their connected assemblage from the muck that, it seemed, comprised the entire Nebraska roadway system. Torrents of splatter produced by tires as they spun free of the muck that said pusher had been kind enough to dislodge them from were happily dispensed head-to-toe on said pusher without remorse. Of this I'd made note and fully intended to speak with Mr. Ford regarding this issue should we encounter him upon our arrival in Detroit.

When Lester bent to dig about in the mud to retrieve his shoe, I, still laughing, scooped up a handful of muck and slogged him back. We were both laughing as we trudged, weighing a full fifty pounds more than we had this morning, toward the Platte River where we were to baptize ourselves for the second time this day.

"Hey John," Lester invoked the name of the Baptist, then pointed at a circling of white doves above us.

I laughed as those particular doves were more likely to anoint *on* us rather than *descend* upon on us. I wasn't at all sure if the Spirit of God or a voice from Heaven was going to occur regardless of the scenario.

"Immersion or sprinkling?" Lester asked.

"Immersion."

We both laughed as we fought our way through the reeds and willows to wade into the slow-moving, bone-chilling baptismal waters of the Platte. It seemed the snow melt that fed it was determined to keep its temperature in spite of the day's heat – not that the frigid water's cooling was altogether unwelcome.

We were waist deep in water and splashing as we rinsed and scrubbed when Lester suddenly inclined his ear toward the road, held his hand out and put a finger to his lips. I watched his eyes shift from one side to the other a couple times. Then I heard it too.

The distinctive creak of a wooden wagon, snorts, hoof falls, and a steady ting of pans swinging into each other drifted our way from the road. Our bicycles along with all of our worldly possessions were leaned against a cottonwood only mere feet from the roadway. "We looked down the road," Lester complained as he trudged briskly through the water toward shore. I was directly behind him, neither of us fully cleansed of our sins.

"We did," I confirmed. We thrashed through the willows of the shallows with frogs jumping clear of us.

91

Two immense oxen stood patiently before the plank-sided wagon they'd been pulling. It was as decrepit, overloaded, and generally nasty-looking as its occupants who had vacated its disarray to surround our packed bicycles. Their hands had already loosed the straps on several packs and lifted the flaps when Lester and I, breathless, cleared the brush. Their greedy eyes met our eyes which were as incensed and fearful as theirs were vile and treacherous.

Gypsies! And if not gypsies, then rascals. And if not rascals, then pure outlaws. And if not pure outlaws, then confederates still waging war – as the battle flag of General Robert E. Lee – tattered, faded, filthy, and no doubt from the war itself – hung limply from a stick just to the rear of the wagon's driver's seat.

This was danger, pure and simple and the gun we'd brought for our protection against such evil was not in our hands but in a pack, the strap of which was in the hand of a man as gaunt and gray and straggly and emaciated as a man could be this side of being a corpse.

"What do you think you're doing?" Lester demanded as I came up to his side.

"Well, we just found..." began a woman, middle of years, short on hygiene, and as immense in girth as the oxen.

"You didn't *find* anything," Lester snapped, his momentary halt, now a forward march as bold as Sherman's assault and the scoundrels' retreat just as quick as his drive. At this moment, everything about Lester was nothing less than fierce and his advance successfully accomplished their rout. "What do you have in your hand there? Give it." The fingers of Lester's outstretched hand beckoned toward something grasped in the hands of a girl of about ten years age. She was ragged, smudged with filth, red hair askew in all directions who, while in retreat, was yet defiant in eye.

"I found this." She clutched it tighter and held it to her chest.

"Pike, get the gun."

I'd just pulled the second strap free on the pack the old man had been at and pulled the Colt from its contents. The instant I got it turned around, its barrel was even with my eye, the hammer cocked, and my finger was on the trigger.

The woman of great girth was going to be the first to go as a charge from her would likely turn the tide. The old man would be next – and that order was based just on the general principal that anyone who resembled a corpse as much as he, should commit one way or the other and since he had yet to decide, I was more than willing to choose for him.

The girl continued to clutch whatever it was that she had in her hands when the wagon creaked and a curtain at the rear of the rolling tenement opened to reveal what was damn near the biggest man I'd ever seen – fully bearded, pink of face, and great of gut. He snorted just as a bull would at the color red and put one foot down on the step. I raised the gun skyward and fired a shot.

He froze and remained that way as my barrel was now aimed at the heart of a threat far more dangerous than the others. Even if it would likely take the remaining five bullets to stop him, the expenditure of lead would be well spent.

"Now hold on," the corpse began, his sole hand outstretched along with a stub where the other ought to have been. "Now we don't need to take to shootin'. We just come acrost these here bicycles layin' in the road an' picked 'em up for y'all."

"Don't think that was the case," Lester corrected, "but I don't see any point in arguing. Give back what you *found* and you can be on your way and we can be on ours."

A curtain pulled back from an opening meant to be a window on the side of the wagon. The double barrel of a shotgun protruded from it, aimed at yours truly. I swallowed, not at the specter of death, but at the wretched woman whose eye was squinted at the other end of the barrel. Even in the dark shadows of the wagon, she was a visage so abhorrent that I was grateful the light of day had chosen not to reveal her.

I changed the order and allotment of bullets by turning the barrel to a point just north of the hag's squinted eye. The next bullet was to be inserted between the giant man's eyes. I would go from there to whoever moved next. I was as fast with a gun as I was with a basketball and every bit as accurate.

"I see we have a stand-off." Lester spoke with reason rather than anger in his tone, nonetheless adamant. "Give us what you *found* and you can be on your way. Nothing to be gained for any of us by any other outcome."

"Bessie," the old man barked sharply, "give them what you found and get back in the wagon."

The girl flung what turned out to be a shaving kit onto the ground, snarled hatefully, then squeezed around the big man who remained motionless, one foot still on the step and the other inside the wagon.

As the great, huge woman who had thankfully not yet charged us, began to back away at the urging of her man's stub arm, Lester pointed at her. "What's that around your neck?"

The only thing clean enough to have caught the sun continued to glisten, but only until her round, filthy hand clasped it tightly. "That's a locket from my dear mother. Don't you…"

"That's Pike's compass. Take it off."

"I will not…"

"*Myrtle*," the corpse commanded.

With that the woman ripped it from her neck, the chain breaking in two places, flying in sparkling arcs through the air. The instant the brass case hit the ground it was covered in tobacco spit. She wiped her chin, the whiskers upon it continued to hold the juice that even now seeped downward from the corners of her toothless mouth. The woman turned, and with a great heaving of flesh that made her buttocks look like two bison in a tussle, waddled back to the wagon. The springs gave and wood creaked as she ascended to the seat and plopped down upon it.

"We was jus' tryin' to be neighborly," the old man lied, turned and followed his woman muttering to himself.

The big man lifted his foot from the step and disappeared behind the curtain.

I kept my aim on the window and shotgun barrel that remained extended from it. The oxen took up the slack of their harness. The wagon's great wheels began to turn in the muddy ruts. As the beasts came into the same stride as a lazy man's walk, the pans, buckets, and junk festooned to the sides of the wagon began to clang together. I held the gun shoulder high and aimed until the sound grew distant and the wagon was small in my view.

My eyes, not having blinked for several minutes now, burned as I closed them. I lowered the gun and eased the hammer back to home. After I'd rubbed and moistened my eyes, I opened them to find Lester staring down the road until the wagon disappeared around a bend. "We need to be more careful."

I nodded, not that he saw me, as his eyes remained on the empty road.

"I've done my share of pushing motorcars out of mud this week. We aren't stopping again – I don't care what it is."

I nodded, then as I bent to pick up the shaving kit, I considered the irony of its theft by a man, woman and child that had no use for it. I looked over at the compass, glistening not from its brass, but from saliva and tobacco. I attempted to swallow my gag while I debated its retrieval.

Lester picked up the broken strands of chain, then pulled his wet handkerchief from his wet trousers and recovered the compass. As he wiped it as clean as he could. "Don't think they were ever going to go the right direction regardless of knowing the way."

I nodded. "I wonder where they were going. I can't imagine there is anyplace west of here where they'd fit."

"Don't think they are people that go toward something. I think they are people that move on from something." He handed me the compass. "Sorry that happened. They must have been bivouacked somewhere along the river and that's why we didn't see them."

I took my compass with utmost disdain – the preciousness of it forever altered by the woman's vile act of contempt. I shook my head, imagining her disdain likely extended to anything honest or true. What possible need could she have of a compass?

Chapter 14

On Migration

Nebraska's towns had become as meaningless as the miles between them. The only things of interest to Lester or me were amusing attempts at drawing commerce from those traveling the great highway. Signs affixed to fenceposts advertised penny and nickel attractions for the curious and road weary. Who could fail to be enticed by an offer to see a giant ball of twine, deformed ears of corn, a two headed pickled piglet in a jar, or last fall's immense but now somewhat wrinkled blue-ribbon pumpkin?

We kept our pennies and nickels. Water and food were our only interest and then only enough to satiate and sustain us. Endless turns of the crank and rotations of our tires were our only goal. Ruts, chuck holes, and mud beneath our ever-turning tires were the only things we saw as few stretches of road were level and hazard-free enough to allow us to take our eyes off its surface. The ever distant, ever elusive horizon had long since lost its appeal.

Although we still heard them, we no longer listened to the song of birds. When we did look up, it was only at the sky as we were always on the lookout for storms that might be, and as the afternoon grew long, were likely forming in angry hues of black and gray.

An unrelenting sun crept east to west and we, along with our shadows, crept west to east beneath its blazing rays. We sweated out the water we drank nearly as fast as we took it in. We no longer spoke unless it was with regard to the direction we ought to ride, and then only briefly. The joy of adventure had unfortunately been replaced with shared determination to get every mile we could behind us as quickly as possible.

Simple things such as meeting a fellow traveler on a desolate stretch of road or encountering a passenger train brought us nearly unspeakable joy. So, when a lonesome black plume that had been visible for miles and its accompanying train at last came into clear view, Lester and I greeted its vestige with giddy excitement. The train's whistle began its greeting while still a mile distant. As it grew near, we began to wave our arms wildly. An assortment of hands and arms started to extend from the coaches' open windows, all waving just as wildly as our own.

Our laughter was spontaneous as we coasted to a stop still waving madly, now spitting distance from the tracks. The great engine's weight shook the ground beneath us. Oh, how we marveled at the mighty throb of its pistons, rush of steam, gracious whistle, clatter of wheels. We returned shouts of greeting to the happy friendly faces of men, women and children – our outstretched hands and theirs coming so close that we could nearly touch.

Then as quickly as it had come, the welcome breeze (and nourishment for our road weary souls) the train had brought was replaced with a choking stench of burnt coal. Its blackness seemed to stick to our tongues. Subsequent spasms of gagging, hacking and spitting turned our laughter upon ourselves. As Lester uncorked his canteen, he speculated the travelers' destination. "Utah and California."

"Denver and Cheyenne," I countered as he swished water in his mouth, spat soot, and handed his canteen to me.

"Not a chance. Salt Lake and Los Angeles. They looked like Mormons and movie stars to me."

I swished and spat as well. "I disagree. They were definitely cowboys, sod busters, and businessmen."

Lester shrugged.

I shrugged, handed his canteen back to him, put foot to pedal and pushed downward. A half mile later, just as it seemed it did every time we were making decent progress, the straight road that had paralleled the tracks turned across them. We were forced to leave the railroad and river's more or less direct path, again destined to ride the excess miles caused by section lines.

Gosh, how I hated section lines. And if we should happen to come across one of the Good Roads people on our journey, I had an

97

earful of discontent in store for whomever that might be.

I came to a stop on the crest of one of Nebraska's rolling hills only moments before Lester came up beside me. Both of us were panting, not from the minimal ascent, but because of our mile-long trek over a muddy, pulverized roadway. Ahead lumbered the source of our distress – a hundred head of cattle embarked upon a drive. The distant *heeyas* of the half dozen cowboys moving them along blended into the snorts and loud, unhappy bawl of the herd. Oh, and excuse me if I failed to mention the copious amounts of dung they'd left behind. Gobs of it was stuck to our tires and splattered on our shoes. As we had not managed to avoid a single stinking particle of it, the rest was baking onto the frames of our bicycles under the hot sun.

We may have planned to stop for no man or no thing, but we hadn't considered this. I looked to my side and found Lester already looking at me. We both dismounted, then careful of where we stepped – *not that it made any difference* – pushed our bicycles off road and leaned them against a post of a barbed wire fence. Cattlemen, as we had come to find, cared very little for travelers upon the highway. They cared even less for the idea of a highway and disliked motorcars with a vehemence. They tended to become quite riled should anyone dare interrupt their drive – especially two young men riding bicycles for no purpose other than to irritate them. God forbid we spook one of their smelly, shit covered wards. Cattlemen seemed abnormally territorial in nature, so, like it or not, Lester and I would be waiting however long it took for the cattle to get to their destination.

Lester opened his canteen. I pulled a few lengths of jerky from a tin. We both looked at the sun and cloudless blue sky. Our skin was already as crisp and brown as bacon sizzling in a pan. I could hear the tips of my ears spitting and popping as we stood under the relentless sun. I took a clean kerchief, soaked it in water from my canteen and laid it over my head.

Lester smiled not only at my sigh of relief, but my appearance, then knelt to clean dung from his Cyclometer and inspect the slack of his chain. "We'll need to get out wrenches and do some adjustments tonight."

I nodded. "Yeah, and some cleaning." Then a ruckus of shouts and whinnies drew our attention back to the drive. Lester stood and shielded his eyes. A horse had gone down and its cowboy had been thrown. Another cowboy was hastily moving cattle along and out of his way so he could get there – hence the shouting. We watched the downed horse writhe but not stand as its rider had. The thrown cowboy attempted to come near it, but repeatedly had to jump away, repelled by its thrashing and kicking.

The drama continued to unfold before us. Like spectators in a theater audience, both of us continued to drink water, gnaw on jerky, and chew raisins. The other cowboy dismounted and tried as the first one had, to come near the downed horse. He pulled a six-shooter from his holster. A distant pop of gunfire sounded and the downed horse ceased its writhing.

The two cowboys then struggled with its lifeless bulk to un-cinch its saddle and remove its bridle. The drive continued on down the road as they worked together to tie a second saddle onto a single horse. With it hanging sideways off the rear flank they mounted up two to a saddle. Within a few minutes, they had rejoined the drive. The coat of the dead horse left on the roadside glistened in the sun.

No words needed to be said and saying any would have made no difference anyway. Lester and I looked at one another, up at the sun, and pulled another piece of jerky from the tin.

The now-distant drive eventually began to flow like boiling brown and black water onto a bisecting road. Before the days of fences and homesteaders, the entire prairie would have been the cowboy's domain. The advent of irrigation farming now forced them to follow roadways and fence-lines. What was progress for the rest of the world was hindrance to them.

Lester and I mounted our bicycles. Doing our best to avoid the larger splatters of dung, we enjoyed coasting the slight, though bumpy downhill before us. The breeze of our own making began to evaporate our sweat and take heat from our bodies.

A third mile further lay the dead horse. Without having agreed to do so, we both came to a stop beside it. The gopher hole it had stepped in had been torn into a gaping crater. Bone protruded from the horse's badly broken leg. The scraped and turned earth it lay upon revealed the extent of its panic and suffering. Flies crawled in and about its nostrils and open mouth. They swarmed its lifeless eyes and the single bullet hole between them.

"What a shame," Lester commented.

"So beautiful a creature to meet such an ignoble end."

He nodded. "By tomorrow it will be bloated. In two days it will be crawling with maggots."

I nodded. "And pecked by buzzards."

Requiem for a dead horse on the side of the road.

We kicked off.

The herd and its mournful, defiant bawls of distress were well northward of the Lincoln Highway by the time Lester and I reached the solitary figure left behind.

He walked east along the highway, a forward lean to his gait in order to offset the weight of the saddle and blanket he carried on his back. I reckoned him to be a little younger than myself, maybe fifteen or so. His face, as we pulled alongside him, was as baked by the sun as our own, but of a ruddy complexion, smudged with dirt, cut, and smeared here and there with blood. His eyes were nearly vacant and fixed straight ahead as we rolled along at his side.

He never stopped walking as we spoke. "That was your horse?" Lester asked.

An answer was unnecessary. A momentary shift of the boy's eyes confirmed not only its redundancy, but his ownership.

"Sorry," I offered. His only acknowledgement was the scuff of his boots upon the road. My eyes were drawn to his hand holding the saddle's straps, its flesh made white by the resolve of his grip. It was then that I noticed his other arm dangling more than swinging at his other side – clearly broken.

"Where you headed?"

His eyes remained ahead. His boots scuffed along step-by-step. Eventually, defiantly, firmly, "I'll find a place."

I looked at Lester who was already looking at me.

"Where's home?"

At this, he turned his face full toward me, still walking. His expression caused a surge of fear to shoot through my soul. In his eyes was not only the pain of the moment, but of his past and I suspect, of home. He didn't have to answer, but he did. "Ain't goin' home. I'll get a whippin' for this an' I ain't havin' it."

Beneath grime and blood, I observed several scars on his face. I saw even greater scars deep within his eyes. I wondered, if not for the shirt and pants he wore, if I would see scars all over his body. I suspected I would and wondered if the whippin' he spoke of might actually be done with a whip. I nodded, knowing instantly his plight, his flight, his reason.

"Anything we can do?" Lester asked.

The boy shook his head only enough that we could perceive it, then turned his eyes forward.

"Can we offer you water, jerky, raisins, anything?"

His continued footfalls and the stubborn side of his face communicated that our conversation had ended.

"Sorry." I put my weight on my pedal and pressed downward.

Another couple towns came and went before we found one with a park and shade trees that beckoned us to enjoin their coolness. We'd scarcely leaned our bicycles against the trunk of a tree when Lester pointed toward the road. A motorcar with the young cowboy and his saddle in the back seat rumbled past, eastbound.

"I sure hope he finds a better place."

"Sounds like that won't be too hard to do."

I shook my head slowly. "You know he's headed the wrong direction."

Lester looked at me.

"Cowboys are supposed to go west."

Lester laughed. "He'll find his way. Tough as nails, that kid."

"Tougher."

Lester nodded.

"Lester, the more I see, the less certain I am about this world and the people in it."

Lester swatted me on the back. "It isn't Little London; that's for certain." He set about unfastening the straps on his pack of food and added as an afterthought, "He'll be all right."

"I see now that we've had an easy life."

Lester looked sideways at me.

"I've had an easy life," I corrected. His attention went back to the pack. I leaned to stretch my muscles. "Our town was planned and built by a millionaire. I have a family, a home, and a job. I can go to school and even play basketball. I don't have to be afraid of anything from anyone."

Lester slapped a couple lengths of jerky into my filthy hand. I bit into the meat, pulled off a chunk, and spoke another of my blessings. "And I have teeth."

Lester laughed, then inclined his head toward the cool grass below our feet. As we stiffly lowered ourselves and laid down, a brown and orange butterfly fluttered past overhead. The travails of the road began to leave me, making way for civilization's comforting sounds to enter my consciousness – a regular sputter of motorcars, beeps of their horns, conversation of passersby, doors slamming, doors opening.

I felt the bumps and slopes of the phantom road as if it were still beneath me. I closed my eyes, giving them rest from the eternal sun.

"You're right about our lives," Lester admitted.

I knew I was, said nothing, rolled my head, listening to my neck pop and snap, then opened my eyes at Lester's nudging. He held a closed fist out to me. I opened my hand and he dropped a handful of raisins into it. I couldn't help but notice the filth on his hands. In my previous life as a city-dweller, I would have been repulsed. On the road, it made no difference. I let a few warm raisins fall into my mouth. Several more butterflies happily bounced through the air above us. I closed my eyes again and continued to feel the flow and bumps of the road.

Bit-by-bit my muscles relaxed. Breaths began to flow rhythmically in and out of my chest. My ever-present thoughts became still. I was very nearly asleep when Lester spoke.

"All the ruins of history were once the ideals of men."

I opened my eyes and turned my head full sideways. I stared at the man beside me who I believed to be Lester but after that comment, sounded more like Plato or Socrates.

Without looking back at me, because this was indeed Lester and Lester always looked straight ahead, I watched a very slight smile form on his lips. He shrugged, possibly as confounded by what he had said as I was. More butterflies, some near and others high in the sky, fluttered past.

Was this a truth revealed, lying in the grass of a park in a town, the name of which I didn't know, coming from the lips of a man who only existed in the here and now and who usually spoke only of the yet to come?

Like a waft of colorful smoke, twenty or so butterflies flew over us. I finally had to ask, "What's with all the butterflies?"

Lester laughed. "Those are Monarchs. They're migrating north. This group is a little late. We'll probably see more up around the Great Lakes – masses of them."

I turned about, blades of grass tickling my neck and ears as I did. How hadn't I noticed the scores and scores of butterflies all around us until then? Hundreds, maybe thousands, of butterflies were flying through the park, around and through the trees, resting or feeding for a moment or two, but all going the same direction in waves of color.

"I've never seen this," I marveled.

"Not one of them that starts the migration north ever sees their journey's end. Not even their offspring's offspring will see it. They will all live and die on their trip. I don't know how they all know the way to go."

I didn't acknowledge what Lester had told me. I was lost in wonder. Butterflies were flapping through the air in rolling cascades – all completely oblivious of me or even of the concept of wonder itself. They knew not their own significance or beauty. As soon as one wave had disappeared, another came from behind.

Here Lester and I were, embarked upon a journey, traveling a road of others embarked upon their journeys. I remembered seeing the names and dates of a few who had perished along the way carved into a wooden panel on the side of a Conestoga. Forgotten. A date and their name were all that remained and that too would eventually fade to nothing and pass away as well. Those known and those unknown, all passed each other either on earthen trails or in time, not knowing where the other had been or where they were going – or where they would end up. All of us simply going where we have to go to do what we have to do. Maybe none of it mattering beyond that we got where we needed to be at the time.

Then I lost myself in the flutter of wings and the jagged, random, purposeful, beautiful flight of butterflies.

Chapter 15

The Oddest Things

It was coming toward us at a clip we'd not yet encountered upon the great road. If its motor was straining, it could not be heard over the joyous shouts and laughter of the half-dozen young men and women about our age, aboard. They stood inside the speeding vehicle – arms outstretched, clothes flapping and hair flying.

I pulled over to one side of the road and Lester to the other, then realizing the berth we'd allowed may not be wide enough, we swung our legs over our bars and scrambled to get as far off the roadway as possible. We had no sooner done so than the motorcar's brakes began to squeal. Its progress slowed and came to a halt. Between gales of laughter, excited speech, friendly waves our direction, gears grinding, and the revving of its engine, it turned, not in a circle, but in a series of lurches: forward, backward, forward, repeatedly in an about-face as comical as it was protracted.

I looked across the roadway at Lester who looked back at me. The motorcar – that we could now identify as a Packard – at long last got turned about. Then with a great roar, it sped away. As its engine and the shouts and laughter of its occupants grew distant, Lester turned to me. "What do you suppose that was about?"

I lifted my shoulders. "Nothing better to do?" I began to push my bicycle back onto the road. "I thought for sure they were coming straight for us."

"Me too."

"Wonder why they turned."

Lester shrugged. It wasn't the oddest thing we'd yet seen in Nebraska and being as we were just over two-thirds across, it appeared that it wouldn't be the last.

We'd ridden only a very short distance before coming upon the reason for their speed. The road was paved with concrete! The joy that entered my heart and mind was nigh unspeakable. Tracks of mud from the road stained the dazzling gray surface for a short distance. Ahead, the concrete became a bright and shining roadway that beckoned Lester and me to the same degree of joy and speed as the young people in the Packard.

This was Heaven – smooth, flat, and – *praise the Lord* – free of mud!

We whooped and laughed; our otherwise weary muscles revived by newfound enthusiasm. We pedaled as fast and as hard as we could and then just as our speed was at its greatest – mud.

The concrete ended as abruptly as it had begun. We slowed and stopped, looked backward, then forward, then backward again.

"Well, isn't that the oddest thing?" Lester scratched his head.

"Why would someone build a stretch of concrete roadway that goes nowhere? Why didn't they at least take it on into town?" My inherited logical and well-ordered mind could not accept the cruel anomaly before us.

"I don't want to ride in the mud. I want to ride on this," Lester complained.

I darn near shed a tear as I begrudgingly accepted reality and eased my bicycle back into the ruts of mud that would lead to the next town upon our journey. Trees and steeples had by now come into our view, promising a larger municipality, possibly one with an actual restaurant. To ease the pain of riding in mud, I added, "We're having a sit-down lunch of real food."

Lester looked down at his mud-splattered trousers, then ran his hand over five days of scruff on his face. "We look like hobos."

"Don't care. I need something good."

"Then, Amen brother. A sit-down meal sounds like a mighty fine thing to me, too."

One Nebraska farm town is as much like another as two peas in a pod. Not only do all the folks in one town look exactly like all the other folks in any other town, but they also talk the same, walk the same and dress the same.

"Bet the peapod people of this town have themselves a wheelbarrow parade every fourth Saturday," Lester quipped as he and I rode at a leisurely pace along main street. Refreshingly, this town was several blocks in length. Some of the water stops we'd thus far ridden through had only a blacksmith, a post office, a church, and maybe a dry goods. Of course, the folks in such places were so darn happy to see another living soul that we'd yet to pass through one where at least one of the townsfolk hadn't offered the hospitality of a meal, and as often as not, a night's lodging.

As I considered the humor provided by a wheelbarrow parade, I noticed a couple buildings with cut stone façades. The standard of construction over the past few hundred miles had been weathered wood planks that had generally shunned the concept of paint. "These folks do seem more progressive than most."

And then because we'd seen a tractor or two along the way, Lester added another spectacle to complement the comical parade he was envisioning. "And probably a tractor."

"It'd have to be pulling a wagon filled with hay and young-uns."

"Well, if all the children are in the wagon, who's gonna ride in the wheelbarrows and wave at the crowd?"

"I guess the old ladies." We laughed and just as we did, my eye caught sight of the mysterious speeding Packard now parked haphazardly down a shady side street. "Lester." I pointed, turned my bar, and circled back. Lester turned as well. We'd both been quite vexed to have observed only a moment of something so mysterious and exhilarating and now, like detectives, we'd stumbled upon a clue. Lester and I well understood the joy, exhilaration and temptation posed by a paved roadway free of pedestrians, trolleys, other motor cars, and dogs. Now we had happened upon the Packard and hopefully its discovery would lead us to the culprits. If it was at all possible, I sure would like to go for a ride like that with those culprits as it looked like more fun than I'd had in quite a while.

But there was no one out on the street except a disinterested dog that hadn't the gumption to bark, much less get up. A lone cat was hunting beside a cottage so encircled with junk that one would hope it had been abandoned – but as I've come to know people – realized it most likely was not.

"Doesn't look like the kind of neighborhood where someone would own a Packard," Lester commented as he looked around.

"Maybe they ran out of gasoline."

"There was enough of them to push it and why wouldn't they have stayed on Main Street if they had? How do you know this is even the same car?"

His argument was sound and considering my stomach was burning for that sit-down lunch, I shrugged and circled around. A proper meal, not to mention chair and cushion, was sounding mighty good to both ends of my anatomy.

I knew it was them the instant I walked in. They were loud, windblown, and imbued with the kind of energy that only a daredevil ride on a road to nowhere can give a person. Lester waved me off after I'd nodded his attention toward the young people seated at a table in the far back corner and whispered as much into his ear. "Now Pike, are we going to accost every young man, woman and parked car we see today?"

I sneered at his chastising and took a seat where I could keep my eye on the laughing, excitedly talking kind of people I'd love to spend the rest of the day with – and maybe, if at all possible, go for a ride with. I can shout and laugh with the best of them. I can. I really can. And after a week and a half on the road with Lester, I sure would like to have some fun – not that I wasn't already having the time of my life – or nearly so.

"What is it about diner food that makes it the best damn food you'd ever had every time you have it?" I asked ten minutes later while eating with the same manners as a pig loosed in a trough.

Lester was about to answer when his eyes lifted well above me. I'd heard the door behind me open. Now I felt the authority of his footfalls. I knew who it had to be without having to see who it was. Lester gulped. I turned. The law in Wheelbarrow Parade (as I'd dubbed the town) stood well over six foot tall and was as broad of shoulder as the door he'd just come through. The black ten-gallon hat atop his head, shining star upon his vest, and suspicious shift of his eyes brought the activity of the establishment, its voices and laughter, to an abrupt halt.

His eyes locked ahead. His footsteps shook the floor as he headed toward the table in the corner. As he sat down with the formerly laughing, formerly exuberant kind of people I just knew I'd like if given the chance to meet them, I heard one word of their hushed conversation rise above the others: *"Joyride."*

"That *is* them," I whispered while leaned clear across the table so that my mouth was nearly on Lester's ear.

He too was intently watching the drama unfold. "I'll be damned. I knew that Packard didn't belong where we saw it."

"He's gonna slap shackles on them any minute and march them out of here in chains." This was going to be a story I could tell for years to come. But then we began to hear nervous laughter come from the table in the corner. I strained to look above and around the other turned heads in the diner. The boy who had been at the wheel and the Marshall rose together. With the big man's hand upon his shoulder, the boy walked ahead of him – embarrassed but smiling – through the diner and out the front door.

I twisted around. Lester rose from his chair. Out on the sidewalk stood a white-haired gentleman. He wore the coat, bowtie, and wide-brimmed straw hat of a traveling salesman. The sample valise in his hand confirmed my assumption. The three spoke for no more than a minute before the young man turned and opened the door. I promptly turned to sit straight. Lester plopped down. We both looked at our plates as the boy strode around our table and over to his friends.

"I have to go fetch the car," he said quite distinctly, then turned and caught me and Lester looking directly at him. I didn't know what sort of hellion he might be. Since I felt he was likely a caliber above that of my companion, my eyes widened. The guilty generally don't like to be embarrassed by the idle prying of strangers. This brand of lawless individual may very well decide to do something about it. He walked up to us and stopped. Even after having been caught by the law, a decidedly devious sparkle remained in his eye. "Was that you two we saw out on the road?"

"Yes," I answered, then added, "Looked like fun."

"It was." He grinned. "But illegal, irresponsible, selfish, short-sighted and that's not to mention, stupid and inherently dangerous." He grimaced. Maybe I did have a certain affinity for hellions, as he was, at least to me, instantly likeable. I smiled. He pointed at me as if we'd meet again someday, made a click in the back of his throat, and exited the diner.

Lester and I twisted and lifted off our chairs to watch as best we could, the boy leave one direction, the marshal depart another, and the white-haired gentleman open the door. We sat abruptly as he came inside to the ting of its bell. We continued to observe him as he took a seat at the counter, laid his valise on a stool next to him and beseeched the waitress. "I've had a trying day. Might I trouble you for a glass of water?"

Lester leaned toward me and whispered. "What a story. If that wasn't the oddest thing."

We departed the diner as bloated and lethargic as two old dogs, and I might add, looking nearly as mangy. Lester and I mounted up and struggled on down Main Street, the unrelenting sun now directly above us. Two blocks later we came upon a park with shade trees and cool, soft grass. I chanced to think for a moment that Lester might point us that direction and we might just lie down and call it a day.

That moment came and went as he didn't and we continued to pedal toward the outskirts of town. I sighed. Chasing the horizon – and losing to it – was already turning my pleasantly full stomach, sour.

Then, as if the Good Lord above had heard the groaning of my soul, we were greeted, not with the elusive horizon, but an excited throng of mankind. Women were holding parasols, automobiles were parked haphazardly, men in hats were bustling about. As if that was not enough to indicate something of interest – some had cameras! I looked at Lester. Lester looked at me. We didn't need to say a word. We both pushed down on our pedals. If there was one thing we would not be late for on the endless Nebraska plains, it was something of greater interest than a hundred-pound squash. Our abject lethargy became a furious churn of cranks.

As we neared, we discovered every other person to be holding a camera – but for what – we could not tell. All we could see was the crowd and it formed a wall between us and what we now, oh so desperately wanted to see – regardless of what it was.

A distant beeping of a horn caused the crowd to erupt in cheers. We tossed our bicycles to the ground, ran into their midst and plowed our way to the front.

A motorcar was traveling at full speed toward us upon another patch of concrete roadway mysteriously placed in the middle of nowhere. My well-ordered way of thinking concluded the crowd was foolishly cheering what seemed likely to be their own demise. With physics being what they are and given the speed and trajectory of the wheeled missile straining our way, I figured we had one-minute tops to, pardon my language, *get the hell out of the way!*

Then I noticed what my eyes had overlooked.

The specter of death had an albatross in tow. Its wings extended a good twenty feet either side of an exposed pilot. They began to bend upward as the motorcar gained speed. The contraption rose and fell, tilted and corrected, then lifted a full five feet into the air. The crowd shouted with delight. The glider's ascent continued, ten feet, then twenty. The tether that had towed it aloft was released and fell back to earth. I gazed openmouthed and motionless, inattentive to my earlier computation of trajectory and speed. The motorcar's brakes were now fully applied and squealing as the crowd parted for its progress. Its radiator was about to introduce me to my Maker when a variety of hands pulled me stumbling from danger's path. I acknowledged none of them. The glider soared above us in silence, sunlight shining through its cloth wings, exposing their wooden framework.

I heard the speeding motorcar bounce off the concrete, burrow into the mud roadway and come to a stop, but never looked its direction. The glider remained wondrously aloft, camera shutters snapping all around us. Then just as it had gone up, it began to come down: fifteen feet, ten feet, then five. The crowd gasped when it snagged upon a fence, lurched terribly, flipped and expelled its pilot –

111

arms and legs flailing. He had no sooner landed, his crumpled form nearly concealed by prairie grasses, than the craft tumbled over on top of him.

I couldn't breathe and neither could anyone else. The motorcar, which turned out to be an Oakland, continued to idle. Its driver stood from his seat, hands to the sides of his head, gawking in horror along with everyone else. My father's frequent warning that my brothers and I were always about to, *"break our darn necks,"* rang in my ears. Oh, how I hoped this wonderful thing had not ended that way. The wreck shifted. A wing began to rise. From beneath it, rose the young man who had been its pilot – neck intact – arms raised in triumph. The crowd's cheer was immediate and twice as loud as before. The driver looked heavenward, blew out a breath of purest relief, sat, and put his vehicle into gear. The Oakland rumbled as it began to bounce across the field.

Neither Lester nor I had ever seen live and in person any sort of areoplane before. And here, in the middle of the day, in the middle of Nebraska, on a patch of concrete in the middle of nowhere that existed for no apparent reason, one had flown over us.

I was exhilarated beyond comprehension.

Had we had the time I'd have liked very much to stay and speak with the two souls adventurous and daring enough to attempt such a thing. But we had fifty miles yet to travel and I'd already bargained for and received a sit-down lunch.

Lester and I worked our way through the crowd, found our bicycles, mounted up, and forged onward. The blessed mile of concrete eased my pain for a short while. All too soon, we were riding abreast in ruts of mud, un-cheered, anonymous, turning a crank to make our wheels roll upon a road.

The day's events continued to play through my mind. I'd witnessed two inspiring occurrences and although they'd gladdened me, my joy was short-lived. They had highlighted my adventure's drudgery and shouted my ordinariness. They snickered at my nature of cautiousness. This tedious road and I were more alike than I wanted to admit. In all my toil I had not sought exhilaration or attempted anything lofty. Maybe it was fitting that Joe Wheeler Bruce aspired to nothing greater than riding a bicycle. They say it's not the destination that counts, but the journey undertaken to reach it. *They* never rode a bicycle over an endless highway – hearing laughter only at a distance and seeing only from below those who dared go aloft.

Then, as if to add insult to injury, Lester and I were forced to come to a complete stop about five miles outside of town. A dip ahead was not merely a bog of mud; it was a pond. Lester's mouth pulled up beneath his nose in a pucker of disgust. "They can lay down concrete where it isn't needed and then we have to navigate this goddamn hole when there's no other..."

I pointed out a detour of tire tracks worn over lumps of prairie grass to our left. Its entrance was denoted by coils of cut fence wire hanging in loops from a post.

Lester muttered something under his breath, then shouted at no one in particular – you know – as there was no one around except a couple birds and a distant motorcar coming toward us, "Fix the damn road!"

Lester and I dismounted to lift our bicycles over a gully between the highway and improvised detour. While walking our bicycles over terrain that may have been as difficult as traversing a pond, the oncoming car heaved off the road. It then proceeded to test its suspension limits as it bounced toward us. Once again I had to credit Mr. Ford on his Model T's durability. Upon meeting, it stopped. We stopped. It's driver, a clean-shaven man of middle years, smiled, deepening laugh lines that ran from his eyes down to his jaw. "Ahoy fellow travelers."

Lester was still in a mood about the road and not projecting much courtesy at the moment. I imagined the driver's out-of-place nautical greeting was due to our close proximity to a pond. "Ahoy."

"Don't you just love it?" The driver motioned at the sorry state of both detour and road.

I assumed sarcasm. "Does it get any better?" I asked and shooed a fly away from my face.

"Somewhat. This part is worse than anything east of here."

"I've got a question for you," Lester interjected curtly. "Why in the hell are there patches of concrete where the road is fine and then where you need a road, *any semblance of a road*, there's only this pathetic…"

The man laughed and held up his hand to stop what might well have become a tirade. "Seedling miles. You're talking about seedling miles outside of towns."

"Huh?" we asked in unison.

"You can thank the Good Roads people for them. They're to make people *want* to vote for road taxes by letting them experience how wonderful this whole highway could be if they did."

The scheme was nothing less than brilliant. Lester was dumbfounded – clearly torn between remaining angry at the Good Roads people or shaking their hands. It was a remarkably sinister plan but a plan destined to become successful. I waved appreciation for the motorist's explanation. "Well, that explains it. Thanks."

He went on his way with a purr of pistons and valves. We went on ours with a sigh and a grunt. Twenty paces later my eyes landed upon a black fender laying in the grass, ensnared in fence wire. "Is that what I think it is?"

Lester considered it a moment. "Well, I'll be damned. That's from the Vagabond's motorcar."

"The only way that could have been pulled off is if they were the first ones who drove through that fence."

We laughed heartily and we sorely needed to.

Lester turned west, cupped his hands to his mouth and shouted, "Vagabonds! We found your fender!"

It was truly a day of just the oddest things.

Once back on our journey, hearing only turns of our cranks and rolls of our tires, I began to think about random patches of concrete placed in the middle of nowhere – seedling miles. I considered laughter, exhilaration, temptation, perseverance and those to whom I'd judged myself and my journey so unfavorably.

Why had I compared their sprint to my marathon?

A weary salesman's long days had earned him a Packard. A moment's want of exhilaration and laughter thought nothing of taking it from him.

A pilot cheered for having glided aloft was in no way an innovator of design. He hadn't spent long years of trial and error as Orville and Wilbur had. He'd only mimicked their hard-won achievement.

I considered my quest, *our quest*, to see Liberty standing in New York's harbor. It wasn't the most thrilling of destinations but it was what we had undertaken and were working to accomplish.

The road I'd chosen was longer than a mile. Its surface was nowhere near smooth. Still, I was undeterred. And that is not at all ordinary.

Chapter 16

Menace and Threat

"Mosquitoes."

"Biting flies."

"Arguments," Lester challenged.

As we pedaled along, keeping our tires on ridges and out of the ruts of eternal mud, I began to list the offenses of biting flies. "Welts. Instant pain. Swelling. Bleeding."

"But you have the satisfaction of killing them in the act."

"True, if you're fast enough."

"And you can feel them when they land on you."

"Usually, but only if you're not otherwise distracted." I continued my case. "Their buzz is annoying. They shit on your food and fly in your mouth – but only after having feasted on a rotting corpse or a steaming pile of shit."

Lester nodded, then proceeded to present his case for mosquitoes. "Stealthy. Can't feel them until it's too late. They also fly in your mouth, up your nose, in your eyes and in your ears. Their sting itches for days, mostly at night. They carry disease and were the South American culprits responsible for nearly killing Teddy."

"Irrelevant. You can't include Malaria or South American expeditions." I looked over at Lester smartly. When he turned his attention to me, his temporary distraction caused him to slip off his ridge. His tires sunk into slop. But as he was still moving, he stood to power through it. He had managed one stroke and was halfway through a second when I heard a snap. His pedal went straight down. His progress came to an immediate stop – unless you consider his torso – which nearly went over the handlebars.

Then when all forward motion had come to a halt, he was forced to catch his balance with both feet, plunging them ankle deep in muck. There it hung, half on the cogs and its other half seeping into the mud. The noble chain had met its demise after a mere thousand miles or so.

I half expected a tirade, but was pleasantly surprised when Lester simply bent, retrieved the remnants of his chain, and stood aright. He wiped mud from broken links, curiously inspected them, then looked up at the position of the sun. He slung the broken chain into the weeds beside the road, looked again at the sun's position, dismounted, and began to push. I said nothing. Figuring that a tirade might yet be on the way, I was determined not to be its antagonist. A sucking slosh of mud beneath Lester's feet was the only sound – other than the buzz of flies, of course.

Omaha *had been* our day's destination.

I dismounted and began to push my bicycle until we had cleared the bog. There was no hint of mankind or help in sight. In our many previous journeys Lester had often wired chain links back together. Because of this, I naturally figured some sort of repair could be executed on the offending chain had it not been so hastily flung aside. But given the black cloud forming over Lester's head, it didn't seem wise to mention that possibility. And if some kind of patch had been practical, he likely would have already seized upon it as *Patch* could very well have been Lester's middle name.

Being well-acquainted with the side of Lester's face and the stubborn determination now cemented to it, I looked at the sun's location and made a quick calculation of my own. I mounted and pedaled rapidly until I had put a city block between us. Then I stopped.

I was untying a length of sisal rope from the eyelets of our canvas when Lester caught up with me. The determination on his face was more like a scowl at this point. I promptly tied one end of the rope to my seat post, then extended the other end to Lester. "I'm giving you a tow."

As expected, he waved me off and he began to push past. I blocked his way.

"Tie this to your handlebar stem."

"You can't tow me."

"Do it."

Lester looked aside, took a long breath, rolled his eyes, looked back at me and slowly released his breath. "Between my bike, my packs and me, that's two hundred pounds – on top of the two hundred you're already moving. Don't be ridiculous."

"Well, I'm damn sure not going to walk forty miles to Omaha." I shoved the rope's frayed end into his scowl. "Do it."

Lester narrowed his eyes.

I narrowed mine.

He grabbed the rope, angrily tied it to his stem, then mounted up and looked at me with purest dare.

I pushed my bicycle enough to make the rope taut, straddled my machine, took my crank up to the top and stood on the pedal.

Aside from my bike tipping to the side, nothing happened with regard to forward propulsion. I righted my bike, stood on the pedal again, this time pulling up on my handlebars to increase leverage. I *had* to pull this off for I was not about to listen to one second of Lester's haughty *I told you so*. The first few turns of that crank were an agonizingly slow experiment in leverage, fulcrums, sinew and sheer determination. Then like a locomotive pulling out of a station, a turn of the wheel became turns of the wheel and we were moving. Praise God because I am no fan of Lester's derision and I would have had to endure it the remainder of the day had I failed to budge this particular train out of the station.

As proud as I was to have managed this feat of strength, about a mile and a half later, I felt I might actually die. But the Good Lord above smiled on me a second time and sent from behind, my salvation. Lester had heard its approach and so had turned about and seen it. "Hey Joe, you better pull over and let this thing pass." Our traverse was so tedious and my death so immanent that I gratefully heeded his advice.

It was recognizable as a Model T, but only in that the lights, radiator and front fenders resembled one. Not only was the contraption crafted by hand, but it was clearly crafted by hands without much crafting ability. A huge packing crate had been wired to the frame in lieu of conventional coachwork – apparently removed in its favor. Across sheets of black, brush-painted tin nailed to the crate, lettered in a flourish more akin to childlike scrawl than refinement, were the words: *Dr. Love's Tonics and Elixirs.*

The contraption slowed, but instead of passing, stopped in order for its driver to survey our situation. This would be the venerable snake-oil salesman my father had warned me about. Although Father had speculated they would be as numerous as ants on an anthill, this was our first encounter. *"Worse than Gypsies!"* had been Irvin's warning.

But when the driver – who resembled Abraham Lincoln in that he was not much more than bones, whiskers, and craggy features – smiled upon us with pity, I decided that judgment of character was the Lord's domain. At least on this particular day, it would be a duty from which I would abstain.

"You boys want a ride?" he asked, then set about using his tongue to push out an assortment of gray-black whiskers that had curled into his mouth upon its opening.

His spectacles were so smudged with grease, fingerprints and soot that I doubted he could actually make out who or even what he was looking at. However, he got two things right: we were boys and we were in a predicament. *"Yes!"* we both cried.

He undid the wire that held the – um, let's call it the driver's door – nearly closed. The black-suited driver unfolded himself from what turned out to be wooden kitchen chair he'd somehow decided to be better than a proper seat – and given the sorriness of his conveyance – a decision that was at least in keeping with its theme.

Lester and I dismounted. Dr. Love completed his Lincoln impersonation by slapping a rather distressed top hat on his equally distressed head of hair. He came around his contraption with long lanky strides. I winced at his approach and took a step away. He smelled like a campfire and if he had come closer, probably a whole lot worse. He looked between my bicycle and Lester's with a hand brought up to his chin in thought. "Reckon we'll tie one to each side."

As he had been considering our transport, I had also been

considering his. The rear tires of his machine were running about flat, but only on the bottom. This seemed not so much from lack of air as they looked about to pop at the top. The crate they supported was ponderous and leaned distinctly to one side. It curiously had a stove pipe at its summit – I would imagine from a cook stove – as it appeared to be the man's year-round dwelling.

When Dr. Love opened the rear – we might as well call them doors – of the box to retrieve wire with which he intended to string up our bicycles, we discovered he was not hawking snake oil. Dr. Love was making moonshine and the stove pipe atop his conveyance was from his still. Around a cut-off steel drum that housed glowing embers beneath a copper kettle, lay a heap a gross of filthy bottles of various shapes, colors and sizes – all apparently salvaged from trash heaps. Doubtless, Dr. Love's *potions and elixirs* possessed the octane to sanitize them. And if not, at least enough to dull one's sensitivities to grime and the bits and pieces of expired bugs.

Since on this particular day, judgment was going to be the Lord's and not mine, Lester and I looked at one another with wide eyes, said nothing, and proceeded to wire our bicycles to the sides of the crate. I offered a prayer that the tires would not pop, and then upon opening the "door" of the passenger side of the vehicle, faced our next challenge. The contraption possessed only the one driver's seat.

Dr. Love handed Lester the crank, and between them, the wreck eventually sputtered to life. Then Lester and I crowded together on our haunches beside our smelly chauffer. If we had at any time thought the temperature of Nebraska in the summer was hellish, the interior of Dr. Love's truck easily doubled it. The still radiated as much heat as the sun but was mere feet away. The fact that there was no floor in several locations, no windshield and substantial gaps all around us, only permitted the hellish heat outside to blend with the hellish heat inside and bring to my imagination our slow, agonizing deaths in a rolling smelting furnace.

But we were moving and my lean quadriceps were not the source of our propulsion. "Colorado went dry, didn't it?" our host asked or stated – I wasn't quite sure.

"Yes. On six months now."

"Folks will be needing my tonics." He raised a crooked finger. "Thought of heading out that way but am a little apprehensive about the church ladies smashing up my laboratory."

I sucked in my lips and nodded.

"Omaha, now that's a drinkin' town there I tell you – a dozen times as many bars as churches. Folks there favor my tonics and their church ladies ain't all that churchy or all that dry."

I responded with an inadvertent raise of my eyebrows.

"You don't think I'm a moonshiner, do you?. Oh Lordy, that's illegal. I'm in pharmaceuticals. This here is medicine to help you get over the shakes caused both by excessive drinking and prohibition. Folks need medicine." He pushed more whiskers out of his mouth with his tongue, then concentrated on coordinating levers, gears, wheel and throttle to propel his lurching vehicle out of the ruts in order to accommodate the progress of an oncoming motorcar. Lester and I grabbed for anything we could hold onto. Behind us, bottles clanked together and mash sloshed. The crate creaked and groaned.

After friendly waves and obligatory honks, the expected mores and pleasantries of passing, our driver plunged his tires back into the ruts. A second great lurching, sloshing and creaking made me doubt whether the Good Lord had indeed sent salvation, or if death had maybe come for us all. Dr. Love seemed not to notice. "In addition to curing the shakes, I distill the finest gout and rheumatis medicine in all the land. Thinking of taking it public on the New York Stock Exchange." He moved his bony hand in an arc where the windshield should rightly have been. *"Doctor Love's Tonics an' Elixers – for all what ails you.* What do you think?"

Thinking grammar is the province of schoolteachers and not me, at least on this particular day, I nodded. "Sounds good."

"Personally, I got no use for liquor. It dulls the mind and makes derelicts of good men. My tonics sharpen the mind and enhance the wits. That's what they does."

Conversation then drifted to Dr. Love's curiosity about our destination. Moments later we were back to his greater concern, the eventuality of prohibition and the need of the populous for medicine – two subjects that apparently occupied Dr. Love's every waking thought. But as long as miles were passing beneath the holes in the floor, I could humor just about any topic of conversation.

Traffic began to increase the nearer we came to Omaha. Unfortunately the road seemed never to accommodate more than one motorcar abreast at any place where one might encounter another headed the opposite direction. Hence the great lurching in and out of ruts and the resultant heaving, clatter and slosh that accompanied such encounters became routine.

Then along a stretch of straight road with only one motorcar in sight and yet quite distant, Dr. Love reduced the throttle, pushed pedals, pulled levers and came to a stop. Nebraska's hellish heat doubled with the cessation of movement. Our driver squinted at the very distant vehicle, manipulating whiskers with his tongue as he seemed apt to do when deep in thought.

"Is that motorcar moving?"

"Doesn't appear to be," Lester answered.

"That's what I thought."

There was a pulling and pushing of pedals, levers and throttle, a grinding of gears, and we began to bounce backwards down the road we'd just come up. Panic sounded in Lester's voice. "What are you doing?"

"We passed a crossroads a bit back that I think is going to be your end of the line."

"Why? What? No!"

"That up there is the mayor's boys, that's why, what, an' how come. End of the line. Sorry boys but there's a battle brewin' up the road that might get a little rough. Don't need me no more casualties than necessary."

The whine of gears, bumping, creaking and clanking reached crescendo, then faded as we slowed, stopped, and the engine's sputter became the only sound – well and that of the breaking of my heart.

"Why is there a battle brewin' ahead? Why would the mayor's boys be waiting for you?"

A prolonged squint of Dr. Love's eyes revealed he wasn't sure reason had much to do with it. "Because I'm a sovereign man and I do what I damn well please. That's why." Then he muttered something about government interference. "An' I ain't havin' it." He undid the wire that held his door. "Get movin' boys. This is my battle an' one I'll fight to the death."

Lester had already unwired our door, crawled out on legs that had gone numb from lack of circulation and wobbled a bit. I followed. Without another word, we all worked together to take down our bicycles.

The man's huge dirty hand was extended along with parting words of direction and advice. "Take this road north until the second right – just follow the ruts. It'll bring you into Omaha, but not the Omaha the Lincoln Highway people intended to greet you. You don't mind Negras do yas?"

I shrugged – never having thought about whether it was my prerogative to mind the existence of another human being.

"Well, follow the road and it'll bring you into the colored part of town an' by colored, I mean these is black negras, not caramel negras like y'all might be used ta. They is black as night an' straight outta Dixie. A smelly bunch," added the pot in reference to the kettle. "Scads of them but the ones not practicing Louisiana voodoo is good God-fearin' folk that'll help you get repaired an' back on the road."

The man then opened the rear doors of his contraption, flung in the wire we'd removed, reached in further and pulled out a double-barreled shotgun. He gripped the barrel with one hand and wiped soot from its stock off onto his trousers (that I now understood may not have been black when purchased). He began to rummage about the bottles with his other hand. I felt the Bruce family crease come to my brow. Not only had we been rocking down the road with distillings that could have blown us sky high, but we'd also have had our asses peppered with shot along the journey. Shotgun shells lay haphazardly scattered among the bottles. Many nested directly against the steel drum of embers. Dr. Love retrieved a handful of shells and stuffed them into his pocket.

I took a step backwards as Lester had already done.

Then Dr. Love rested his shotgun on the ground and leaned again into the box. He took down a cloth sack hung from a nail – the contents of which I had already discerned. I therefore took two steps back and pulled Lester along with me.

The sack that looked like it contained bundles of dynamite, did indeed hold T.N.T. – two sticks of which he removed and stuffed into his other pocket.

"The mayor's boys got a little surprise in store if they think they're gonna bully J.D. Snodgrass around today."

"Snodgrass?" I questioned over my shoulder as Lester and I were by now hastily pushing our bicycles up the northward road.

"At your service." The man heretofore known as Dr. Love – but now proven to be anything but healer and far more scoundrel than lover – bowed. He waved his hand in a flourish akin to the scrawl on the side of his vehicle – that I now understood would be his eventual coffin and certain pyre.

He wired the rear doors shut, picked up his shotgun, and saluted us as he walked back to the driver's compartment and folded himself up inside. "Good luck with your journey and give my regards to Wall Street when you get there!"

The engine revved, gears ground, axles clunked, and the box began to creak and groan as Lincoln's far less worthy twin charged eastward to his or someone else's untimely demise.

"The curse of the sovereign man," I commented dryly to Lester, grimaced, and raised my eyebrows.

"Good Lord Almighty." Lester shook his head.

"Amen," I added to what sounded somewhat like a prayer. I turned full to Lester. I again handed him the length of sisal rope. We began to tie its ends between our two bicycles.

I had my leg halfway over my bar when Lester interrupted.

"I'll take a turn." He offered me his handlebars as he reached out to take mine.

I accepted the trade without argument and as we passed, I caught in his eye, the purest mercy of a friend. He was not merely taking a turn; he would pull me into Omaha – however far that would be – and I would let him. I nodded, smiled, then took his mount as he took mine.

Lester, although not remarkable in stature or in heft, was

remarkable in strength. Coiled steel described his muscles. As he powered down the road with me coasting behind, I looked back. Dr. Love's black coffin was hurdling toward either glory or disaster – with odds favoring disaster. I cried out as hawkers and snake-oil salesmen are apt to do: *"Doctor Love's tonics and elixirs – for all what ails you!"*

Lester laughed, then slapped his neck.

"Biting flies," I cried victoriously. It struck me then, their similarity to the sovereign man. Both inflicted welts upon their hosts. Neither possessed any degree of insight in matters of right or wrong. One was a fly. The other was a man who thought only of his own rights and lacked any concept or vision for the common good of the nation that granted his sovereignty.

Chapter 17

A Swath of Destruction Long and Wide

"I reckon," she said slowly, thoughtfully, but not at all certainly, "at least sixty, don't know. Could be seventy. Chattel don't gets no date of birth. We gets dates of sale an' I was sold back in eighteen sixty-two. That's my date. I do remembers me that. Could figure it out ifin I knowed how old I was when I was sold." Wet began to form in her eyes that she allowed to well and then to spill. This was her great hurt. We'd known her but only two minutes and in that time she'd asked us not our names, only our ages, and then began to speak about her own as if it had been our inquiry or the reason for our meeting.

Her eyes were gray, her hair white, her skin black. She looked a hundred. Since it was her great granddaughter who had eagerly introduced herself as Lila Mae and just as enthusiastically brought us to her, I figured I might not be all that far off. *"White boys, Queenie. I found me some white boys,"* Lila Mae had shouted the instant her great grandmother had come into sight. She'd managed this exclamation in spite of being breathless from having run in front of us for darn near a quarter mile.

I doubted the old woman could see for gray is not the color of a sighted eye and both of her eyes had the cloud of the blind. The dry, hard-baked dirt road we rolled in upon was stark contrast to the lush green of her tiny patch of front yard. She sat two steps above us on a gray enameled porch and rocked upon a rocker that was at least twice whatever age she happened to be. Beyond her rocker was an open front door from which sounds and aromas of dinner cooking taunted our hunger. It was late, the sun mercifully nearing the western horizon, casting long shadows along a row of compact homes that in some cases looked more like shacks than dwellings, but were dwellings just the same.

Faces so black they could not be seen if in shadows and eyes so white they appeared to glow, peered at us from every place we turned. We were an anomaly at least as great as a circus elephant – two white boys in a colored neighborhood.

As great grandmother wept, I looked with curiosity at the numerous uneven parts on Lila Mae's scalp. Her shiny, coal black hair was braided so tightly it strained her skin. It had to hurt, but pink ribbons adorned their ends, as if maybe to soften the pain. Lila Mae was a girl maybe eight years of age, but as I watched her stroke Queenie's arm and comfort her, "It's all right, Queenie. It's all right," I believed her wisdom likely exceeded her years.

Pain this deep is sacred. I did not know what to say and so I dared not interrupt. I waited, wondering why this girl had brought us to her Queenie and not to a shop where we might purchase a chain and afterward be on our way. But then, if you happened upon a circus elephant wandering the street, would you not want to bring it home?

Lila Mae turned to us and smiled, now patting the back of her grandmother's hand as if this bout of sorrow were about to pass. The old woman wiped one eye and then the other, one cheek and then the other. She began again to rock her chair. "What brings two white boys to this part of town?"

"Passing through," Lester explained. "I need a chain for my bicycle."

"One is pulling the other, Queenie!" Lila Mae laughed. "You should see it! An' they's loaded up with packs and bedrolls and all!"

And Queenie did laugh – her head tilted back, no teeth, great cavern of mouth, nose flat to her face and nostrils as round as a pencil but three times the size – as though she could see us in all of our comic glory. As I was watching her, I realized she was still sighted – maybe not in reflections of light, but in a heart of reflection. I felt her joy as I had felt her pain and so could not help but laugh with her.

"Oh chil', you is one funny girl bringing me such a thing!"

Lila Mae beamed to have given her grandmother the gift of laughter on a sweltering summer afternoon.

"Where's you boys headed?"

"New York City, Ma'am."

"Now don't be callin' me Ma'am an' such. I ain't no Ma'am. But my oh my, New York City! What takes yous two there?"

I shrugged. Lester spoke. "It's something we need to do. A place we need to see. A trip we have to take."

The woman stopped rocking and sat utterly still, her lips now an "O" and her mind at least as far back as the days of the selling of human beings. Eventually and slowly, she began to nod. "Why is this a trip you haves to takes?"

Lester and I looked at one another. "To see the green lady, Liberty Enlightening the World," Lester offered.

Her lips formed another "O" and she nodded.

"My peoples didn't come through no gates of liberty. I s'pose yous knows that."

We nodded, then said, "Yes."

She nodded. "Well, that be a mighty fine thing you boys do. Everyone should see liberty in their life. You is sojourners, then."

I hadn't thought of myself that way but nodded, then said, "Yes."

"I's a sojourner myself. May God bless you on your way."

The blessing of God is fine and dandy, but it isn't a bicycle chain. I was tempted to say as much but could not for as I stood there, I began to realize the depth and meaning of the blessing I'd been tempted to overlook while mired inside my own predicament.

I was in the presence of something, or more accurately, *someone* close to the Lord. I felt it in the air. I heard it in her voice. I saw it in her clouded eyes. It was then that I remembered the words of Jesus – *I live in the least of these, your brethren* – and as I stood before a woman who dwelt and flowed easily between laughter and tears, and maybe between the eternal and the present, I knew what Jesus had said was true. I was near God.

And then she smiled – apparently having discerned the worldly part of my thoughts and remembering another of Jesus' words – that a blessing to be well-fed without a serving of bread is useless. She instructed Lila Mae, "Take thems around back. Tell your papa to fix them up. Tell him they is sojourners and I said so."

Around back, on a lot that while narrow, was so deep that it seemed to have its own horizon. I saw no end of gardens of flowers and vegetables. I glanced at a dozen or so chickens milling randomly about. They were so pathetic and pecked featherless that I felt a mercy killing might be in order. Then my eyes drew back from the horizon and the motley lot of poultry. They landed upon a black face and white eyes filled with apprehension.

Papa, it turned out, was a man probably only ten years our senior. His very black skin glistened with sweat. He looked up from the axe he was sharpening upon a whirling stone. The action of his feet propelled the device much like a seamstress propels a treadle sewing machine. He ceased and the stone began to slow. He stared with purest suspicion at the sudden appearance of two white boys being led into his yard by his daughter.

"Queenie says you is to help them," Lila Mae interjected as I caught the man's very white eyes shift between us and a collection of knives on his bench – not that the axe in his hand wouldn't do the job.

"Hello." Lester stepped forward with his hand extended. "My name is Lester and this here is Joe."

The whites of the man's eyes completely disappeared as he squinted at us. I was thinking we should leave and was about to say as much when Lila May stepped between Lester's hand that remained extended and her Papa's hand, still upon the axe, that was not. "Queenie says to help them. They gots them a broken bicycle chain and they is sojourners."

The man's full lips puckered at the relayed instruction. The previously whirring stone at last coasted to a stop. The axe in his hand was laid among the knives. The man stood. Lester stepped forward. I stepped backward. Hands shook. Lips remained puckered. Eyes remained narrow. Words were grunted. "If Queenie says so."

"She do."

Nostrils flared. Papa nodded, released Lester's hand and wiped sweat from his brow with the back of his hand. "Let's have us a look."

Lila Mae danced ahead of us as we headed back around the house. Hunger panged in my stomach as we passed by an open kitchen window. Air moving through the screen was heavy with pepper and pork. A snap and splatter of grease teased my ears as well as my stomach. And as if that wasn't already bad enough, I caught an aroma of cornbread mingled among the other aromas. I wanted to stop and eat the air.

Papa observed our packed, mud-splattered bicycles as warily as he had beheld us but said nothing – for who knows what two white boys in the colored part of Omaha might be up to.

"I have parts waiting for us in Galesburg," Lester began to explain. "Tires and a chain. But..." He shrugged. "Guess I miscalculated the wear." The man kept his eyes on Lester's bicycle.

I glanced at the front porch and now empty rocker. Two white eyes inclined upon a head tilted in curiosity peered back at me from shadows beyond the screened door.

"Iver Johnson," the man commented. "I should'a knowed." Lips puckered. Head shook. "Bring them 'round back."

"Lila Mae!" We all turned toward the screened door and squat woman holding it open. "Get me some greens." The woman's other arm produced a tin bowl, jutted forward as sharply as her command had been issued.

"Yesum, Mama."

"An' don't bring in no snails er slugs er pinchers with 'em." Then white eyes set in a face so black I could not discern its features in the fading daylight, landed on Lester and me. "You's stayin' for dinner. Queenie says."

Then she muttered something about white people under her breath and disappeared back into the shadows. The door slapped rudely closed behind her.

The early morning sky was just beginning to change from black to gray when Lester and I awoke, possibly more tired than when we'd finally gone to sleep and definitely more sore. We rolled our beds,

130

stuffed them in their canvas sacks, tied them to our bicycles and relieved ourselves in a two-seater at the rear of the lot – the horizon of which we'd become familiar with as it had been our night's encampment.

Lights were on in the house as we pushed our bicycles past Papa's Iver Johnson, now missing its chain. It seemed that a sojourner, even if they be two white boys in the colored part of Omaha, took precedence over the transportation of a working man. We pushed our bicycles past the kitchen window, which was already alive with the sounds of morning, and then upon coming around front, leaned our mounts against the porch.

Two bowls of corn flakes and a pitcher of milk waited on the rail as had been promised the night before. Lester and I downed them in the silence, quickly, but not as swiftly as the steady brightening of the sky above us. Lester stepped up on the porch, cupped his hands and shouted through the screen, "Thank you! Thank you for everything!" He was barely off the first step when a thunder of footsteps began from inside. The squat lady had never warmed up to us much. From the impact and haste of the footfalls approach, I feared her white eyes were about to appear at the door. I was fairly certain we were about to hear her mutterings about white folks a little more distinctly than we had before.

To my great relief, Queenie appeared at the screen, opened it and stepped out onto the porch. She looked at us, sighted in the dark more so than two white boys sighted only in the light.

"Yous so welcome. If yous two be through this way comin' back, stop in an' tell us 'bout yer journeys. Yous always welcome."

"We appreciate it ma… Queenie, and we'll do that."

And then Queenie broke all the rules she'd not yet broken. She stepped forward; hands outstretched to grasp Lester's. Black hands took white. "God bless you on your way."

Then she came to the rail where I stood below and reached over to take my hands. "God bless you on your way."

Between her voice of velvet, silk and honey and the firmness of her grasp, I heard and felt the unmistakable presence of the Lord. Her hands were rough, yet smooth; dry, yet soft; strong, yet tender.

They communicated not a touch, but a lifetime and more than a lifetime, a people. And – I add to my shame – a people whom I had seen but never known – and before this moment – had never touched.

She said not another word and neither did we. What can you say when you have suddenly and without warning found yourself so blessed? We mounted and rode away per instructions given us the night before: *"Two blocks over – then left – follows the trolley line until yous see the bridge off to the right, then goes that way to the great Missouri. You can't miss the great Missouri."*

Two blocks over, then left, we rode into a landscape of torn and twisted trees – their broken arms black silhouettes against a haze of sky about to lean from gray to orange. Homes lay in rubble and if not in rubble, then in disrepair, some merely foundations filled with rainwater. Throughout the instruction of where to go, no one had mentioned the destruction we now saw all around us.

We rode abreast, wordless, in awe, in wonder, in confusion. "What do you suppose happened?" I finally asked.

"Don't know. Some disaster."

"Tornado! I bet it was a tornado!"

"But when?"

"Sometime back," I ventured noticing a tree's green shoots and estimating the seasons it would have taken to grow them.

But life went on in disaster's scars as it did anywhere else. In the dim light of predawn, people – black people – emerged from their dwellings, lunchbox and bags in hand, walking, going off to work as if everything around them was normal and if not normal, then what it was, rather than what it ought to be.

Since Lester and I had already broken all the rules, we rolled upon a black man waiting at a trolley stop smoking a cigarette. We stopped. Lester waved his hand at the broken landscape behind us. "What happened?"

"What do you mean, what happened?"

"The destruction."

He laughed. "Oh, you never seen this before?"

We both shook our heads.

He looked at our packs, assumed our journey and laughed again for our surprise was his reality. That in itself was odd enough to bring forth a laugh – not of humor – but of irony. "Tornado, back in fourteen. Quarter mile wide. Left a path three quarters mile long through this place. Killed a score. Injured more. Cut this city in half."

We nodded. "Thank you."

We put our feet on our pedals and were about to push down when he spoke again, not in conversation, but forcefully, as if this was something we needed to know. "Resurrection day."

We faced him, puzzled.

"It happened on Easter Sunday; resurrection day."

We nodded again and pushed off. We rode in silence until streets became streets like any other street and trees grew like any other trees and homes looked like any other home. The sky above was now orange and the sun just about to break over the horizon. Bird song enveloped us all around like any other morning of any other day. Still riding abreast, I turned to Lester. "How many people do you think lived in Queenie's house?"

"Hard to say, but quite a few."

"They filtered in all evening long, dog tired, walking home from work from all directions."

"Sure did. All evening."

"How did they have the energy to dance? It seemed to me that they danced all night."

"They heard the fiddle. Hell, as tired and sore as I was, I wanted to get up and dance with them."

I laughed. Maybe we hadn't broken *all* the rules – two white boys eating at a separate table in the backyard of the most hospitable home we'd yet come across, yet a home we never entered for it would not have been proper to do so.

Then Lester added, "Queenie explained to me that they danced every night, not because they had the energy, but because they were free."

"How come white folks don't dance like that?"

"We dance every day, Pike."

I looked over at Lester's half smile, a riddle begun.

133

"You and I dance every day. We go where we want. We do what we want. We go to Robbins on the Corner for ice cream. We sit in the front of the trolley. Our fathers are tradesmen and businessmen. Your brother is a detective. Your sister is a nurse. Our income is measured in dollars, not in pennies from sharpening knives or cleaning homes or cooking or taking care of other people's children. I'm welcome wherever I go. I can shake the hand of everyone I meet. We dance every day, Pike. We just haven't noticed the fiddle."

I nodded, hearing one pull of a bow across strings as I did – a sour, haunting sound it seemed to my waking ears. For as I thought about it, the fiddle had always played just as the dance had always been danced. Neither were heard in the hearing of those who assume their freedom rather than relish its novelty in the ways and annals of man.

Sometimes great masses of air traverse the land and in so doing, meet in places and at times and in a way that great masses of air are not meant to meet. They then leave the violence of their resettling in scars across the land – twisted, broken arms reaching for resurrection against an ever-brightening sky, but a sky the sun has yet to pierce.

Chapter 18

June Bug

They are terror from the sky, pure and simple. Evil with a flurry of wings, a clatter of shell and a landing akin to the deathly grasp of Satan's right hand. I might add that Lester hasn't stopped laughing about it for nigh on two days.

We crossed the mighty Missouri into Iowa – the breadbasket of this great land. Whereas the west is, with the exception of two months in the spring, basically shades of dust and dirt, Iowa is green with shades of deeper green and a side order of green just to be sure. Everything not only lives in Iowa but grows to the proportions of bones chiseled from rocks that date from prehistoric times.

Spiders in Iowa are the size of silver dollars. Centipedes are as long as your hand. Cockroaches are the size of a Model T. Then God looked upon all that he had made, said that it was horrible, but decided he could do worse – so he made June Bugs.

It was evening two days ago in the barnyard of a kindhearted farmer when I became acquainted with June Bugs. Our host had allowed us not only a patch of grass on which to lay our bedrolls but use of his pump and trough for sorely needed bathing. I had just come up out of the water when I heard it: thunder on the move, plowing through the twilight, at first a shadow careening wildly in the distance. It floundered like a bat, growing louder, legs silhouetted against a gray-black sky. Its aim like a torpedo, determined as a bird of prey, lurching wildly yet on course – until it landed upon my head with the firm grip of Satan's right hand.

Yes, I screamed.

Yes, I swatted at the creature now tangled in my hair.

Yes, I jumped naked from the trough.

Yes, I ran helter-skelter about the barnyard, still screaming, still swatting, jumping and howling in purest fright. The evil of a June Bug is not to be compared to its size. Although only an inch in length, it is an inch of black disgust – terror from the sky.

Lester had fallen to the ground, laughing so hard that the farmer's entire family was drawn onto their porch – gaping at my distress, covering their eyes at my nakedness – but laughing along with him. And two days later, even when Lester isn't still laughing about it, a smile of his delight at my predicament will not, and absolutely cannot, leave his face.

On this Sunday morning, day of the Lord, we have left our bicycles and packs at the Y.M.C.A. where we had spent the night. While walking toward the nearest steeple to bow our heads in reverence and thanksgiving to the good Lord above, I happened to turn to Lester. The smile that simply cannot go away had returned to his lips. His eyes shifted slyly toward me.

"What?"

"Since it's Sunday and all, I was just thinking about when Jesus came out of the water and the Spirit of God descended upon him like a dove."

I pushed Lester sideways with all my might. He laughed as he stumbled. But since that was kind of funny, I found myself laughing along with him.

I'd noticed, even if I had not paid attention, a peculiarity ahead. Motorcars were allowing a berth around something sprawled half on the road and half in the gutter. Other churchgoers were leaving the sidewalk as they came near, then crossing the street to avoid it. "What is that?" I pointed.

"I don't know. Looks like a great lump of fabric. Maybe some bolts fell off a textile truck."

"Why would people avoid rolls of cloth like that?"

"Maybe it's calico."

I laughed. Calico was *so* out-of-date. Since this was Sunday, my hair was slicked to the side and due to a late-night scrubbing in the Y.M.C.A. lavatory, my clothes were as clean as they could be. I didn't yet smell, but even the slightest exertion in Iowa's heat would likely change that. Lester, proper citizen that he is, should we happen to come across an obstacle sprawled in the path of progress, would likely be inclined to volunteer us in the task of its removal. "Shouldn't we cross?" I innocently indicated the altered path taken by those ahead of us.

"I'm kind of curious to see what that is," Lester replied.

"I'm clean so let's not change that by getting stuck tidying up someone else's mess."

Lester frowned at me.

I made a face in return.

We continued only a few more steps before Lester stopped. I stopped. At closer observation, it was quite unmistakable. We looked at each other, then once again ahead. The obstruction was nothing less than the body of a great, large woman. We came a couple steps nearer. She was quite dead, blood dried upon a gash on her head, flies encircling her corpse. I looked up and around wondering which edifice she might have jumped from but found none in the proximity.

We watched with puzzlement the total impassivity of those who walked and drove around her. Neither their pace nor conversation were altered in any perceivable way upon encountering the scene of morbid death. "Shouldn't someone ring the constable?" Lester finally asked.

I shrugged.

"Could we at least pull her out of the road?"

I made a face. Had I *not* just stated my desire to avoid physical labor?

"We should do something. We can't just leave her there."

I rolled my eyes, sighed, and walked forward at Lester's side. This was a great mound of flesh, but assuming we possessed the horsepower, Lester bent to grab one arm and I stooped to take the other. We set our feet, engaged gear, eased off the clutch and had pulled her about a foot when the lifeless body in our grip convulsed. Her head, heretofore dangling from its neck, rose up, opened its great cavern of a mouth and screamed.

Lester and I screamed in sheer horror, flung the woman's now flailing arms from our grip and jumped away.

137

"What in the Sam Hill do you think yer doing?" she demanded.

As I now fully understood the saying: *eyes popped out of one's head*, I remained speechless. My lack of response seemed not to matter to the corpse who was now quite occupied in pulling arms and legs together. She rolled about trying to rise up from the street. Might I add that as she thrashed about, the cause of her sorry state of affairs began to work free from folds of fabric and flesh. Alcohol scented brown glass bottles clinked against pavestones and spread out in ripples around her

"Well don't just stand there," came a second screech. "Help me up!"

Do! Don't! Pardon me on the Lord's Day, but what the hell? Lester and I stepped forward to the rolling, thrashing, somewhat indecisive corpse and grabbed her hands – you know – the ones we'd just been ordered to fling aside. The great mound of fabric began to rise, eventually stood, wobbled, then pulled her hands from our grip. "Let go of me!"

Her eyes, deeply set in flesh, glowered at us as a belch punctuated her heartfelt contempt. She turned toward the sun now well above the horizon, squinted, and scowled.

Lester looked the woman up and down, glanced at the various bottles laying on the street and raised his eyebrows. "You going to be all right?"

Her eyes penetrated us and her cheeks shook with outrage. "Who the hell do you think you are asking me if I'm gonna be all right?" Then she not-very-discretely nudged a few bottles from sight with her foot.

Lester lifted his hands in surrender. Both of us were now fully knowledgeable as to why she had been left lying in the street un-assisted by churchgoers on a Sunday morn. We were in full retreat when she began to pat her expanse of clothing. Then she looked around in confusion as if she'd lost something – you know – other than her mind.

A toll of church bells began to ring. The warm embrace of stained glass, consecrated sanctuary, and fellowship with likeminded people of the Lord were mere steps away. I felt the Bruce crease come to my brow. "Lose something?"

Eyes set in way too much face looked up at me, then shifted side-to-side. The thought that evaded her had to be around here somewhere. She puckered her mouth to one side, returned her eyes to the here and now – at least more or less – then began to lurch unevenly a direction that seemed yet to be determined. My shoulders sagged as I looked at Lester and gave up the thought of sanctuary.

"Ma'am," Lester offered, walking toward her, his hand outstretched, "can we help you get somewhere?"

Mouth shifted to the other side. "Maybe." A short finger on a pudgy hand came to her mouth, the lips of which she drew up beneath her nose. Her eyes shifted upward, inadvertently toward the sun, which brought another grimace to her otherwise unpleasant countenance. She swatted the sun aside. Her eyes again tracked side-to-side looking for that elusive thought.

She turned about and with great determination, began to walk the opposite direction. Three paces later she stopped and turned to us again. "Last night is a little fuzzy in my mind. Don't know exactly how I got here and havin' a little trouble remembering where I belong."

Thinking she arrived by way of a proprietor of liquor, I looked up and down the street for the shingles of such establishments – only briefly as she was once again on the move. Although she was moving forward, she was also listing to the side, veering left so that given enough territory, she might well have circled around. Lester began to sheepdog her progress – which once again came to an abrupt halt. Eyes rolled up in her face. "Detroit Electric, Series Sixty Brougham!" She raised her arm and short finger in victory, then took to looking up and down the street for where she might have left one.

"Is it red?" I asked.

"Red!" Her arm raised in triumph once again.

"This way." I pointed us back the way we'd come. Every motorcar caught my eye, but a maroon Detroit Electric with steel spoked wheels and whitewall tires had lodged in my memory – well that and the fact that it had been parked much as we'd found its owner – half on the street and half in the gutter.

It was a gorgeous motorcar, essentially a coach fit for Cinderella's ball, but with a rounded stub in front instead of a team of white horses. This machine of refinement was somehow owned by its antithesis now lumbering toward it, still listing left with Lester still sheep-dogging her progress. The Detroit's door had been left open from her apparently drunken disembarking the night before. As I beheld in awe the curved glass and graceful lines of its coachwork, I scarcely noticed her entry until its springs gave way. Entry was followed by her subsequent plop upon the driver's seat.

We watched as the woman struggled to arrange an assortment of bars that apparently controlled the machine. Then without warning or sound, the sculpture of refinement began to propel itself backwards – might I add just as the great girth of woman rolled off the seat into a heap upon the floor. Lester jumped on the running board and leaned into the still open door, masterfully took the levers in hand and brought the vehicle to a stop only moments before it would have plunged into a tobacconist establishment across the street. I smiled to imagine the shop's wooden Indian might then have replaced the woman at the Detroit's controls, for it may well have been a better driver – and possessed a more agreeable personality.

Lester peered down at the heap of fabric. "Could I drive you somewhere?"

The woman's face turned about, looked up from the floor and nodded. "Might be a good idea."

Once we got her up and nestled into the sofa-like seat in the rear, she stretched out her arm like Custer leading the Calvary to its last stand. "Forward!"

Never mind that we were full sideways in the street and *forward* would have taken us over a curb and into a clothier's window. I watched with amazement as Lester not only figured out how to control the silent vehicle but drive it as expertly as if he were her chauffeur.

"Left. Right. Over there! What are you doing? Left I said! Slow down. Back up! Oh, the Sun! Circle the block. Up the hill. That one! I said stop! My God, what are you doing?"

By the time we reached her destination, a magnificent hilltop

Victorian, I'd about had it with the wretched one. I would gladly have left her seated in her Detroit and rotting until Christmas or possibly even Easter. I could see Lester considering the preponderance of steps the listing one would have to navigate, then ever the Good Samaritan, he looked at me. As this was the Lord's Day and a curse from my tongue could very well land me in purgatory, I snarled discretely and committed myself to completing the parable we'd begun.

After extracting her wobbliness from the Detroit, we began our trek. As we trudged along the winding path I couldn't help but notice the contrast of her mansion to her neighbors. Not a single blade of grass grew from the dirt we walked upon. Whereas her neighbors homes were encircled with flowers, shrubs and trees, hers was stark, but the structure itself as well kept and ornate as all the others. Peculiar, but then given the day so far, not totally unexpected.

Her front door of oak complemented with leaded, stained, and beveled glass, swung open to an entryway of deep walnut panels. With the wretch firmly wedged between us so as not to lose control of her bulk, we stumbled past fluted columns with ornate cornices.

A staircase as magnificent as any I had ever seen, greeted us. A lead crystal chandelier above was equally spectacular. But what caught my eye and was obviously meant as the hall's focal point was a canvas. I'd never seen a painting so large, well not outside of the Antler's Hotel lobby in downtown Colorado Springs – but then it had been of a life-size twelve-point bull elk. This was a portrait of a most beautiful young woman attired in Edwardian finery – corseted waist, boddice, a preponderance of lace, shawl and parasol. She was surrounded by a garden that would make Eden look parched by comparison.

My mouth fell open. Was that angels singing? Perhaps the wretched one had a daughter whom we may soon meet and possibly spend the day with. One never knew what reward might await a Good Samaritan who had given up sanctuary for a stranger found sprawled upon the street.

"Who is *that?*" I allowed my arm's sweep to encompass the entire beauty – already in my arms. I could feel her breath on my lips as we whispered sweet nothings to one another between soft...

"What do you mean, who's that?"

"Well, I mean, who *is* that?"

"Are you daft? It's me, of course."

The Bruce crease pinched my brow so hard I nearly cried out. My heart shattered. I gaped at the abomination that had destroyed my fantasy. "Huh?"

"It's me. Who else would it be?"

I looked at the woman, now attempting to strike a pose identical to the painting. She was five times her previous size and dressed as if she'd rolled in wallpaper paste and then thrashed about on an acre of tapestry. Her attempt did not replicate well. I could not prevent a raise of my nostril.

"Well, I was younger then."

That didn't explain the half of it. My nostril remained in a position of disbelief and my brow kept its crease.

Her attempt at a smile to imitate the demure tease of the beauty preserved in oil above us approximated a silent cackle. My eyes widened in horror and my pinched brow rose.

"My father was a banker and I was his only daughter, the apple of his eye. He doted on me and gave me everything I could ever want." The woman abandoned both her pose and the grotesque smile she had spoken through. "Some say he spoiled me." She winked coyly as if spoil was not the same as rot, and obviously only an innocent and harmless expression of affection.

My grimace was nearly identical to the smile she had spoken through.

She waved her hand at me. "Ah, what do you know?"

Lester cleared his throat and gestured toward the door that we had left ajar behind us. "If you're going to be all right, Pike and I will be going."

"Pike? What kind of lunatic names a boy Pike?"

"Joe," I explained. "Joseph is my name. Pike is my nickname."

"Ha! You want to hear mine? Well, first I gotta tell you what my parents came up with for my given name: April May. Can you believe that? Well, I said why stop there? Why not add June and July?" She laughed. "April May June July! Now that's a name don't you think?"

I shrugged. So did Lester.

"My folks got a laugh outta that but then shortened it to what became their pet name for me, Junebug."

Lester laughed with an outsized guffaw – which pleased the wretch as she believed the source of his delight was her wit and not my embarrassment – which of course it was. "Junebug!" he repeated enthusiastically. Then he winked at me to add, *what a great nickname for a gal!*

I scowled at Lester as Junebug had scowled at the rising sun.

"You boys want to stay for breakfast?" Her eyes rolled up. "Or maybe lunch. I'm not quite sure. I just know I'm hungry and there should be some reward for the two chivalrous heroes who got me home."

While I hesitated, Lester closed the door behind us. As the hall was then illuminated only by scant light filtering through elaborate designs of stained glass, we were plunged into near darkness. "Absolutely!" he exclaimed. After two weeks of pedaling one hundred miles a day, both he and I were *constantly* hungry – the Lord's Day being no exception.

"I'm sure I've got something in the refrigerator we can devour. That's right," Junebug raised her finger, "I said *refrigerator*, not ice box! Electricity! Now that's the way of the future I tell you. That's a commodity to invest in."

Then apparently revived by the idea of devouring whatever the refrigerator contained – and given her girth, possibly in its entirety – she led the way stumbling through the corridor, all the while reminiscing of who she had once been. "Let me tell you, I had suitors standing in line around the block. I rejected them all!" She waved her arm as if she'd vanquished invading hordes instead of the possibility of true love and a lifetime of commitment. She turned to us, victorious in loneliness as we entered the kitchen, again only illuminated by light filtered through stained glass windows. She smiled proudly as if we should congratulate her on her spitefulness.

I didn't know what to say. Lester didn't either, so he changed the subject. "Where does your wealth come from?"

She laughed. "Daddy! Well, that and oil. Oil! Now that's the way of the future I tell you. That's a commodity to invest in."

She again laughed.

"But I thought you said electricity was the future." My comment was intended to prompt a thought that perhaps one might indulge in its convenience by switching on a light or two.

Junebug blinked. "Well, yes. Electricity is the future."

I glanced at Lester who glanced at me.

"Well, several things are the future: oil, electricity, steel, coal, wheat, barley – it's all the future."

My slow nod expressed doubt more than understanding.

She cleared her throat. A smile worked its way to her lips and her eyes chanced to sparkle. "Whatever returns a profit is the future, my boy."

"But isn't the purpose of investment to build a fledgling industry and make it the future we *ought* to have and then make it profitable? I mean, if it's already profitable, it's the present, not the future."

Smile fades. Formerly sparkling eyes squint. Lips part. Mouth says nothing. Hand waves me away. "Ah, what do you know?"

Then our hostess began to look about her kitchen equipped so that it very well could have been that of a restaurant and yelled, "Cook!" A stomp of her foot set glasses rattling on shelves. *"Cook!"* She stomped again, her residence's shudder causing me to doubt the integrity of its floor. "Where is my damn cook?"

"It *is* Sunday." Lester chanced to explain Cook's lack of response and possibly prevent the floor's demise.

Lips puckered, then pulled up beneath the woman's nose. "Augh. *Sunday.* Worst day of the week. Her day off. A true travesty of justice." She opened the refrigerator door and bent at the waist – or at least where I imagined her waist might be. She pulled from the electric wonder, a pan and thrust it into Lester's hands. A covered dish was then shoved into mine. "Probably something there you can eat." She waved us away with the back of her hand and stood aright. Her eyes rolled up in her head, then shifted to one side. "What's today?"

"Sunday."

"Glory be!"

She swung the refrigerator door shut with a sweep of her arm, turned about, went to a counter, then lifted a cover from a platter. My mouth salivated as I beheld a two-layer chocolate cake revealed beneath. *Oh my,* do I *love* chocolate cake – especially on a Sunday!

But my salivation was nothing compared to her drool. While quite literally licking her lips, she pulled a handful of forks from a drawer, picked up the cake and strode to the kitchen table. Forks clattered upon its top as she set the cake before her, tongue sweeping side-to-side across her lips. She sat.

Realizing she had forgotten a knife with which to cut the cake, I pointed toward the drawer she'd grabbed forks from. I'd just opened my mouth to offer to get one, as well as perhaps some plates, when she plunged her fork into the cake's center. My well-ordered way of thinking tumbled over. I gasped as she began to shovel an entire cake into her mouth. My eyebrows may very well have reached my hairline while my jaw fell to the floor.

She ate with a hum that never ceased but only changed tone and cadence with the rhythm of her fork. Chocolate crumbles and dollops of icing spewed out across the tabletop as Lester and I placed leftovers before us and began to inspect toothmarks in the sustenance that had been given us.

Had we not been as hungry as we were, we might have abandoned lunch and left with our pride, but a burning stomach trumps pride. We began to scavenge what we could of cold food that ought to have been served hot, scraps that ought to have been servings – guests in Junebug's mansion of inherited wealth.

A sweat had broken out on her forehead by the time Junebug leaned back on her chair exhausted and tossed her fork onto the debris that remained of the layer cake. She drew a breath. *"Cook!"*

Lester cleared his throat. "Cook's off today."

Junebug's eyes rolled up in her head. "Oh yeah. Get me a quart of milk." Her arm rose from her side and her finger pointed impatiently toward the refrigerator.

It was with purest resentment that Lester rose, fetched a jug of milk and set it before her. She seemed to notice nothing except her desire's arrival – which she grasped with both hands, emptied, then slammed down, chocolate drool now running from its neck. She wiped her mouth onto her sleeve.

I forced down a gag.

Then, as if to punctuate my distress, a noon symphony began. Apparently every room of her mansion possessed a chiming timepiece – all of which began to sound within seconds of one another but disturbingly not in unison. It was a hideous cacophony that by the last chime, had been enjoined by Junebug's snore.

Both arms hung limp from her sides. Her head rested upon its chins and her chins lie deposited in layers upon her heaving chest.

"I believe she's done."

I laughed at Lester's dry comment. "I believe she is."

"What do we do now?"

I had an answer for that. I rose, went to her cupboards and started opening doors.

"What are you doing?"

"Looking for dessert."

"You can't do that."

"Why not?" I closed one set of doors and opened another.

"That's stealing."

"We were invited for lunch, barely got that, then she ate dessert and we got nothing." I moved a few boxes and sacks to look around them. "There's got to be something sweet in here somewhere." Opening a third set of doors revealed the motherlode – three cookie jars – all full! I said nothing, took down and opened all three, filling my pockets as Lester looked on slack jawed. I returned lids to jars and jars to cupboard, then looked square at him. "She'd still be lying passed out in the street had we not hefted her up, supported her on our shoulders and taken her home. She owes us."

It wasn't exactly completion of the parable as Jesus had told it, but even good Samaritans are commanded to seek justice. I looked again at Junebug in her chair, nose whistling as she drew breaths and lips sputtering as she released them. Drool continued to seep from one corner of her mouth.

When Lester frowned at me I brushed his disapproval away with a wave of my arm. "Ah, what do you know?"

He laughed.

I did too.

"Sorry we missed church."

I shrugged. "I guess if we did the right thing, that takes the place of church."

"Doing the right thing is church." Lester gestured toward the stained-glass windows. "At least you got to experience sanctuary."

I considered windows of ornate, symmetrical, meaningless patterns and shades of colored light that glowed from them. They were beautiful indeed. I couldn't help but think it odd that their scant light contributed more to the mansion's darkness than its illumination. "I think this sanctuary is more about avoiding the light of day than understanding the meaning of light."

Lester looked at me strangely, smiled oddly, then nodded. He and I began to walk back through Junebug's mansion, past carved woodwork and its grand staircase, lastly to the portrait of a beautiful young woman. Spite had destroyed her beauty. Gluttony had altered her figure. What a shame, for once upon a time, she had been a beauty.

When a June bug is in larva, it lives in the ground where it feeds on the roots of grass, severing them from the blades that bring nourishment from the sun. As an adult, it comes out at night and eats leaves from foliage, taking away their light and eventually killing the June Bug's source of food.

Then it moves on in a jagged cacophony of flight, determined as bird of prey, landing not by intent, but wherever it happens to find itself – to devour – for its only drive is to devour.

Chapter 19

Of industry, gods, and fodder

"Twenty-two seconds. Eighteen seconds. Twenty-six seconds. Nineteen seconds. Twenty-nine seconds." We watched in amazement, Lester looking at his watch and calling times at each passing. Brand-new automobiles, purring on first firings of their cylinders, were driven under their own power as they rolled out of Mr. Ford's vast plant. I was absolutely transfixed, my brain overwhelmed by the sheer magnitude of everything I'd seen today.

Mr. Ford had created a wonder. Not only was a Model T reliable and the strongest built automobile a man could own, it was affordable and with a network of dealerships, easy to obtain.

We stood outside the world's largest, most modern factory. Within a decade of implementing his vision, Mr. Ford was already the richest man on earth. The equation by which he had accomplished all this was opposite mainstream rules of commerce.

Doublehalf.

Mr. Ford had doubled wages of his workers. Then he cut prices of automobiles in half. In addition he changed a 6-day, 55-hour work week into a 5-day week of 8-hour days. It made no sense, yet here we were, watching proof of Mr. Ford's unique accounting roll off his production line, shining, smelling of paint, rubber, and combusted gasoline. It was wonderful and I inhaled it deeply.

Detroit was our well-earned holiday, a halfway mark on our journey, a renewal for our bodies, an expansion of our minds, a place not only of ideas, but of industry. Perhaps most importantly it was Lester's city of birth and home to his paternal kinfolk. And not to sound self-centered or cheap, but Detroit signified two things very dear to travelers – free room and board. *Hallelujah!*

Detroit was so unlike anything I'd ever known I could not have conceived of it. Here in brick and mortar, not merely printed on a label, were names of products everyone knew, stenciled boldly across buildings in which they were made. Men who made them passed us on the street as if they were mere mortals, common men, and not gods. Even if their task was merely tightening a nut onto a bolt, they were building mankind's future – not in some ethereal idea, but in steel, solid, a thing within our hands, thus changing how we lived. They were gods without knowledge of their divinity – walking anonymously in hordes, all looking the same – nameless faceless gods transforming not only this generation but all yet to come.

"I'm hungry."

I turned to Lester whose hunger chime, as regular as clockwork, had just sounded. Mine sounded in concert. "Me too."

We'd packed salami and cheese sandwiches, water and apples that morning. Our rations would be quite warm but hopefully not yet spoiled on a day as bereft of shade as it was of breeze. We sat on a curb, resigned ourselves to dining in sweltering heat, opened distressed waxed paper and began to consume our sustenance. Nourishment in no way prevented us from observing everything we could about Ford's wonder of efficiency. Steam engines belching black smoke, boxcars, and men at siding switches operated as an extension of assembly lines and conveyors humming away inside. New motorcars passed in front of us, driven immediately to boxcars and absorbed into them as quickly as water is sucked into a sponge.

Everything was clockwork: precision, planned, executed – a symphony, each note of every instrument doing its part and no beat unnecessary. Opposite the railyard was another operation conducted with similar precision. Certain automobiles left the line, turning right instead of left. These changed hands between factory workers and teams of dealership drivers waiting to receive them. They then drove them away in convoys. Most of those shiny new machines had already been purchased. Their buyers in whatever town or state were waiting with baited breath – their entire lives and those of their families about to be changed by this wonderous invention.

Twenty-seven seconds. Twenty-two seconds. Twenty-eight seconds. Twenty-

149

three seconds.

We watched America change before our eyes, eating warm salami, greasy cheese, bruised apples, while breathing the acrid air of progress.

Our hats off to the President
who has kept us out of the war!

It was a massive sign, painted on canvas, hung across the factory wall awaiting a visit of Woodrow Wilson whom it honored. While Mr. Ford was a man of creativity and foresight, a captain of industry, he was also a man of opinion and conviction – none which he felt obligated to keep to himself. Mr. Ford fully intended to affect America's policies and ways of thinking as much as he influenced their lives. Mr. Ford had opinions on war, isolationism, roads, and nations. His agreement with President Wilson's stance on Europe's great war couldn't have been stated more clearly – or on a larger scale.

Lester and I would miss Mr. Wilson's event scheduled nine days hence, hopefully having moved on by then to Toronto – the home of Lester's maternal kin. But today as we strode around Ford's complex, we were at least witness to preparations for a visit of a president of the United States of America.

Windows were being cleaned, awnings brushed clear of soot, smokestacks whitewashed, handrails burnished. Woodrow Wilson had indeed kept us out of the war and was therefore a hero to those who had suffered and lost homes, limbs and loved ones in the still very raw memory of war between the states. And Misters Ford and Wilson may have had a point, keeping order in Mexico and the Caribbean seemed enough distraction for an infant nation still working to reconcile its own brokenness.

According to Mr. Ford and others of his same mind, we had no business in age-old conflicts of nations as dedicated to tyranny as we were to freedom. Let them fight it out if they so choose. We were a nation where all things would be new. More so, we were a nation kept safe by oceans on both sides. What had we to worry about?

150

America was a new world order. Here gods walked as mortals and here the voices of mortals had toppled history's established orders. In this U.S. of A., at long last, we the people had spoken. Here we were king and king was servant, voted into office at our will. Yet our president was no less venerated than a king, for we cleaned our windows in his honor of waited on his arrival with giddy anticipation. We raised our hats to his positions – that is – if they agreed with our own. And if we did not agree – our derision was as scathing as our praise was jubilant.

Aside from the day I would see the Green Lady herself and walk New York City's man-made canyons of broad avenues, this day had been the greatest of my entire life. We had walked and stood most of the day, so as Lester and I rode a trolley homeward, we sat side-by-side on an oak slat bench. Every jostle shook us and every turn swayed us. "I am so tired," I confided. "But happy. What a great day."

"It was. Isn't it great to be a tourist?"

We both laughed as much as our remaining ration of energy allowed. As citizens of a state that advertised its scenic wonders nationwide in hopes of attracting sightseers, we had often griped about tourists. Tourists had a tendency to randomly stop, spring from their motorcar, produce a Kodak, and then conduct a photography session as if the road were their studio. Further, they uniformly expected all other traffic to accommodate their whim, and this vexed us sorely.

"I got so excited at one point today, Pike. I wanted to hop on that assembly line and start turning bolts."

I laughed. Lester had come a long way from his days of string and bailing wire repair. Nowadays he could figure out just about anything mechanical. He also seemed to possess a sixth sense about how to operate anything with wheels, but to imagine him manufacturing an automobile tickled me.

"What's so funny?"

"Nothing. I think this is our stop."

We rose from our seats and made our way up the aisle. When our trolley slowed, we made our leap. Detroit, not unexpectedly, had

151

an abundance of motorcars of all shapes and sizes that – as all motorcars were apt to do – came at pedestrians with murderous intent – or so it seemed. Hence we scrambled onto the sidewalk.

Every city block had at least one market, most of them spilled half onto the sidewalk where passersby could not help but be enticed to make a purchase – well that or tormented if they were hungry.

"I'm starving."

"Me too."

I pulled my watch from my pocket. "What time did your aunt say supper would be ready?"

Lester leaned to look at the watch face I turned toward him. *"Five minutes ago!"*

We took off running. If they saw us coming, pedestrians leapt out of our way. If they didn't, we veered around them. We simply hurdled small children and dogs – laughing all the while. Our objective was a five-story apartment building that housed the cramped, dismal quarters that had been cheerfully billed to us in prior correspondence as "plenty of room." Aunt and Uncle lived up three flights of stairs from street level. Our race still on, still laughing, neck-and-neck, we skidded from the sidewalk, thundered inside, and bounded up a wooden staircase that seemed more a depository for milk jugs, children, cats, and sacks of trash than egress – jostling intensely for position in the home stretch.

Lester burst from the staircase, clearly in the lead, but not *fairly* in the lead, as his last shoulder nearly sent me over the rail and would have plunged me to my death had my reflexes not been what they are. My near demise and his preeminence brought forth from him, an abrupt about-face, victorious crow, and finger pointed at me in mockery.

I would gladly have knocked him on his keester but for two reasons. One: it would not have appeared good sportsmanship. Two: Detroit housing's preeminent rule was that no apartment hallway door was ever closed day or night. One would suppose in vain hope that somewhere a breeze might stir, come through an ever-open window, and bring hellish heat from one cramped quarters across the hall to exchange it for hellish heat in that apartment, and ultimately, wishfully, expel it into a great outdoors of equally hellish heat.

As no breeze ever stirred to any noticeable degree and it would have made no difference if one had, open doors served then only to bring irritated housewives into their frame with frowns upon their faces should two boys from out-of-town be too loud or rambunctious – which we had apparently been – as three doorways were promptly filled with irritated housewives, curlers in their hair, and frowns upon their faces.

Lester and I sucked in our lips, nodded greeting, tipped our caps, and walked past them without a word. An unintended aspect of open doorways is that they allow every cooking odor – *and odor is the word I mean to use* – to mingle with smoke from every cigarette, cigar, and pipe and then fill the lungs of yours truly with a veritable potpourri of national origin. It only took a single sniff to determine whether the occupant of any given apartment was Italian, French, English, German, or Spanish – not that most of them didn't speak in their native tongue and if not that, then with thick accent, and usually at a volume intended to carry to the homeland – or so it seemed.

Screaming children, crying babies, yelling couples, crackling phonographs, clanks, thumps, and crashes at all hours completed city dwelling's trifecta of sensory misery. This, in turn, inspired Lester and me to be gone from his kinfolk and their "plenty of room" every possible moment we could manage.

But now we were late and entered the kitchen as bad dogs about to be scolded, our heads already hanging and tails between our legs. Conversation that was never more than minimal, became non-existent as we offered a humble apology for our lateness, then silently took our plates to the stove and began to fill them.

We called him *No Fingers Fred*, not to his face, but in private conversation and laughter when well away from home. I barely understood designations of first cousin, second cousin, great this and great-great that. Therefore, I wasn't sure to what degree, if any, No Fingers was related to Lester. In Detroit, it seemed people of any relation, no matter how distant, lived together in cramped quarters the city offered its working poor. No Fingers was one of five adults and – I don't know – twenty or thirty children living or at least passing through the two-bedroom abode at any given time. Another rule of Detroit was that all children were required to have snot perpetually dripping from their noses and encrusted on their upper lips. The sight of them at mealtime made me gag.

That's why Lester and I watched No Fingers. His struggles with a fork and spoon were quite beyond anything Charlie Chaplin could have devised. Bring a knife and a tough portion of meat into the act, and neither Lester nor I could look at one another without risk of falling to the floor in laughter. What makes *good* comedy *great* comedy is the complete oblivion and unwitting participation of the person providing said hilarity.

Now, in all fairness, Fred did possess three one knuckle fingers, two no-knuckle stubs, two two-knuckle fingers without tips, one complete finger, and a partial thumb. He worked in steel, operating a shear, and over ten-and-a-half years of doing so, had nearly removed all possible interferences with his duties.

His hands were calloused, strong, and his fists – used often – were as solid as the iron that had removed their digits from them. Fred did not smile. He never laughed. He scarcely spoke. The entire household steered clear of Fred on a good day and kept a safe distance from him on dark ones – especially if a bottle had been involved – and as we had been warned – usually was.

Tonight's meal of boiled cabbage and potatoes included a sheer indulgence – meat, in this case lamb, which meant bones, which meant greasy fingers and gnawing. Whereas gnawing was easily accomplished with hands that possessed fingers, No Fingers basically would mash a chop to his face and hold it with his stubs as his teeth attacked its southern front. With grease smeared all about his face and hands and his jaw and tongue working in frenzy, I feared a complete collapse of my composure. Lester must have as well as he and I turned away from our favorite form of amusement and began to speak of our day's excursion.

"It was so amazing – utterly amazing – to see it in motion – to see automobiles built from parts to complete motorcars just as fast as that." I snapped my fingers, looked at No Fingers and found him looking back at me from under his brow. I swallowed and turned my attention back to my plate.

"He's paying them twice the usual wage for manufacturing. Twice! There's no talk of unions at Ford and no need for them. What there's talk of is workers buying the Model Ts they make, of workers buying homes – not renting – buying! They have savings! It's amazing. Clockwork. You have to see it to believe it.

"Mister Ford is changing the world. Everyone works side-by-side and everyone knows what to do, exactly how to do it. Efficiency. That's what it is. Every motion of every man goes directly into making an automobile. And Mister Ford is getting rich."

That was when No Fingers took his handkerchief, wiped his hands and mouth, pushed his chair back, stood and walked out of the apartment. I wondered what was wrong with him when I happened to notice disapproving expressions of everyone at the table were oddly aimed at me rather than at Fred's departure through the perpetually open hallway door.

We located Fred an hour later, sent by Lester's aunt with a stern admonition to find him and bring him back in whatever state we found him. Fred was sitting on the roof under a sky made orange by twilight refracting through layers of smoke that hung over the city. Ever-moving trains below pushed smoke into the sky both day and night, their chugs and whistles as much a part of the city as their bellows of black. Fred must have sensed our presence and seemed to have expected us. He didn't look our way until we settled in next to him on the brick edifice where he was sitting.

We said nothing. He said nothing. We waited.

"Sounds like you had a good day." His words were measured if not forced, Irish of accent.

"We did. I'm sorry that we offended you."

If he had had fingers, they would have risen from his hands that rested on his legs in a gesture to dismiss our offense.

We waited.

He held up his hands in the dimming light, looking at their deformity, shaking his head so slightly as to barely be noticeable. "Can't work at Ford. Can't work anywhere but where I work. Got no choice. In the land of opportunity, got no choice."

My heart panged.

A wry smile tugged at his mouth. Hands went back to his lap. "I don't blame you. You meant nothing by what you said. It's just hard sometimes to realize that my future isn't going to be what I imagined it would be. I came to this country expecting opportunity, but bit-by-bit, finger-by-finger, it went away and now the future I dreamed of, saved for, sailed across the ocean for, has become my fate." He drew a deep breath and released it. He laughed a little. Bitterly. "I was fourteen when I came to America. Lost my first finger at fifteen." He shook his head.

"Figured I'd learn to keep my hands clear after that, but working ten, twelve, sixteen hours a day – hungry – cold – hot – sick – fever – throwing up, you lose focus and make a mistake and another finger is gone."

Suddenly I felt guilt at my laughter, regret that I had found comedy in his predicament.

"I'm about to turn twenty-six." He looked at me, then at Lester. "Twenty-six."

I had thought him to be forty.

"Deaf in my right ear. Bet you didn't know that."

I shook my head.

"Steel banging on steel all day every day. Deaf as a stone in that ear and not so much left in the other ear. So, this is what I do. I operate a shear and hope one day it doesn't take a hand and I end up in soup lines with the vagrants."

We listened to a nearby whistle of a train, chugs of steam, a clank and rattle of cars on tracks.

"Sometimes I see the owner. He comes to visit driving his Cadillac – no – *driven* in his Cadillac. Fat. Bald. Smoking cigars. Rich. I'm still working for the same wage I earned five years ago.

"And I think what would it take – how much would it take to raise my pay a dime a day? Why has no one ever said, 'We're sorry Fred, about your fingers. Let's try to put some kind of plate in front of the blade where your hand can't slip.' What would it take? How much would my protection impoverish that man?

"He doesn't know I exist. He walks through with his managers never a glance my direction, talking all the while – *Why isn't this?* – *What about that?* – *Why not this?* Every question based on how he could get another dollar out of his operation. In ten-and-one-half years, he's never spoken to me, never even looked at me. Yet I hear that he is a philanthropist, a generous man, a donor to the arts.

"I am fodder to him, fodder of his wealth, fodder of his industry. I count for nothing. I am food and he is fat."

Fred held his hands up, stubbed silhouettes against a darkening sky of orange, blood red. A train's distant whistle joined arguments in thick accents coming from open windows as if playing the score of his lament. "This is my life – my one and only shot at life."

I couldn't help but think of Katherine Bates standing wind-whipped atop my Pike's Peak in Colorado's pristine crisp air. Blue sky overhead – snow-capped mountaintops and plains spread out before her in all directions as far as an eye can see.

O beautiful for patriot dream
That sees beyond the years
Thine alabaster cities gleam
Undimmed by human tears
America!

America.

Chapter 20

Ring the Bells

"Unless you want to spend tomorrow cooped up in here or find yourself in the hospital with flesh wounds and broken ear drums, you better get yourselves out of the city."

Lester looked at his aunt and blinked. To our knowledge, Independence Day was a family day: an all-day picnic, singing, dancing, bands playing in parks, neighbors, friends, and when the sky became dark – *glory be* – roman candles and skyrockets!

"But what about you and all the kids?" Lester asked.

"Aw, this is what we're used to. The kids don't know no different and I'm not inclined to pack everyone and everything up just to spend a hot day with a thousand other people swarming all around us, losing kids, then stumbling home dead tired and hoping some lunatic hasn't burned the place down. You go. Have fun. We'll stay here and guard the home front."

Explosions, pops, and crackle of fireworks – or more accurately – detonation of miniature bombs and discharge of firearms – had been an ever-present, all-night prelude to Independence Day since we'd arrived in Detroit. Tomorrow would be the grand finale of hooligan behavior that had been politely rephrased by newspapers as *over-patriotism*.

Maiming and death had traditionally claimed thousands of lives each Independence Day, particularly so in big cities, of that Lester and I were well aware. We agreed without a word of argument.

Shortly after dawn the following morn, we set out on foot to find a place to spend the second greatest day of the year – you know – next to Christmas.

"It feels different this morning," I commented while walking to catch the trolley.

"We can actually hear our footsteps."

I smiled. We could. Industry's ever-present clamor usually obliterated footsteps. "And birds," I added. "I can hear birds."

Lester inhaled deeply. "And do you smell this?"

Dew had washed it of yesterday's smoke and made it sweet. Morning's cool allowed it to be damp and pure. Soon it would be humid and suffocating – unless we could get away from brick and steel to claim a shady spot somewhere near water where a cool breeze might blow on us all day long. We carried small packs of provisions, intending to spend the night wherever we ended up, without a clue as to where that might be, but knowing it would be somewhere strange to us.

Now three weeks into our journey, most nights a surprise, some of them distressingly so, we'd become accustomed to the unknown, often reflecting on Jesus command: *take nothing with you, if you find hospitality, stay there, if not, shake the dust off your shoes and leave.*

We were disciples – but of what – we weren't sure – which pretty much dispelled any notion of disciplehood and reenforced that we were nothing more than vagabond tramps.

We hopped one trolley, rode it to line's end, then another, then another, walking in between, looking for a place where we could spend our day, each time moving on, hopeful of a better place. As heat set in and crowds began to build on city streets, more often than not, we no longer heard our footsteps or birds. We'd about come to realize that the better place we imagined might indeed exist only in our imagination.

"It isn't too late to go back," Lester offered, looking at me out of the corner of his eye as we walked along streets of another place we didn't belong, but had come to explore regardless. I looked at fine homes set back from the street by shaded lawns – all fenced with iron pickets or walls of brick – all of which implied, *Keep Out.* "Maybe someone will get a whole carload of company and we can sneak into one of these fine homes with them unnoticed."

Lester laughed, gesturing up and down himself, for we hardly possessed the trappings of the wealthy.

"Maybe we can sneak in the back and tell the servants we had been hired for the day."

Truth was that anyplace a person would want to be was behind fence or wall with windows and doors closed and locked. Inside superb homes were furnishings and dishes beyond our dreams. We had a place in the world and it was not in homes we walked past, dreaming to be invited into, but knowing we never would.

"Do you hear that?" I asked, ear inclined to a sound carried on the day's heat. We stopped and listened.

"Sounds like a drum."

"Yeah, snare, I'm pretty sure."

Its short riff no sooner stopped than it started again, ran its length, and started again.

Lester's eyes shifted toward me. Not much of a repertoire.

I shook my head. "Not much at all." Then I smiled. "Sounds like whoever is playing it needs company."

"Well, what is music without a celebration? And what is a celebration without guests?"

We began to walk, briskly now, toward the distant sound like a homing pigeon on the wing, certain of where it would go, but unaware of why it went other than it was compelled to go.

We found the beat of the drum coming from a park of grass and cool shade. A lonely, ragtag boy of maybe ten or eleven stood in an empty gazebo nestled beneath the trees, idyllically beside a pond complete with lily pads. His eyes locked on us at our arrival and stayed on us as we began to cross the grass, his riff never faltering.

Now one might assume that after we had come face-to-face, he may have stopped playing to exchange a pleasant hello. He did not. His eyes remained focused beyond us, toward the streets – not so much hopeful of more being drawn in by his playing – but demanding their presence – his sticks never losing their vigor, his tempo uninterrupted.

I cleared my throat. "Why don't you stop for a minute, have a drink of water, take a rest?"

He continued to look straight ahead.

"Just for a minute or two. We'd like to talk to you."

His riff ended, then started again. If he blinked, it wasn't noticeable.

I looked around. Lester and I were alone here. My ears were starting to ring from incessant drumming so I nudged Lester, angled my head toward the pond, and we began to walk that way. "What's wrong with him?"

"Apparently he's on a mission."

"He is never going to fill this park playing that one little drum and that one little tune over and over."

"He got us."

"True." We found the shady spot we'd imagined and sat on its grass, our legs and feet instantly relieved.

"How long do you think we'll be able to hear that same beat over and over again?"

I laughed. "I think we could tie him up if we needed to."

Lester laughed. "I don't know. He has pointy sticks and he looks pretty determined."

I laughed, but as I did, I noticed others coming as we had come, maybe a dozen more, drawn to the beat that refused to quit, its entirety little more than a refrain. "Maybe we'll have a nice little gathering after all."

"Maybe so."

We laid back looking up through tree branches at a sky that didn't seem to know blue, only gray summer haze. We said nothing, our eyes alternating between open and closed and then deciding on closed. Dreams began to distort my consciousness. The drum's beat was crude, sharp, uncomfortable, yet it did not prevent sleep from taking me into its pleasant embrace.

"Pike. Wake up." Lester had turned about, now propped up on his elbows, and was nudging me. I was about to insist that unless heaven and earth were about to… "I think our little drummer boy has incurred the neighbor's ire."

It may not have been the end of heaven and earth, but this sounded interesting and that was close enough. I struggled to pull cobwebs from my head and rolled about to rest on my elbows. I looked the direction of Lester's still-pointed finger.

161

She was wearing a lavender dress and a wide-brimmed hat roughly the size of Montana. Its ostrich plumes – also lavender – ruffled in the breeze of her own making for her stride was more that of a worksite foreman than a lady. Her leg's thrust tested limits and seams of her flowing skirt. Had she been wielding an axe, her determination was such that she may well have cleared the park – which was now, surprisingly, a quarter full.

Nonetheless, her beeline toward gazebo and drummer boy cleared a path.

The drum's beat stopped. Then he who had not deigned to even look at us put both sticks in one hand and bent to speak with her. I'd expected shouts and wild waving of lavender arms, but I heard and saw nothing of the sort. They conversed civilly. Lester looked at me as I looked at him – you know – having expected fireworks but gotten a dud. The boy stood aright, woman turned, boy began to play, woman began to walk – her stride and determination unaltered.

"You woke me up for that?"

"Well, it looked like trouble."

"Someone needs to stop that kid."

"I don't know, it's kind of catchy."

"It's annoying."

"Makes me want to get up and dance."

I hit Lester's shoulder with the back of my hand, then rolled back onto blissful cool grass. Dreams and sleep refused my invitation so I listened to a drumbeat now accompanied by sounds of laughter and conversation from those it had called.

Several minutes later Lester nudged me and pointed my attention to a truck, piano in its bed. It lurched over a curb, the piano in back rocking violently and nearly tossed from its bed. "That's something you don't see every day."

Not only was it something you don't see every day, it was also something unheard of. "Who brings a piano to a park?"

"Personally, I was hoping someone would show up with a fiddle or a trumpet." Lester and I watched the truck turn, then back up toward the gazebo.

"All we need now is a piano player."

Lester pointed the opposite direction. With music sheets in hand, the lady in lavender was striding back across the lawn.

"Well, isn't this a most unusual thing?" I mused.

But Lester wasn't musing. He was rising. "Come on, Pike. We need to help unload a piano."

It took six of us grunting and stumbling up wooden steps we were none too sure would hold both us and a piano. We'd no sooner positioned the piano and put its stool put in place, but the lady in lavender sat, arranged her music, flexed her fingers and began to play. Of course, it had to be The Star-Spangled Banner – to which the crowd, heretofore in clumps of their own scattered about the expanse of park, stood and came together – cheering, applauding, as grateful as Lester and me for real music and not just a beat.

She played mightily and her repertoire proved extensive. As she played and the crowd swelled, others with trumpet, string and even blocks of wood joined her. Then when she sought rest, they played on. What had started as a day of doubt, searching for a place neither of us were sure existed, was becoming a day of celebration – for what is music without a party and what is a celebration without guests?

We laughed and clapped, forgetting ourselves, feet tapping until dancing began, then dancing – taking hands of strangers, not only hearing music, but feeling music throughout our bodies as if we were one with it.

Then food began to appear as magically as the music. Neighbors whose homes we would not have been allowed into, not only came to the gathering, but brought with them food for the wayfarer who had brought only himself.

Given it was Independence Day, we'd imagined any music we would hear to have come from a proper band – men in striped suits wearing straw hats, broad smiles upon their faces, rehearsed – music from performers, not improvisors. We had followed a snare drum beat to anything but a practiced affair.

One ragtag young man had come as we had come, maybe seeking sanctuary, maybe seeking refuge, but unlike us had come with a drum. He only knew a march, and he had played it over and over and over again until his call had been answered.

We happened across him late in the day when off by ourselves for a moment of quiet, looking for a place just to sit and reflect on the celebration going on behind us. He was standing alone, his drum hanging at his side from a strap, sticks in his pocket, looking now not beyond the park with fierce eyes, but at the park and his creation alive in it.

We approached the lad and found him different, human, friendly in his smile of welcome, recognition in his expression.

"You filled the park."

He laughed. "There's still room."

"We would never have found it if we hadn't heard your drum."

He patted its side. "She's a good old drum."

"Is this what you wanted?"

He nodded, looking again at his creation alive all around us.

"Thanks for playing the music and bringing everyone together."

His friendly eyes turned toward us sharply, as fierce as they had been before.

"I don't play music." He pointed toward the impromptu band and the woman in lavender who was again playing the one instrument that no one ever would bring to a park. "That is music. They brought everyone together. My drum only brought people here."

The boy's eyes demanded my acknowledgement. I nodded and had just opened my mouth when I was interrupted by a huge boom.

The music stopped.

People gasped and turned toward the explosion, a sound we knew well from our nights in the city. It was a bomb disguised as a firework, destruction disguised as celebration, detonated somewhere among riverside crowds of lost children and strangers who would never dance together. Words I'd intended to speak left me. I instead remembered words I'd read used in newspapers to describe such destruction. "Over-patriotism," I said aloud.

"*Ha!*" The boy's eyes penetrated me, but it seemed with accusation rather than correction. "Patriotism has nothing to do with it. Hooligans just want to make the loudest noise and be heard above everyone else. They don't care about the music – never have and

164

never will." He looked at me until I nodded that I understood. Then he looked away.

He didn't laugh again nor did he return his eyes to us. He was only a boy but he looked as if he would fight the entire world if he had to – until they understood his clarion call – his march.

Music from the gazebo started anew. Conversation and laughter returned. Gradually the park became our little drummer boy's creation once again. Yet his gaze remained beyond it – maybe at those who should have answered his call but had not – maybe at those who never would – maybe at those who had yet to hear it.

Since that day when I've looked up at Old Glory gently waving in the breeze – its red, white, and blue so clear and vibrant under the sun – I remember the day I saw its colors as one. I see the lady in lavender. Though I remember the music she played that day, I've never heard it since. Those clamoring just to make the loudest noise have drowned it out. But I still hear the incessant beat of that little drummer boy. I smile to think that Guy and the cripple might somehow have heard that ragged lad's march as well. Or maybe it had been a grainy black and white photograph of the torch of Liberty Enlightening the World that had called to them. But one thing I know, one day all mankind will be drawn to that little boy's call – that Green Lady's torch – as I have to think that all mankind aches for liberty.

Chapter 21

Beneath the Surface

Running, jumping, shrieking, splashing. We were surrounded by more children this sweltering Sunday afternoon than we'd yet encountered along our entire journey.

Lester gave his head a mad shake as we strode out of Lake St. Claire's sparkling, dancing waters, back upon her sandy shore. We'd frolicked in the water so long that our heavy legs had forgotten how to bear our weight. I shook my head and returned the spray of water Lester had just pelted me with. Then I scooped a double handful from waves splashing around my knees and drenched his already drenched self.

Ignoring my childlike behavior, he stopped, rolled his head backward, drew a long breath, and closed his eyes. "Pike, I don't want to go back to the real world. I want this to be the real world."

I laughed, turned toward him, noticing distant silhouettes of ships that all day, every day, traversed waters beyond the buoys. I spread my arms to the sun above and closed my eyes. "I heartily agree my friend. I heartily agree."

We'd been in Detroit nearly two weeks and had daily hopped trolleys to go exploring. Our fascination with industry had lost its luster due to the grime, smoke, noise and general bustle innate to progress. Being boys used to genteel strolls through Colorado Springs' quaint downtown where everyone greeted everyone with a smile and a proper hello, we eventually found ourselves out-of-place in a city of busyness. We missed the hum of a breeze sifting through mountain pines, birdsong floating over windswept plains, and the delicate twilight song of crickets. We had therefore found ourselves drawn to any refuge we could find. The beach, *any beach*, as they seemed beyond number, became our refuge. In the Midwest there was a body of water darn near everywhere you looked. Such refuge became our inevitable destination nearly every day since our curiosity with progress had succumbed to industry's tarnish.

A heat wave which had settled over the entire eastern half of the nation cemented our commitment to water. Water was our only relief – well, maybe I should say – *everyone's* only relief – for we were but specks in a swarm of humankind that had flocked to the beaches this fine Sunday afternoon.

After a month on the road and being the largest and often only thing in our world, it felt a comfort to be just one of many – mere grains of sand on the beach whose individual destinies and plans mattered not on a scorching afternoon. I thought of the real world that existed in what seemed another place and time somewhere beyond the buoys. Like freighters and passenger ships, it seemed always on the go, always about its business, unstoppable.

We held to our ideal of existing in Lake St. Claire's carefree waters with our heads tilted back, arms outstretched and eyes closed only mere seconds longer. Then Lester uttered the more pressing of our desires. "I'm hungry."

I laughed. Smoke of roasting hot dogs wafting over us had summoned us hourly to patronize their vendor. And this hour would be no different than those that came before it. Even if we were on vacation and not riding one hundred miles a day, we were still *always* hungry.

We emerged fully from Lake St. Claire weighing a thousand pounds each. With the hot dog cart's umbrella in our crosshairs we headed its way like sluggish dryland torpedoes over sand, the heat of which, our feet became sharply reminded of.

Our sluggish trod quickly became an animated tiptoe as pain displaced lethargy. While nothing is quite so American as baseball, apple pie and hot dogs, it was a Chinaman's cart we'd frequented so often this fine day. He broiled our delicacy of choice over a handful of charcoal that he was tending when he looked up at us with a broad smile of Jack-o-lantern teeth. His smile was due not only to his familiarity with us, but likely also our vigorous and somewhat comical approach – knees and elbows akimbo.

Without asking, for he already knew, he whipped chopsticks from his apron pocket, plucked two juicy frankfurters from the grill, and plopped them into buns his other hand had simultaneously retrieved. Brown skin stretched in creases from his eyes and mouth back to his ears and coal black hair. His jagged and somewhat toothless smile remained as he bowed slightly and extended the hot dogs to us.

"Thank you," we said in unison, taking them while Lester deposited fifteen cents in our vendor's other hand. I looked over at Lester with a smile like that of a child about to receive a present. The extra nickel and Lester's wordless pointing at a pitcher meant Lester was treating us both to a waxed paper cup of refreshing lemonade.

We shooed flies away from a sticky bottle of catsup and open jar of mustard while the Chinaman plucked three dead bodies of their fallen compatriots from the lemonade he'd soon pour. A glance passed between us – but as we'd already discussed – that which did not kill us would only make us stronger. The Chinaman's grimy hands, questionable food storage and dubious preparation had not yet killed us. And really, could anyone with a smile that sincere harbor a serious or lethal disease? We chose to think not and the delicious aroma of roasting frankfurters reassured us, if not of the correctness of our decision, then at least our excuse for having made it.

Another brisk sprint across the sand, again looking as if we were being electrocuted, brought us at least partially into shade now being cast by one of many resorts that lined this portion of shore.

It took but a few bites and mere seconds of mastication until both aroma and taste of those flavorful hot dogs were but fond memories. Then Lester looked disdainfully at his Dixie cup of lemonade and asked what we always did after having fished dead flies from beverages. "What's the last thing a fly does before it dies?"

"Takes a shit."

Lester raised his cup in salute. "To the humble fly."

I raised mine to meet his. "To the humble fly and the flavor they add to life."

"In God we trust."

"E Pluribus Unum."

We partook of our precious refreshment with all due reverence for those who had lost their lives in it, crinkled our cups and dashed them aside like robust and daring men — as we indeed were.

But as urgency of one need passed, insistence of another began. "I need to use the bathroom." Lester was displaying both expression and posture of a toddler actively engaged in filling his diaper. This was not a false alarm, nor was it one that I supposed could outwait a beachfront traverse to public restrooms with any degree of success.

We turned toward the resort's wide porch filled with well-dressed guests sipping icy drinks from crystal glasses and picking idly with silver forks at delicacies fanned out on fine China.

Lester looked back at me with the kind of determination displayed only by the poor and desperate of circumstance. "I'm going in."

I raised my eyebrows and looked Lester from head-to-toe. He would never pass for a person of wealth — but then again — bathing suits were a great equalizer whereby the wealthy often looked far worse than the poor. He had a chance, so I shrugged. "Good luck."

He saluted, climbed up to the wide porch, vaulted its rail, which was daring in and of itself given his present predicament, then strode through deck chairs and tables, not with arms and legs akimbo, but with a short, brisk, purposeful stride, his ass clenched tightly on his bathing suit. I couldn't help but laugh. While I wanted another six or seven hot dogs and a gallon of lemonade (sans flies), I settled for an idle stroll anywhere relentless rays of sun were not baking sand to temperatures of a steam radiator in the dead of winter.

This restricted me to a one-foot-wide path along the resort's porch. I committed myself to a treasure hunt for dropped coins. A small fortune could very well await the tenacious and observant. But then, departure of a group from their table drew my curiosity. A gentleman had left upon his now vacant chair, a newspaper.

Although it had clearly been discarded and was headed only toward a garbage can, it was forbidden gain. I nonchalantly edged that way, cleverly reached through the railing and nabbed it like a toad's tongue gloms onto a dragonfly. I tucked my treasure under my arm and skedaddled out-of-sight with a short brisk stride and my ass clenched. Like Billy the Kid, they would never take me alive – or had he simply grown old and died a natural death – I was a little fuzzy on details – but I had nabbed a newspaper and thus far, no one was the wiser.

It was a little distressed and splotched with food, but still news to me. I eagerly shuffled through its pages until I found the front, refolded the mess and stared dumbstruck at the horror it presented. Time stopped. Shouts and laughter coming from the beach grew distant as I began to read.

"And don't come back," were the words that eventually broke my spell. I looked the direction from which they'd come and found Lester being shoved unceremoniously toward the resort's beachfront steps. His banisher was a youth somewhat younger than myself but dressed in a bow tie and white shirt. He possessed an air of authority that even Lester didn't choose to defy. Instead of being chagrined or ashamed or angry, Lester's eyes were dancing. His lips pulled into a smile that revealed damn near all of his teeth as he strode toward me – somehow victorious in his vanquishing.

"We better get out of here," he said with a laugh, grabbed my arm, and pulled me along.

"What happened?"

"Well, after I finished my business, I decided I wanted to see how the other half lived. I started to walk around and peek in doors and such." Lester pointed over his shoulder. "Then Sherlock Holmes back there caught on and started following me. I zigged and zagged and went upstairs and down and thought I'd lost him. Then just when I'd grabbed a handful of mints out of a bowl on the check-in desk, his hand landed on my shoulder. I was nabbed in the act." Lester was all out laughing when he opened a pocket on his bathing suit to reveal a stash of candies. "Yeah, the illustrious Mister Holmes pinched me on my *second* handful!"

We were back on the hot sand, attempting levitation by springing along with knees rising as high as our hips – as if that would make us lighter or the burning of our feet briefer. The shade of a nearby, but not *nearly* nearby enough, tree rescued us whereupon the gay pirate Atkinson produced a handful of now quite soggy and sticky confections from his pocket and thrust half of his treasure into my hand.

Now accessory to a crime, I shared momentarily in his gay pirate cackle and filled my mouth. Both our cheeks were bulged with ill-gotten loot when Lester gestured curiously toward the newspaper I'd tucked under my arm. I couldn't speak and didn't need to. Lester's happy countenance faded within moments of my handing it to him. Front page photos, tragic and quite graphic explained far better than I ever could. He read as I did with lips slightly parted and brow creased.

These things didn't happen.

Yet they had.

New Jersey's coast had been terrorized for weeks. When Lester finally cleared his mouth of candy enough to speak, he looked at me and uttered but one word. *"Sharks?"*

We turned, looked with dread at Lake St. Claire's sparkling water that we'd frolicked in all this day, then looked again at grainy photos of a boy and a young man, the latest victims of a man-eater.

"It was twelve miles inland?"

I nodded.

"Swimming in fresh water?"

I nodded.

We looked over at gentle waves lapping on a sandy beach, sun sparkling off dancing waters, children laughing, shouting, screaming, splashing. Lester's eyes went back to graphic images, his lips remained parted, brow still creased. Never looking up, he read as he spoke. "Clear back on July first was the first attack. We never heard about this. Why didn't we hear about this?"

"They didn't believe it was a shark. Biologists claim they're docile." I shrugged. "They didn't know what had done it and they didn't want to scare folks – you know – unnecessarily."

Lester bunched the paper aside with a sharp crinkle, then emphasized his words with swinging arms. "Cows are docile. Goldfish are docile. Any idiot can look at a shark and know they're not docile." With another loud crinkle of paper, Lester began to shake it at me. "With rows of razor-sharp teeth, a fin that moves silently through the water, dead eyes, and its sheer size, they couldn't believe the only creature capable of biting off someone's legs had actually bitten off someone's legs?"

"They do now. Witnesses saw it pass under a bridge as it swam up Matawan Creek." Lester's scowl seemed to accuse me. I didn't know whether to defend myself, a nebulous them, or plead the fifth. "Well, they didn't want people to panic," I excused. "You know how people can get."

"You mean they didn't want to lose business. The resorts hushed it. You think for one minute they didn't know it had been a shark attack? You think for one minute they didn't know that if they told the truth their beaches would be closed and their rooms empty?"

We both turned to look at bathers dashing about the surf, swimming out, hanging onto buoys, diving from them.

"Maybe we aren't the only ones who want to be suspended from reality, exist in a world of make-believe – where all is good and we aren't even required to bear the weight of our own being."

Lester grunted.

I pointed at the paper bunched under his arm and offered words of redemption. "But did you read that President Wilson has put out a bounty to rid the waters of the man-eater?"

Lester smiled bitterly and shook his head. "He did nothing when a torpedo glided underwater and sunk the Lusitania – *killing I might add* – nearly a score of Americans. Political maneuvering is what this bounty business is about. It's a semblance of action. A semblance of concern. It is election year, after all. The Lusitania was sunk at mid-term so he didn't have to do anything – and he didn't."

I knew better than to argue politics with Lester. His passion for what he believed to be right or wrong, true or false, could be quite biting. This discussion was no longer about sharks swimming in fresh water, but about right and wrong, truth, and Lester's opinions to that regard.

As I've come to find in life, truth is not something that can be disavowed, it is only something that can be put off – and then only for a time. Arguments engaged in on truth's behalf seemed only to bulge veins on foreheads and turn otherwise recognizable, friendly faces red with anger. Veins on Lester's temples were beginning to pulse. My stance – not that I had one – would have no impact either on Lester's opinion or President Wilson's actions. I did the safe, smart thing. I nodded and said, "Uh huh."

Hunters took both to inland waters and open ocean to rid them of terror and threat. For some this was civic duty, for others, for payment of a bounty. In the hysteria, it had been supposed that our nation faced a multitude of man-eaters. As it turned out, we'd faced only one shark gone rogue. It had acquired a taste for human blood, then became relentless, mad, frenzied, in its quest.

A lone shark had mobilized a nation. It seemed a world war raging across the Atlantic, deaths numbering in the hundreds of thousands, ships being sunk, and decimation of entire towns might have spawned like unity and action at some point over the past two years.

But the war wasn't on the New Jersey shore.

Chapter 22

Stained Glass

"Good morning."

"Good morning."

"Fine day."

"Yes, it is."

It was Sunday morning. As we passed open apartment doors, neighbors who we'd only heard yell and seen intoxicated or trying their best to get there, were this day sane and sober human beings. Footfalls sounding from the otherwise quiet hallway brought them into their doorways with smiles and pleasant hellos. It was a difference so remarkable; it was as if someone had flipped a switch.

Leading the way were Aunt and Uncle dressed in their best Sunday go-to-meeting clothes. They cordially returned their neighbor's smiles and greetings. No Fingers trailed sullenly but obediently behind them. No Fingers' only concessions to Sunday were to attend church and *try* not to get in a fight. Friendly greetings and pithy comments about the weather were, shall we say, not in his forecast.

Lester and I brought up the rear of our churchgoing procession. Our reasonably good pair of knee pants and white short-sleeved shirts were not only clean but pressed. My hair was parted and slicked to the side. Lester's, because it tended toward having a mind of its own, was heavy with styling wax and combed straight back. We looked as sharp as brand new two-dollar bills. We smiled politely, nodded, raised our hands in greeting, and tried not to push each other when no one was looking – you know – as the irreverent and disobedient are apt to do on Sunday mornings.

The miscellany of distant relatives, in-laws, outlaws, and their dozen or so snot-nosed children, had remained crammed into the "plenty of room" back home – which was fine with us as we had long since tired of their company. Our one-week Detroit visit had turned into two. Why? A brutal heat wave had settled over the eastern seaboard, northeast, and upper midwest. While Lester and I might have braved heatstroke, Auntie refused to be responsible or accessory in the demise of yet another of her brother's hellions – *excuse me* – sons. She mocked our schedule, refuted our protests, then gave our itinerary's significance a rather firm kibosh.

Feral stairway cats that had languished or hunted mice all night dashed for safety as we began a thunderous three-story descent on wooden steps. We emerged into bright sunlight already breaking a sweat. Church was three blocks down and one over. According to our calculations, maximum armpit saturation would be achieved at two blocks down. We walked in silence as is natural for churchgoers on a Sunday morn.

A motorcar sputtered past. A clack of steel wheels on tracks sounded momentarily as a trolley traversed a cross-street ahead. Sidewalks in front of markets were clear and swept. Doors of businesses were shuttered. It seemed as if even commerce was taking a badly needed breath.

"Wonder what that's about." Lester gestured ahead. The trolley's passing revealed a small cluster of churchgoers assembled on the walk. A newsie near them was waving a paper, shouting its headline in shrill prepubescence like a carnival huckster. Sunday mornings demanded a degree of reverence and this sort of weekday hawking of papers was *not* appropriate – you know – unless Jesus himself had been spotted coming on the clouds and we had but mere minutes before his arrival.

No Fingers, who was as deaf as a stone and had a personality to match, noticed nothing, but Aunt and Uncle were as drawn to the scene as we were. Others in their Sunday best were crossing over and the lad was doing brisk business. A glance passed between all of us. We needed to know, so after a check for oncoming automobiles and cyclists, we crossed. A half block later I was able to make out the newsie's herald.

Bombing in San Francisco! Four killed! Dozens wounded!
Bombing! Read all about it! Get the story here! Five cents!

An Indianhead nickel that had been destined for the offering plate was already in my hand. Lester and I had overtaken Aunt and Uncle for the lead.

Preparedness Day parade route bombed! Tragedy and chaos in
San Francisco! Read all about it!

We secured our copy then promptly joined the growing crowd. Auntie peered over our arms as Lester and I held the paper between us. Uncle leaned in sideways. It had been carnage: arms and legs lying in the street, blood-splattered, pockmarked buildings. Shrapnel wounds were extensive from nails and bullets a suitcase bomb had shot into innocent families simply come to view a parade. As infection would invariably set in, these injuries would likely take more lives. *This* was an act of war. *This* was an act of treason. *This* had happened on American soil.

As we read in horror about the previous day's events, a ringing of distant church bells began to sound.

"We need to get to church. Put that away and we'll read it later." Auntie had spoken – which was pretty much the same as the law – so we folded the paper, its images fresh in my mind, then double-timed it to church.

The sanctuary was dim but not as hushed as a Sunday morning ought to be. Heads were turned. People leaned forward and backward over pews. Their quiet but agitated conversation competed with the organ's protracted notes. A hard oak pew creaked as we sat. While Aunt and Uncle bent their heads in prayer and No Fingers gazed idly around, my eyes were drawn to windows of stained glass aglow from sunlight beyond.

Jesus stood in resurrected glory above the altar – a halo around his head, a lamb and lion lying together at his feet, his arms were outstretched, crimson wounds in his open palms.

Sanctuary sidewall windows were of the twelve he'd chosen to follow him, all immortalized in their own window. Eleven had halos. Eleven were radiant in glory. Eleven were examples of holy self-sacrifice. The twelfth window was dark and brooding – nearly black. Judas was crouched, a bag of silver in his hands, Satan on one shoulder and him looking over the other. The posture of a traitor.

The traitor.

Even Jesus had selected and trusted a traitor. I found myself looking at the traitor, knowing one thing of Judas: he thought he'd followed a leader who planned to vanquish Roman oppression and lift Israel to its destiny as God's chosen people. He'd believed Jesus to be a redeemer of a nation. But on the night of Judas' fateful decision, Jesus had donned a servant's towel, knelt and washed Judas' filthy feet. Jesus revealed his destiny was to be a redeemer of souls, not nations. Judas was a patriot ready to take the sword for the highest of ideals: nation, honor, destiny. Then on the precipice of true justice, Jesus spoke only of humility and sacrifice. It had disgusted him. The one they had called Lord *intended* to rush headlong into failure.

The organ continued its dirge as more worshipers filtered in, women already fanning themselves and men loosening their collars. Ushers started opening windows, pulling top sashes down and pushing bottom sashes up – breaking up not only the righteousness of the saints but a traitor's wickedness. Windows that had told our stories of good and evil became a senseless kaleidoscope of jagged glass. Stark light entered our sanctuary like flash powder ignited in a photographer's trough.

I looked again at Jesus, lamb and lion at his feet. I shook my head and snorted to myself. Not on this earth. Maybe in Heaven, but not here. Maybe there was no such thing as sanctuary just as there was no such thing as peace. Closed windows colored light in familiar shapes that confirmed our ideas and soothed our souls. But their light was not the stark light of day. When opened, those same windows allowed light that showed every crease of skin, flash of eye, and shape of mouth. It struck me that sanctuary was not so much a truth, maybe not even *the* truth. Sanctuary confirmed *our* truths.

A final peal of church bells began to ring. Congregants sat

straight in their seats, preparing, turning pages. Lester had his songbook in hand, already turned to the first hymn.

The organ's dirge ceased. There was the usual coughing and clearing of throats as organ bellows filled. It was a joyful hymn, one of hope, one of victory. Once through – only organ – first verse – so everyone knew the melody – could prepare to sing on-key – and would be ready. At its conclusion, the congregation came noisily to its feet. Oh, how I loved a hymn I could sing with all my heart and this was one of my favorites.

Lester offered to share his book, but I pushed it away. This morning I listened to lyrics of hope and victory in doubt rather than in faith.

There's a land that is fairer than day
And in faith we can see it afar
For the Father waits over the way
To prepare us a dwelling place there.
In the sweet by and by
We shall meet on that beautiful shore.

I'd like to say that in the refrain I saw only Christ, arms open, on River Jordan's banks. I'd like to say that I saw Mankind coming from all directions toward him. All in white. All finally above Earth's strife. But I did not.

Images flashed through my mind – cubist nightmares like those of Picasso and Dali. I saw sharks swimming in fresh water, traitors blowing up their fellow countrymen at parades, lifeboats rowing away from the Lusitania's sinking hulk, laughing swimmers diving off buoys, black and white photographs of dirigibles raining destruction on London, an old negro woman's tears streaking down her face, a bowl of ice cream being set before me at Robbins on the Corner, rolls of barbed wire laid across heaved battlefields, Fords rolling off an assembly line, trenches filled with soldier's twisted bodies, trees broken on the day of redemption, maimed fingers silhouetted against a sky of orange – blood red, a young cowboy walking – saddle on his shoulder, Guy's casket being lowered into his grave, wheatfields

178

undulating under winds that herald a storm, clouds – dark and foreboding, forming on Earth's horizon.

While the congregation sang its final *sweet by and by* I heard widows wailing, the joyous laughter of children, bawling cattle, cries of newborn babes, morning songs of birds, a thunder of bombs, the babble of a pure mountain stream.

I heard wind winding through a forest of pines.

Chapter 23

On Horizons

The heat wave we'd been, um, *convinced* by Auntie to wait out in Detroit had broken decisively, with afternoon rains for two days now. This relief presented a window for travel. Although we'd loathed every aspect of close city living, I couldn't help but feel a bit melancholy this predawn morn.

Lester was saying his last goodbyes to Aunt and Uncle just inside their doorway. I waited in the hallway, just enough distance between us to allow them privacy. My fully packed bicycle was leaned against my legs. Lester's was propped against the wall. I had offered a guest's brief and sanitary farewell. I couldn't help but overhear Auntie, a hard woman of unquestioned authority, squeaking with emotion to say goodbye to her brother's now oldest son. Given distance and hardships of travel, Lester would never see his aunt and uncle again, nor they, him. I hated the loss inherent to moving on but every day is a moving on for men on a journey.

When Lester at last emerged from their apartment door, it was with a stiff smile on his face and a nod. I leaned his bicycle toward him. We wheeled our bicycles along the dim hallway and carried them down the stairway of feral cats in silence. We met the milkman who was busily exchanging dozens of empty bottles for full on the stoop, greeted him succinctly, mounted up, and began to ride.

Streets this time of morning were absolutely silent and all windows dark – save the baker's storefront and light that spilled from its window, washing across both sidewalk and street. We pulled up beneath its transom windows and inhaled deeply. Is there any aroma more wonderful than that of bread baking? I have to think there isn't. Between us, we must have inhaled an entire loaf – enough to assuage the sorrows of goodbye – and then we were on our way.

We were on schedule. If all went to plan, sunrise would coincide with our arrival at the Detroit River shipyard docks. This morning, a ferry would take us across a mile of water, to Canada's shore. It's funny how one dilemma always seems to give way to another. Ever since Guy's drowning, deep water and passage on boats had become a quandary for Lester. He knew full well that such passages would be necessary on our journey, yet his carefree countenance changed each time one was forthcoming. He didn't have to say a word. In fact, he hadn't said much at all during our ride through Detroit. Now as we were standing in line to pay our fare, he began to gnaw at his fingernails.

"It'll be all right," I consoled.

Lester's jaw muscles flexed as he continued to chew his thumbnail, eyes riveted on a ferry steaming our direction. We were standing in line with horses, wagons, trucks, motorcars, and those traveling on foot. It would only be a mile's journey to Canada, but for Lester, a mile's journey over deep, cold, moving water was a mile too far. That half our journey would be made over Canadian waters sat in Lester's stomach like a stone.

Further up the shoreline was a constant commotion of crashes, squeals and clanks of train cars. As there was no bridge, they had to transfer onto large ferries to get across. This hubbub did not serve to comfort Lester's unease. Might I add that *unease* is a kinder word for what I saw. Fear shown in his eyes as he stared at the ferry.

"That's a big boat." He licked his dry lips and swallowed so hard I could hear his Adam's apple thunk deep inside his throat.

"It is, and it makes this trip across the river twenty times a day. Safely."

Lester's nod was barely perceptible but matched the degree of comfort my statement had provided, or more accurately, had lacked.

At this point I'd had about enough of my own pandering to his apprehension. "You know, a ferry ride isn't quite the same as Guy paddling a canoe in rushing waters of a spring thaw."

Lester's head turned toward me in a snap.

I hastily sidestepped, then pulled my bicycle across weathered dock planks, back up to my side. Lester's head remained turned toward me. He no longer chewed his nails. His eyes blazed. His jaw continued to flex. But he said nothing.

Sometimes you have to say the thing that needs to be said.

The ferry bumped and slid into its berth, jolting the dock beneath our feet. Deckhands scrambled to affix the ropes to moor it in place. Ramps were let down and commerce began to roll from its belly with sputter and whinny, clank and rumble. While I felt anticipation and excitement for this next leg of our journey – *Canada!* – for others, this morning's crossing was routine.

Drivers of horse and wagon, truck or automobile waiting around us continued to smoke and converse unhurried, knowing both rhythm and pace of the process. I marveled at a Cadillac a couple conveyances ahead that was started with the flip of a switch. I was tempted to make small talk about it but Lester was again looking fearfully ahead, chewing fingernails.

When the ferry was emptied of westbound traffic our eastbound line began to creep forward, Lester and I along with it. We'd observed many freighters and barges in our explorations but it's hard to truly appreciate the size of even a ferry from its outside and especially so from a distance. I marveled as we entered its cold superstructure and became engulfed by it. Harsh echoes of wagon wheel, car tire, hoof fall, and engine resounded off its steel, amplified, it seemed, in volume.

I found myself smiling to consider the engineering and skill of men, but also smiling to think that we were now like Jonah, in the belly of a whale – headed to a land of an unrepentant people who had not yet heard liberty's judgement – a vestige of the crown – an antique of old ways in a new world.

"What's so funny?"

I turned to find Lester staring at me, clearly annoyed at my mood's evident lightness.

"Oh nothing. Just musing about Jonah and the whale."

For that I received a scowl.

I raised my eyebrows, puckered my lips, rolled my eyes and turned away. Lester wasn't going to be Lester until we reached the river's other side and were once again on solid ground.

We were soon settled in place, listening to last traffic rolling over ramps behind us. Deckhands began calling out to one another, preparing for departure. To my right was a shadow of a lazy black plume rising from the ferry's stacks. As ramps began to clang shut behind us, the lazy plume changed to a billow of churning smoke. Even if our journey across was a short one, a clanging of steel aft was to Lester, akin to shutting a prison door.

Until Guy's drowning, Lester and I had swum in Prospect Lake, a small lake near our homes, often swimming shore-to-shore, carefree, racing one another. After Guy's death, Lester refused to venture into any water deeper than he could stand in, chest deep — even if he could swim like a fish and was as safe in water as a bird is in the air.

"Hey, why don't we leave our bicycles here and go outside and stand at the rail?" My offer was as calculated as it was generous, and since we'd been standing in line for the past hour or so, not entirely selfless, as I'd observed some benches outside as well.

Anxious to leave the whale's belly, Lester said nothing, leaned his bicycle against a steel support column, and took off ahead of me. I watched him weave through a maze of conveyances and drivers who were once again languishing about, smoking and conversing. I didn't try to catch up with Lester, but rather followed at my leisure, savoring any break from his intensity.

The steel beneath our feet began to gently rock as the ferry scraped away from its berth. When I caught up to Lester, he was standing at the rail watching first ripples of the ferry's wake fan out from its bow. I kept my eyes forward as I came up to his side. He didn't turn toward me but out of the corner of my eye I could see him smirk and raise his eyebrows. "I've been thinking of some names Guy would have called me this morning if he had seen how I was acting."

"I think he'd understand."

"Maybe. Maybe not."

I bent to rest my elbows on the rail and felt the steam engine's powerful vibrations rattle my bones. "Sorry to be so harsh earlier."

"It needed to be said. I mean, look at me, afraid of crossing a river on a ferry? It's ridiculous."

I nodded and decided to change topic. "You realize that in a few minutes we'll be international travelers."

Lester nodded, a smile on his face.

Then we just stood together at the rail, wordless, feeling remnants of morning coolness mix with the coming day's heat, smelling night's sweet air give way to the acrid smoke of day. I found myself thinking of the pristine air and blue Colorado sky back home, of rustling leaves, breezes blowing across its prairies. Colorado was more than just a thousand miles away. It was a world away.

As shoreline and docks of our northern neighbor drew near, I felt heartstrings for home, mother, father, brother and sister begin to strain and to my dismay, gently snap – one-by-one. It was just a river, a mile-wide crossing of water, yet I felt strangely alone, as if I was about to leave something more behind that I would never have again. I wasn't certain exactly what that was, but I knew I'd miss it once I realized what it was.

After a passing of no more than a few minutes, docks of my good old U.S.A. had become distant and Canada's docks, near. I slapped the rail and inclined my head. Lester and I headed back into the belly of the whale. As we wove our way through, cigarettes were being flung aside, doors opened and closed, and engines started all around us. A minute or two later we felt a jar. Deckhands began to call out to one another. Ramps clanged into place. Shadows cast by the roiling billow of smoke tamed once again to a plume.

A fully loaded and tarped Mack truck was parked ahead of us. Unlike other vehicles and horse-drawn wagons rolling around us, it remained motionless, sputtering for only moments at a time, then wheezing and coughing before falling silent. I looked at Lester. "Just our luck."

But Lester was once again back to himself. "I think we have time for a cigarette," he offered humorously. "I saw one with a few draws left on it over there." He pointed and kept a straight face as if he was serious. I couldn't help but laugh. Smoking is the very last thing a true bicyclist would ever do. We waited patiently as over and over again the Mack coughed and died.

"We could wheel our bicycles around and be on our way."

Lester looked at me, frowned, leaned his bicycle back against a steel column, and began to walk alongside the truck.

Its driver had raised the hood's side panel on its hinge and was just positioning it in a notch, when Lester, with me right behind, inquired, "What seems to be the problem?"

The driver startled a bit at our near presence and nearly lost his footing on the running board – but his startle was considerably less than ours when a woman's face turned toward us. Green coveralls and a blue and white striped engineer's cap had concealed her femininity quite effectively. Neither Lester nor I could close our mouths. Worse, our eyes about bugged out of our heads. I'd never in all my life seen a woman wear pants and had *never* imagined seeing one as a driver of a truck.

She seemed not to notice our surprise or was so accustomed to it that she answered seamlessly. "It's been acting up for a couple days and getting worse, dying on hills and now it won't even start."

Lester's mind clicked and whirred a moment, then with an air of confidence, gestured for permission to take her place – which she relinquished with a quick step off the running board.

"Have any tools?" Lester asked as he bent to look about.

She stepped around her open driver's door and retrieved a folded leather pouch from the cab. Lester extended his hand, took it, then walked around and opened the hood's other panel.

"He'll have you going in a minute," I assured her. She watched anxiously as the whale's belly continued to clear out around us, impatient drivers leering at her predicament. Perhaps more comfort was needed. I cleared my throat. "Lester's basically an idiot savant when it comes to internal combustion engines. You'll be up and running in no time."

"He's an idiot?"

"Idiot *savant*. Savant means genius – you know – of sorts." Unless reassurance is indicated by raised eyebrows, wide eyes and puckered lips, it appeared I'd missed my mark. Then as if to confirm the other half of my assertion, Lester disconnected a fuel line. I'd seen enough lit cigarettes flung aside by other drivers that I stepped back when gasoline began to drip and spurt. Emollition wasn't the method by which I intended to leave this earth, nor was today the date of departure I had in mind. Lester tapped, blew, tapped and blew again before reassembling the line and pointing our quite concerned driver back to her cab. "Choke it halfway, turn it over a couple times and push it in."

After a doubtful glance at me she climbed up and plopped down on the driver's seat. She turned the motor several times before it caught and roared to life. Since Lester had confidently already returned tools to their pouch, he simply put the hood back in place and latched it down. He stepped around and closed the other side. By now we were the sole occupants of Jonah's whale and diligently observed by deckhands, arms folded across their chests, waiting at the ramps.

Lester hopped up on the running board, presented our driver with her tool pouch, and jumped down. She clunked the Mack into gear and it began to rumble toward daylight.

Lester and I mounted up and rode behind. Had I thought we would simply wave our goodbyes and wheel away – as I had indeed planned to do – I found myself sorely mistaken. The moment we rolled onto Canadian soil, uniformed soldiers with pistols on their hips encircled the Mack, lifting its canvas and peering suspiciously at its crated cargo. As I puzzled at the scene, we became part of it.

"What's your business in Canada?" a particularly humorless middle-aged soldier demanded as he approached.

"Visiting my mother's family in Toronto," Lester answered clearly – almost as if he'd expected this exact situation.

The soldier looked disapprovingly at Lester's packs, then over at mine. "What are you bringing into our country?"

"Just everyday things, clothes and food, bedrolls."

"Any weapons?"

"Just a pistol. We're on the road, you know, so we have one for protection."

A squint and slow nod of the soldier's head was followed by a pointed finger. "Why don't you open a few of those for me?"

186

I might have protested under any other circumstance but given the request was backed with enough weapons to riddle me through with bullet holes I unfastened my straps as quickly as I could. I stepped back as the soldier lifted our flaps with the back of his finger and peered disdainfully at our provisions.

"You American citizens?"

"Yes sir. From Colorado."

"Name of kinfolk you're here to see?"

"Langford Bullen."

The soldier narrowed his eyes even further, seemingly disappointed we'd not uttered a German surname so that he could unholster his firearm and relieve it of an ounce or two of lead. I gulped as his suspicious glower shifted between us and continued to do so for nearly a minute. By the time he finally nodded, the Mack's manifest had passed similar scrutiny and it was rolling away. We mounted up and followed – not too quickly lest we appear in an unnatural hurry and not laggardly – should we appear insincere in our departure.

We'd not much sooner turned onto a boulevard when the Mack trundled aside and stopped. Thinking Lester's repair had not held, we stopped as well – only to hear its engine's healthy reverberation. The driver came around. "I just wanted to say thank you." The woman removed her cap, revealing long dark hair put up in a bun. She wiped sweat from her forehead onto her hand, then off onto her pantleg – again – something I'd never seen a woman do before.

"Oh, you're welcome. It was the fuel filter. Happens all the time. Depending how much you drive, you should probably clean it every couple weeks or so."

The woman laughed easily. "This isn't something I'm used to doing. This was my husband's job."

I inclined my head in puzzlement.

"We're at war overseas. There's a shortage of Canadian men right now. We all have to do our part – you know – what we can for the cause." She looked at our bicycles, packs and assumed enjoyment of summer's carefree days were our cause. "I take it that you are Americans."

187

I nodded. Before crossing to Canadian soil, any aspect of war had been far from my mind. Now as I looked about, I noticed a presence of soldiers both on foot and mounted all about the waterfront, rifles slung over their shoulders, observing movements of everyone and everything.

Always one to keep our progress forefront, Lester took it upon himself to wrap up the conversation. "Well, I hope the war ends soon and he comes home safe."

I watched the woman's mouth straighten, her eyes fall, and her face follow. Lester had said everything except *have a pleasant day*. Women. You just can't figure what might upset them. Then sunlight caught a single tear as it fell from her eye. It continued to sparkle its entire descent. Even with a cacophony of noise around us, I swear I heard it tink against roadway cobbles as if it were the only sound. I suddenly knew more than I could have possibly known. I felt her heart and knew what it knew. He *had* come home.

In a box.

When she looked up, it was with red-rimmed eyes and an iron smile of purest strength – but not a word. I bit my lip as I watched her walk back along her truck and climb up into its cab. Engine revved. Gears ground. The Mack lurched away.

We rode south through Windsor in near silence, speaking only about where to turn. It would have been impossible not to notice calvaries drilling in the parks, women doing men's work, and rarely an able-bodied man anywhere to be seen – unless of course it was ourselves.

Turned heads was something we two wayfarers on packed bicycles had become used to, however now it seemed with accusation more so than curiosity. But then guilt makes its own interpretations.

We were well into farmland and rolling hills of grazing sheep when we slowed, looked at one another, coasted beneath the shade of a massive cottonwood and stopped. We stretched and leaned, then began to drink water and munch on nuts and raisins, I looked up at blue sky and out along a green horizon that encircled us. This was how mankind ought to live – in open vistas, breathing clean air, hearing the song of birds.

"I know what you're thinking." Lester smiled knowingly, then dropped a handful of raisins into his mouth, stared at me challengingly, and began to chew.

"Do you?"

He nodded.

Of course he did, for no one knew me better. I drew a breath, a breath to release what I'd been holding. "She was a widow."

Lester nodded again.

"As we've been riding, I couldn't help but remember that giant banner hung across Ford's plant thanking the President for keeping *us* out of the war. How was that woman one scant mile from our border somehow not one of *us*? Why are they fighting and we aren't?"

Lester swallowed. "We are Americans. They aren't. We vote and keeping out of the war is, right now, the people's will."

I felt blood rush to my face. "We're wearing blinders to think we can be neutral."

"I don't disagree."

"How can we pretend the entire world doesn't exist? How can we think that war will never reach us? It isn't thousands of miles across an ocean in distant lands. It's *one mile* away from Detroit. Hell, it's in San Francisco!"

"I don't disagree. But right or wrong, our country is governed by the majority."

"Regardless of right and wrong?"

"Regardless of right and wrong."

"So, *I got mine, too bad for you,* is what America has come to stand for? Majorities can be wrong. Hell, looking back through history, majorities are usually wrong. It's the smallest voice that's usually proven right."

"Wilson isn't going to get reelected if he doesn't keep us out of the war. Do you want me to rewrite the constitution so that it fits your idea of right and wrong? Not everyone thinks like you do, Pike."

I narrowed my eyes.

"You challenged me earlier today and said things I didn't want to hear but that I needed to hear. So now I'm going to do the same for you. Do you want Irvin overseas fighting the Kaiser? Do you? Do you want him to come home without his eyes or arms or legs? Do you want Nellie bandaging soldiers in a battlefield tent or do you want her working in the hospital blocks away and coming home for dinner?" Lester raised his eyebrows. "Would you want either of them to come home in a box just because other nations haven't learned how to get along and respect each other's borders?"

I'd had enough. Lester enjoyed baiting me, testing me, getting a rise out of me and he'd already gotten all the satisfaction I was going to give him this fine morning. I slapped my pack closed, didn't bother to strap it, mounted up and took off.

I kept ahead of him until I tired of my independence – which was about five miles later, then gradually slowed until we were once again riding at each other's side. Another five miles passed in silence before he added one last thing because Lester always adds one last thing. As we bumped along, he looked over at me. "You still have the passion of youth, Pike. You think in terms of right and wrong – but that will fade. You will eventually learn to settle for what you have today. You will eventually decide to settle for what is in your hand, and once you have, anything that can take that away will become what you fear.

"And what you fear will become your horizon."

Chapter 24

A Name to Remember

I'd forgotten about the desolation and loneliness of a road less traveled – that is until the stark refresher provided by a meandering road that appeared in no hurry to take us around Lake Ontario. "Expect to run into a moose or two," I quoted an old-timer who had imparted his warning from his roadside porch two towns back. "'Specially in the marshes."

"An' iffin you should," Lester repeated the codger's advice verbatim, "git yerselves the heck outta there."

"An' don't you be making no bugle sounds thinkin' yer funny."

"It'll be the las' thing you do."

I was beginning to feel a sense of relevance concerning the codger's advice as we entered a marsh. Grass, cattails and reeds were shoulder high, and that was in low spots. Escape, if it wasn't straight ahead, was pretty much impossible should we encounter the dreaded moose. As we began to traverse the swamp of – um – let's call it *our imminent demise*, we were looking out for and trying not to run into: *"Either an eight-foot-tall ass or a twelve-foot-tall, ten-foot-wide rack attached to the ugliest damn beast you ever did see."* The codger might have been exaggerating, but I didn't think by much.

Here's the thing about a moose: Might charge you, might not. Might trample you, might not. *"Fiddy, fiddy,"* the old-timer had concluded with a smack of his toothless gums and a knowing nod of his head. Well, fiddy-fiddy was enough incentive to get us up on our pedals and through the wetland bog quite expeditiously. We didn't stop to catch our breath until we were a good two hundred yards east of danger and on the crest of a rise – you know – just to be safe.

"How fast do you think a moose can run?" I asked between breaths I was desperately trying to restore now that we were beyond the bog's danger.

"Probably faster and longer than we can ride."

I nodded. "Thought so. You hungry?"

"Am I ever *not* hungry?"

There wasn't a tree in sight so we wordlessly agreed to eat in the sun, leaned our bicycles against one another and began to release straps that held our food packs. "That sprint done tuckered me out."

"Likewise."

"Ever notice how we start talking like bumpkins whenever we're in the country?"

"I notice that *you* do. Thank the good Lord that *I* retain that there city dignity."

We laughed, then filled our mouths and began to chew. We'd eaten about three bites when we heard it. Turning our backs to marshland, we faced eastward. That we could hear its roar while it was yet but a distant speck caused us to look at one another warily.

Lester latched onto the length of jerky he'd been gnawing on with his teeth and handed me his pouch of raisins. He quickly unpacked our trusty pistol and stuck it in his belt – which in hindsight might have been a good idea upon entering the marsh of *our imminent demise* – not after. Anyway, we were as ready as we were likely to be for whatever or whoever this was.

It continued to strain our way and hadn't slowed in the slightest. This maniac was coming straight for us. Lester grabbed his bicycle, I grabbed mine, and we vacated the roadway. Now discernable, this was likely an Indian – not one with warpaint and a feather in his headband who very well may scalp you – but an Indian with two wheels propelled by an insanely powerful three horsepower engine that very well might run you down. As it neared, we could see its rider clad in full leather and crouched so low as to be one with the bike. His eyes were obscured by goggles.

"Probably a scoundrel who just robbed a bank."

Judging by its speed of approach, that seemed a likely scenario – except given a dearth of banks in the area – maybe not. I nodded anyway.

We had not much sooner cleared its trajectory but the

motorcycle shot between us as if ridden by Satan himself. Flames shot from its exhaust with an ear-shattering blast that ancient gods of thunder would have envied. I could utter but one word in its wake. *"Damn."*

"I'll say."

"That was rude. Whatever happened to courtesy?"

Lester shrugged. "I could try to shoot the rogue, but I doubt my bullet would be able to catch up with him."

"What if he had thrown up a stone or lost control? He might have killed us."

Just then the motorcycle's acceleration cut. It began to gurgle, sputter, backfire, cough, downshift, gurgle, sputter, cough, downshift, backfire, cough, gurgle. Then after its rider had turned it around so that he once again faced us, he revved its engine, then idled, revved and idled, revved and idled.

If there *had* been a moose in the marsh, its eight-foot-tall ass would most likely have taken off for the Northern Territories by now. Lester took our pistol from his belt, cocked its hammer, put his finger on the trigger, but allowed it to remain at his side. I was already of the opinion that he should fire it and dispatch this villain. What nerve to speed past us in such a manner…

A spray of muddy water suddenly shot from its rear tire. Once again it was rocketing toward us. Whatever fate this encounter was to hold, we were not going to avoid. I expected another ear-shattering, gut-shaking pass by death's messenger but the Indian approached and slowed to a mannerly stop between us.

Its engine cut.

"Hooo doggie! That was a good run!" The rider lifted bug-splattered goggles and let them rest on his bug-splattered leather helmet's visor. "What did you think of that, boys?"

I'd half expected to meet Satan himself, but it was a boy at least a couple years my junior who flipped the kickstand down and dismounted.

"Boys?" I questioned, my well-ordered way of thinking temporarily stalled. First, this boy had displayed no courtesy. Then, a boy who was barely this side of pubescence had called *me* a boy.

"Yeah. What did you think of that?" Oblivious to my tone of voice, an apparently permanent and clueless smile remained on the lad's broad face. He placed his hands on his hips and arched backward.

Lester released the hammer and pushed our Colt back into his belt, by now confident that bloodshed would not be required. This lad was maybe fourteen years of age. If push came to shove, either one of us could slap him down without having to try too hard. Lester answered for us. "That *was* some run. Are you going for a land speed record or something?"

"Damn straight I am. Speed and endurance. That's the Indian way." He patted his machine, pulled a glove off one hand and then the other. He boldly stepped forward with his sweaty little hand extended. "Vidal J. Pettigrew. Remember the name."

I'd met a few people who satisfied the description of cocky, but this boy exceeded cocky by a country mile, that mile being in the general direction of Obnoxiousville. So far, to my way of thinking, his only redeeming quality was his leading man good looks: sharp symmetrical features with a smattering of boyish freckles spritzed across his nose just for good measure. To say that his expressional qualities exuded life, vitality, and friendliness would be like saying that a whale is big. Lester took his hand and answered humorously and with like formality. "Lester E. Atkinson."

I folded my arms across my chest, debating whether or not to slap some of the pretty off of Vidal's face – just for the hell of it – not out of jealousy.

Vidal released Lester's hand, waited for mine, realized it would not be forthcoming, then stuck his tongue in his lower lip. He nodded slowly. "You don't like me, do you?"

I stuck my tongue in my lower lip – not to mock him – well, yeah, maybe to mock him – and shook my head. "Not in the least."

"Love me. Hate me. But what I won't do is suffer the fate of the timid. What are we eating?" Then he swung the hand he'd offered to me, over to Lester, this time, palm up.

Lester chuckled as much at the boy's nerve as at my chagrin. He dug a length of jerky from his pack and slapped it in the little beggar's hand. The brat gnawed off a hunk but that didn't stop him from speaking as he chewed. "It bogged a little on the incline, didn't you think? I'm thinking either advance the timing some or retard it and lean out the carburation – not that that's the intuitive thing to do, but it just might work with reduced backpressure on the valves – you noticed that right – the way I modified its exhaust?"

Lester's eyes lit up like the rising sun. Talk of things like carburation or timing or valves was every bit as enthralling to Lester as true love. Judging by the look on his face, Cupid's arrow just got him squarely in the heart.

I already couldn't stand it, so I grabbed my canteen, two more lengths of jerky, a mittful of raisins and stormed off to be by myself – not that anyone noticed. Lester and Vidal J. Pettigrew were already kneeling beside the Indian's sizzling hot, ticking twin V cylinder engrossed in animated conversation. I could only *hope* that one of them would accidentally lean into its manifold – you know – with his lightly freckled face.

I was looking out over Lake Ontario watching a bald eagle circle above its waters when, after fifteen minutes or so, Lester evidently remembered that I existed. "Pike, come here."

Seeing as I had nothing better to do, I folded my arms across my chest and walked his direction, an unmistakable flare of disdain tugging at my nostrils.

"Tell him what you just told me." Lester nudged Vidal who popped to his feet at Lester's side.

"I said, I'm a Rough Rider." Vidal shrugged, not realizing his comment's full significance. "You know – not on horseback, but on steel."

"Who's your favorite President?" Lester coaxed.

I was thinking that a Canadian boy wouldn't know any more about American presidents than I would about Canadian prime ministers or their kings or queens when Vidal replied, "Well, Theodore Roosevelt, of course."

I was beginning to suspect that Lester and Vidal were now in cohorts and therefore pulling my leg. "Theodore Roosevelt," I repeated with soda cracker dryness. "You expect me to believe you know anything about Theodore Roosevelt?"

"No man is worth his salt who is not ready at all times to risk his well-being, to risk his body, to risk his life, in a great cause..." Vidal began.

My jaw dropped, but only long enough for me to draw a breath. *"Don't hit at all if it is honorably possible to avoid hitting, but never hit soft."*

When he was able to move *his* dropped jaw, Vidal exclaimed, "You like Teddy?"

"I *love* Teddy!"

"Teddy!" He threw his arms out.

"Teddy!" I threw my arms out. I inclined an ear – did that twang I just heard come from Cupid's bow?

It had been seven years since Teddy had occupied high office and seven years of aimless, uninspired governance as far as I was concerned. I'd only been in the early grades of elementary school when Theodore had served as the greatest president of our time, but I knew every word he'd ever spoken and every speech he'd ever given.

Then as if to prove that I'm not exaggerating, Vidal asked, "Did you read what he had to say about Mister Ford's anti-war views in his April speech?"

I absolutely could not shut my mouth. "I did!"

Only a genuine aficionado of the great man would know and follow such things. Teddy was my hero. No. Teddy was *our* hero.

I think it would be fair to say that a half-hour passed with Lester scarcely getting a word in edgewise. He eventually gave up trying and may have wandered off to watch eagles – who knows – as Vidal and I completely ignored him from that point on.

What a well-rounded, independent, educated, industrious, brave, and inventive young man my good friend Vidal turned out to be! *Who knew?*

But then, as with all things, my eyes had wandered Lester's direction and found his watch cover glinting in the sun. His eyes were looking not so much at his watch as they were at yours truly. I turned to Vidal and spoke with keenest regret. "I'm sorry, but we need to get going."

"To?" Vidal asked.

"Toronto."

"My hometown! Why didn't you say so? What are you waiting for? Let's get moving!"

Lester's eyes rolled back, his head followed, and he stood motionless as an exaggerated sigh of irritation vacated his breast. The subtlety, *not that there was any,* was not lost on Vidal who was every bit as sharp as his looks. "You know Lester, you'd be welcome to ride my motorcycle for a stretch, if you'd want to…"

Lester's face snapped forward, his mouth formed in a reverent 'O', as in *Oh my, would I like to do that!*

After a brief training on how to operate and ride a motorcycle, Lester took off ahead of us. Vidal threw his leg over Lester's bicycle, looked over at me, smiled, and we began to ride. While I had been lost in thought of what topics of current interest or which qualities of our great former president we might discuss as we rode, I found myself about to be learned in the ways of Canadian men.

Seems when not defying death or riding like the Devil, they sing. Not occasionally. Not quietly. But with the robust enthusiasm of frontiersmen and evidently without ceasing. And could Mr. Handsome Leading Man carry a tune? He could not only carry a tune, he could flip it, catch it, and commence to juggle it like a performer in a circus sideshow.

Lester rode a stretch on the Indian, then I rode a stretch, and so the most enjoyable afternoon of our entire journey progressed. We arrived in Toronto not only refreshed and invigorated, but in the company of our mutual, new, and fondest friend – Vidal J. Pettigrew.

Now, meeting and getting to know Lester's maternal grandparents, aunts, uncles, cousins and all that sort of thing is very nice, but not as nice as an adventurous new friend who knew every particular of every place and anything that might be of interest in or about Toronto.

We three were kindred souls indeed. Lester and I did our best to balance family obligations during the week we'd set aside from our travels while still making ourselves available to explore and investigate just about everything Vidal proposed.

Vidal turned out to be an entrepreneurial sort who upon

completion of the sixth grade had gained employment as an early morning deliverer of newspapers and parttime apprentice mechanic at a Ford dealership.

Any free moment he had available, which was generally within minutes of him completing his newspaper deliveries and breakfast having barely landed in our stomachs, he would arrive at Grandmother's front door ready to go. And when he had things to do at the shop, Lester and I eagerly became the apprentice's apprentices.

If hours remained after his workday, we were either tinkering on his Indian or riding it. Together we explored Toronto and points thereabout as we debated any and all matters of modern society. Lester and I met Vidal's friends and family – who welcomed us as interesting and somewhat audacious specimens of humanity. We and our adventure were every bit as intriguing to them as the illustrious and quite worldly in the most manly and daring of ways, young Mr. Pettigrew had been to us.

Sunday, depending on a particular household's degree of piety and one's own leanings, has the potential to be either the longest and most boring of days or the most satisfying and enjoyable of days. Lester's grandparents were of a more modern and progressive variety. Their home was a well-tended white clapboard two story situated on a narrow, deep lot of verdant green grass and fruitful, well-tended gardens. With the exception of a grandparent's obligatory steamer trunk filled with dusty treasures stored in the attic, there was nothing old or dowdy on the premises – which I found quite remarkable for folks born in the mid eighteen-hundreds.

But I digress.

Lester had made the motion. I was standing at his side in the parlor. Vidal, the subject of Lester's proposal, was lingering politely out of earshot on the screened sunporch. Our entreat had been filed and the court was considering not only the propriety, but legality of a houseguest's prerogative to invite a houseguest for an overnight. Counsel wasn't breathing as he waited the court's decision.

"Why of course. We'd be glad to have him." Grandmother

smiled as only old and ineffably kind women can smile.

Lester, at nineteen years of age, hugged his grandmother with the same joyous passion of a five-year-old. Their Honors now had to determine what degree of sanctity would be observed on the Lord's Day.

Court was in recess as Grandmother and Grandfather discussed precedent and considered counsel's well-stated arguments. Grandfather stepped through the front door to join counsel, client, and me, as we had all adjourned to the sunporch during their deliberations.

All rise.

Grandfather cleared his throat. "Dominos are all right. Cards are not. No wagering. No motorcycle monkeying around or riding. You can walk as far as the park. No exploring beyond that and no riding trolleys. You'll watch your language, wash and dry all dishes, you will stay home after supper and lights out will be at nine p.m. Lights out means no talking, no whispering, and no monkey business of any kind."

"Yes Sir. Absolutely, Sir."

His Honor faced the defendant. "Tomorrow, will you be joining us for worship or arriving afterward? We attend the Methodist church and there'll be a potluck after our service."

"If they'll let an Anglican in, I'd like to join you. I should warn you, I sing loud and know every hymn there is, so be prepared."

I watched a slight smile come to Grandfather's otherwise straight mouth. Not only did he love a youth with heartfelt religious leaning, but in case that leaning was not quite right in the Lord's eyes, an opportunity to bring him around to a correct way of thinking.

And so, the inevitable pain of leaving young Mr. Pettigrew's friendship would be assuaged. Our last day and night in Toronto would be with his nonstop company before our departure early Monday morning.

After a full Sunday of Mr. Pettigrew's companionship, at precisely 8:45 p.m., Grandfather stepped through the open front door, out onto the sunporch that had been our quarters for cool, bug-free nights and brisk mornings throughout our stay. Our laughter, chatter and tournament of Dominos came to an immediate stop. Grandfather's wordless but nonetheless effective stern point toward the alarm clock that would wake us tomorrow morning communicated his imperative quite effectively.

A mad scramble ensued. We collected up our game, made last bathroom trips, and after a frenzied arrangement of pillows, sleeping mats, sheets, and a quick undressing, Lester pulled the electric light's chain at 8:59 p.m. and dove for his sleeping mat.

Then, like rodents waiting to come out in darkness, we listened intently for Grandfather's last footsteps, then bed creaks coming from upstairs, waiting our chance to stir.

It is quite unfortunate that not one of the three of us was a man of our word. If one were to mount a defense, I'd favor an excuse of exuberance of youth over that of damnable corruption of soul. At or about 9:17 p.m., if one was to listen very carefully, rhythmic breaths and whistles began to filter from Grandfather's open window. They wafted through the quiet night eventually finding their way into our den of disobedience. Whispers ensued in night's dark shadows at or about 9:18 p.m.

"Vidal," Lester began, "when we were undressing I couldn't help but notice your armband."

Since I didn't know what Lester was talking about, I turned toward Vidal. His face was illuminated by splotches of blue moonlight that had found its way through tree branches, to illuminate the porch. Vidal said nothing. I could see his eyes were open, looking straight ahead. Lester rustled about to look at him as well.

"Edward."

I thought that a queer response to explain an article of clothing and would have said as much but Lester replied as if it made sense. "Sorry."

I lifted my head and raised up on my elbow. Vidal's arms lay atop a sheet pulled over him. There was a band about his upper arm, black even in the night, and I understood at once. We said nothing, waiting for grief to speak in its own time.

"He was my cousin. Went off to the war."

I watched Vidal shake his head, pull in his lips, then smirk with bitterness.

"The Indian had been his."

In our week of laughter, adventure and exchange of stories and ideas, he'd never mentioned his cousin or his motorcycle's origin.

"He was like a brother to me. He'd been a mechanic at the dealership."

We'd never asked how one so young could have come to possess something as expensive as an Indian or how he had gained such prestigious employment as a mechanic's apprentice.

"He'd planned to ride it coast-to-coast, race it, have the adventure of his life from its saddle."

We never questioned Vidal's almost unnatural appreciation for even the most mundane of moments.

"He joined our Expeditionary Force, trained two weeks, then shipped off to the front."

Vidal sang continuously. He wore mourning's black band beneath his clothes. How could anyone have suspected, much less known?

"We think he's buried somewhere in Belgium."

Pale moonlight shone down on three faces of youth, eyes wide open, mouths closed, minds stirring with things we didn't understand and didn't want to, the night's only sound then, the ticking of the clock.

Chapter 25

Dark Tome

I would say that Monday morning dawned early, but our alarm rang at four a.m. so we arose well before dawn had a chance to shame us. Vidal needed to get to his newspaper deliveries and we had many miles to ride before either the day's heat set in, or given weather patterns of the Great Lakes, afternoon rains would begin.

Grandmother – in nightgown, bathrobe, curlers and nightcap – set out bowls of cold cereal for us, then sat with us as we gulped them down. We'd no sooner put our bowls in the sink and rinsed them, than Grandfather, in pajamas, emerged from the stairway with his wisps of gray hair standing askew. We looked at him very much like rodents whose disobedience may or may not have been overheard. He wordlessly checked the time and managed a nod of approval. We shared a guilty glance at one another, then proceeded to take care of our morning constitutionals. Finally, we stowed last items into our bicycle packs.

Grandmother and Grandfather had come together on the front walk and were watching Vidal check oil and gasoline on his Indian when we wheeled our bicycles down the front porch steps. Vidal and I said quick thankyous and goodbyes to our kind hosts. Vidal started his motorcycle; its exhaust sufficiently muffled so as not to shoot flame or disturb neighbors. I mounted up and took Lester's bicycle from his hand.

It was a reverent moment as Lester and his grandmother, the woman who had given him *two* mothers – Mary *and* Adelaide – expressed their mutual ache of parting beneath the predawn sky. After a long embrace with his grandmother and a firm handshake with his grandfather, Lester joined me. I leaned his bicycle toward him. He took it and mounted up in silence. When he looked at me, his mouth was stiff lest he cry. He nodded. Vidal clicked his Indian into gear. We began to ride westward.

Our plan was to ride together until we reached downtown where we would help Vidal strap bundles of newspapers onto his motorcycle's rear rack. Then we would say our goodbyes. Lester and I would ride off one direction and Vidal the other.

I chanced one last look back as we rode along the tree-lined street. Even in the dark, I could see Grandmother standing on the front walk alone, her hand raised in silent farewell, no doubt weeping. I ached for her and for the number of her years. This was not just a visit ended, it was a last look.

Then – *and I should have expected it* – Vidal began to sing. Not quietly with respect for those still asleep in the predawn morn. It was a song, the words and tune unfamiliar to me, but obviously one that demanded the kind of volume and vigor with which he sang. I was inclined to shush him, but instead laughed aloud. If one is inclined to sing, one should do justice to the song. Only irrepressible Vidal would dare such a thing in the morn's sacred silence.

I turned to Lester riding at my side, fully expecting an equally bemused response accompanied by a wry shaking of his head. Instead, I found that same stiff smile of parting on his face that I'd seen before. "You know, we don't have to," he offered.

The Bruce crease came to my brow.

"We don't have to go to New York."

I reversed the turn of my crank and came to an immediate stop. Lester did the same, coming to a halt a length ahead of me, his bicycle skewed a bit sideways in the street.

"We don't have to go to New York?" I questioned, not able to hide the incredulous tone in my words.

"I mean, we've come far enough and I'd be fine with staying here another week or two with Vidal, and then just, you know, packing it up and heading home."

Vidal was now a block ahead, still singing. My head was reeling. This, *this* was not Lester, not *my* Lester, not the Lester I knew. A man's eyes tell far more than his words and I saw in Lester's eyes, not doubt that we could ride to New York, but a yearning for the comfort of the day at hand. It wasn't that he didn't want to see Liberty, it was that he had liberty enough for today.

Laziness is the father of invention as we are always looking for an easier way to complete a task – all in all a good thing. Comfort is the father of complacency – the killer of goals – the nemesis of risk, paradoxically, a bad thing.

Vidal had by now stopped singing. His motorcycle was stopped dead in the street ahead, idling. He was twisted about on its saddle looking back at us. I returned my gaze to Lester and squinted, half considering his proposition, half annoyed by it. "No," came quite succinctly from my lips. I tried not to sneer in contempt, but I may have. I put my foot back on my pedal and began to ride.

Forward.

Again, a man's eyes say it all. When I passed by Lester I caught a glint in his eye – as if my refusal had taken something away from him. I felt a flash in my eyes as if he had attempted to take something away from me – no – away from *us* – and continued riding.

"Park your motorcycle. You're going to need to use the truck this morning." The newspaper man standing on the dock tossed the bundle of papers he was carrying onto the flatbed of a Model T delivery wagon already backed to the dock. There was an air of urgency in the man's tone so Vidal hastily parked his motorcycle, then bounded up the steps to help hoist bundles. Lester and I dismounted but remained below.

"Special edition this morning. You're taking twice the amount to every newsstand. You need to be quick about it and depending on what happens, we might have a midday edition."

"What's going on?" Vidal might ordinarily have just looked at the headline instead of asking, but given the atmosphere of urgency, the dim light of morning and meek illumination of a single electric bulb hanging by a cord from the building's side, he posed the question and kept his eyes on the newspaperman as they worked.

"War has come to the States."

Panic shot through my head and heart. *What had happened?*

The boss man heaved the last bundle onto the bed of the T

204

before he elaborated. "Saboteurs. Saboteurs blew up a trainyard in Jersey City early Sunday morning. Something like two million tons of high explosives and armaments went up. Turned the night sky to brilliant daylight. All the windows have been blown out of lower Manhattan and Jersey City. Shook the ground all the way to Philadelphia. Fires are still burning."

My jaw was hanging slack. When I turned to Lester, his was as well.

"Get going Vidal." His boss man clapped his hands to impart urgency. "Expecting brisk business this morning."

Vidal jumped off the dock. We'd all envisioned a fond farewell, handshakes, laughter, maybe even an embrace but Vidal looked at us for one brief moment as he opened the truck door. He leaned in, set throttle and choke, then grabbed the starting crank from beneath the seat. We watched him go around front, finesse its position and give it a jerk. The engine sputtered and took. As Vidal came back around he looked at us one last time and managed a brief sweep of his hand in parting. He jumped in the cab, switched on headlamps, put her in gear, gave the engine a rev and eased out the clutch.

The newspaperman lifted his visor and wiped sweat from his forehead as he watched the truck turn and bounce onto the street. We listened as it went through gears. It turned and disappeared around the corner.

Vidal was gone.

The newspaperman considered us with apprehension – or scorn – I couldn't be quite sure. "You're Vidal's American friends, right?"

We nodded.

"He's spoken of you every day. Lester and Pike – did I get that right?"

"Yes Sir."

"Well Lester and Pike, maybe this'll bring your country to its senses. You can't straddle both sides of a war. Doing business with both Allies and Germans and God only knows who else…" a disgusted shake of the man's head and a muttering under his breath about treachery completed his statement. His abrupt about-face and subsequent disappearance into the building punctuated it.

I looked at Lester.

He looked at me.

The newspaperman reappeared, this time with a paper in his hand. He bent toward us. Although he didn't throw it, the thrust with which he slapped it into Lester's hand approximated an equal degree of contempt. "Your Wall Street turns on the front's victories and losses – lives of men the same age as yourselves – living or dying in its trenches. And do you know why? Your industrialists make munitions for both sides. *All sides.* Wherever a profit can be made. Your leaders and financiers have become puppeteers of war: banking, speculating, watching, waiting, doing nothing but making money." Then he added derisively, "Neutral my ass," spat, glared at us and went back inside.

We peered as best we could in the dim light of morning at grainy harsh black and white images of twisted steel, raging flames, and churning smoke. So far, war had come only as close as headlines or moving picture newsreels of carnage overseas. Today's headline was from Jersey City, U.S.A.

The shark of war was on the New Jersey shore. How much longer until it was headed inland, swimming in fresh water, crazed and relentless in its quest for human blood? And would we be like innocent little Lester Stillwell, skinny-dipping on his noon break, not a care in the world when it struck?

Lester yanked the paper we'd held between us from my hands. His temper had already been primed once this morning so I knew what was coming. Lester bounded up the dock's wooden steps while rolling the paper. It seemed a bad dog was about to get a thrashing. By the time I caught up with him, he was already inside.

The newspaperman had been pouring tea into a stained tin cup when Sheriff Atkinson, arms waving, had accosted him. More tea was on the table than in his cup when I arrived in the newspaper's dingy, smoke-filled back room – Lester's first volley already whistling through the air. "Oh, like we deserve this. Like we brought this on ourselves? Britain declared war on Germany. Canada could have stayed out of it. Don't blame the States because your country is bleeding for your king and Europe's senseless, age-old disputes."

"We are bleeding to preserve decency and right – something your country has forfeited in favor of profit. How do you not understand the complicity of not only what the U.S. is doing, but what it is *not* doing?"

"Who's to say who's right? When it's all sorted out, who's to say?"

"Who's to say who is right?" the man asked incredulously, veins beginning to pulse on his temples. *"Who's to say who is right?"* He blinked a few times, then slapped his hand down on the desk. "When some pointy-headed Hun is holding a bayonet at your stomach you'll know who is right."

"The British are the only ones who have held bayonets to our stomachs and they've done it a couple times now. The U.S. has never had a quarrel with Germany."

My eyes shifted to the newspaperman who was at the moment, temporarily speechless. "I see your point," he conceded with a tone of reasonableness. "But Germany is the aggressor on this one. They invaded France and Belgium and do you know why?"

Personally, I was a little fuzzy on that one.

Lester said nothing.

"Because of what France *might* do. Because they couldn't afford to take the chance of being in the middle should *'might'* come to be reality. So, they made *'might'* the reality by striking first. And your industrialists are making them the bombs and shipping them the steel to make victory of their aggression a possibility.

"But that's not all you're doing." The man shifted his weight and leaned forward – his finger pointed firmly. "How and why do you think the Lusitania went down from a single torpedo in a mere eighteen minutes when it took the Titanic with four or more watertight compartments ripped apart nearly three hours to sink? A single torpedo doesn't do that kind of damage to a liner that size. The survivors reported a second explosion. Curious, isn't it? Why do you think that is?

"It had a hull packed full of armaments and high explosives, that's why. The U.S. and Britain used innocent civilians as a shield, thinking the Germans wouldn't dare act. And I will say, to the Huns credit, that they gave ample warning they were going to sink the damn thing. And if you don't believe the Lusitania had explosives in her hull, look at the damn paper." He reached over and flicked the paper Lester had previously pointed at him with. "Two million tons of munitions exploded in that shipping railyard. You can bet your ass that two million tons wasn't the first cargo of its kind headed overseas. That's complicity. That's what your precious U.S.A. is doing in the war. Your country isn't neutral by any stretch of the imagination."

The Sheriff's gun had run out of ammunition – or more accurately – had only been half-cocked to begin with. Lester's face twisted like it does when he knows he's lost the day. But Lester had tactics yet to employ – for if one cannot prevail, one can at least evade. Losing tactics numbers one and two: take the dispute to ridiculous extremes and then divert attention away from the real argument in hopes of befuddling your opponent. Lester's face wrinkled contemptuously. "You know, amazingly, I haven't been invited to dinner at the White House lately so President Wilson and I haven't…"

The exaggerated guffaw, head thrown back, and arms flung out from the newspaperman's sides was every bit as biting as he intended. "Tell me this – *young mister it's not in my hands, what can I possibly do?* – you obviously have opinions, and apparently strong opinions or you wouldn't have stormed in here like you did. Whether right or wrong, what have *you* done? All the world is at war. Tens of thousands of soldiers and civilians are dying *daily*. Tell me, what is the opening sentence of your Constitution?"

Lester's answer was soft, nearly inaudible. "We the People."

"Very good."

It was silent a moment.

Lester resorted to losing tactic number three: futility. "We're nineteen and seventeen years old. There's nothing *we* can do. We can't vote. We have no voice."

"Oh really? Women don't have the vote but tell me, what have your women in the suffrage movement accomplished? Our women got the vote and yours are about to get it. What have the prohibitionists – mostly women I might add – accomplished? Vidal told me your state has gone dry. Didn't your black men get the vote without having a vote? Isn't labor scratching at the door of the magnates of industry? Damn straight they are and the Rockefellers and Vanderbilts are quaking in their boots. Americans, common ordinary Americans just like you have the right of conscience but how many of you bear the responsibility of action? Right or wrong, you two boys have more power in this world than the countless millions who have lived and died in total obscurity before you."

The Sheriff's gun was by now hanging at his side. Lester's long exhale was essentially a last clicking through the revolver's empty chambers.

"Listen. This is a mess. Start to finish, this whole thing is a mess that may never get properly sorted out. The U.S. began its statehood on moral ideals. Your founding fathers would be appalled that the principles they fought and died for have been distorted to nothing more than a hollow gospel of Capitalism." He shook his head. "They would be *appalled* that capitalism has become the banner of the United States and that liberty and equality have become its footnotes – footnotes it boasts of to the other nations of the world but deigns to grant fully to its own."

Lester began to gnaw his lip. He shrugged a little and nodded. "Sorry."

"Don't apologize for being passionate. Get the facts, *all the facts*, not just the ones you want to hear. *Then* be passionate." The newspaperman smiled wryly. "I, on the other hand, have all the facts but have lost passion due to the overwhelming despair of it all."

The combatants looked at one another.

"Do me a favor," Lester began, "don't take my argument with you this morning out on Vidal. I don't want him to lose his job over me."

The newspaperman's head angled a little to the side. He squinted. "He didn't tell you?" He looked between Lester's blank face and mine. "Vidal gave notice last week. He signed with the Expeditionary Force. This is his last week here."

I fought the sudden urge to cry and argued, "No. He wouldn't do that. We've made plans for next summer. He's going to ride his Indian out to Colorado, visit us, race in the hill climb."

The man smiled genuinely and snorted kindly. "That sounds like Vidal. Sounds like something he'd want to do. He keeps a lot of things to himself. You must be the one who adores Theodore Roosevelt?"

I nodded.

"It was your conversations with him, quoting the great man, that helped him decide."

"Oh my God. That was just talk. It was *just* talk, just words."

"There is no such thing as just talk, just words."

I blinked.

"He quoted me something you'd repeated about failure and daring greatly – 'so that his place shall never be with those cold and timid souls who neither know victory nor defeat.' Vidal never wanted to be among the timid, or as our Lord calls them, the lukewarm."

I was not above employing losing argument number four: denial. "He's too young. They'll never take him."

"They already have. There isn't a lot of scrutiny when it comes to age. If he tells them he's eighteen, he's eighteen. If he looks like he can march and fire a rifle, he's in."

I could not have been more heartbroken. One look at Lester's drawn face confirmed he felt the same as me.

"Do you know the only difference between us – between Canady and the U.S.A.?" the newspaperman enquired.

I puzzled.

"Words."

I puzzled again.

"We also have a representative government. We vote the same as you. We have freedom of speech and autonomy of the press. But the U. S. wrote in their founding document ideals of equality, life, liberty, and the pursuit of happiness. The men who penned those words changed the world. They were not cold and timid souls who neither knew victory nor defeat. They were men of integrity, head and shoulders above your ever-placatory, *how may I appease you?*, President Wilson."

Lester looked numbly at the paper in his hand and set it on a table. We turned to leave and were passing through the door when the newspaperman spoke one last time.

"You know that *if* Vidal comes back, he won't be the same."

I thought of last night, moonlight shining through the trees, illuminating our faces as we lay on the sunporch floor. I'd thought war and death were something we didn't understand. Vidal not only understood, but he had also already made his decision.

Then I remembered an offhand comment Lester's grandmother had made when first introduced to Vidal. *"Oh, what a great name. Do you know the meaning of your name?"*

Vidal had shaken his head.

"It means life," she had said. *"It means life."*

The ticking clock had done its work as all ticking clocks eventually do.

Chapter 26

Quagmire

We rode in near silence that morning, not the comfortable silence of companions putting miles behind us on the road, but in the silence of eyes abruptly forced wide open. The war had not just come to our shores, it had come into our lives, our plans, and our friendship with Vidal. The distant war now seemed a nefarious shadow of a dirigible creeping across the land, blotting out all in its path, and Lester and I beneath, looking up helplessly, about to be engulfed.

So far on our journey we'd not backtracked. Every road had been new. But today, given the choice of boarding a steamer to cross Lake Ontario or ride the meandering road west, back around the lake, we considered the expanse of water, the tales of sudden squalls and shipwreck, and chose the path we'd already traveled. We knew the turns to take, when to take the high road or the low, but the road we traveled was not familiar to our eyes. This morning we were seeing it from the other end.

I had supposed we would stop, so as Lester and I crested the rolling hill where we'd first encountered Vidal, we coasted to rest without a word having passed between us. Lester smiled stiffly at me and I at him. I took raisins from my pack and he pulled jerky from his. The sun was high above us as we began to refresh ourselves.

When I looked east, I could see the lunatic speeding toward us on his motorcycle. When I looked west, I could see the specter of a phantom moose wallowing about in the marsh. The lunatic became our friend. The specter remained unchanged, unexplored, unseen, foreboding, and I resented not only the specter moose, but the codger who'd warned us of its threat.

I nodded westward toward the phantom moose. "I'm stopping in the bog."

Lester lowered the canteen he'd just taken a drink from and wiped the corners of his mouth with a swipe of the back of his hand. Every now and then Lester smiled at me with the kind understanding of someone older, allowing me my rebellion and permitting me a fall should one occur. He nodded and filled his mouth with raisins.

We were at a funeral and though we had yet to speak of the deceased, talk of the extraneous seemed out of place so we ate and drank in silence as the sun beat down on us a few minutes longer.

Our eyes eventually found their way eastward and the service began. I could see the motorcycle and rider, hear the engine, feel the apprehension of his arrival just as I had before. Lester began Vidal's eulogy. "He's not going to come back."

I nodded.

"He'll lead the charge, find his way to the front line."

I nodded.

"He'll be the one his fellows and comrades in arms speak of in their old age."

I nodded.

"And decades later, still mourn."

I released a long breath. "He'll be fearless."

Lester nodded.

"Do you believe life goes on – in Heaven?"

I shrugged. Before our journey I would have said an emphatic, yes, because before we left Colorado Springs, life was planned, not happenstance. The best was always yet to come. I managed a feeble, "I hope so."

"Maybe someday he, you and I will take a journey together."

"Maybe."

"A wild, crazy journey, laughing and singing the whole way. Never hot, never tired, never cold, never hungry." Lester thought a moment. "Pike, I have to believe that. I *need* to believe that."

I nodded, then raised my canteen. "To Vidal."

Lester raised his. "To Vidal."

We drank, wiped our mouths, capped our canteens and slung them back around our necks. I faced west, hearing again the powerful revving of the bike's engine, seeing muddy spray kicked up from its acceleration, imagining the worst and Lester cocking our gun just in case it came to be.

If I'd allowed myself another moment of remembrance, the quiver of my lower lip and burning of my eyes may have taken me into despair and sapped me of my resolve.

But I had an engagement with a moose.

The road we'd raced across in fear for our lives was upon a slower traverse, a quagmire – a word whose meaning I now more fully understood as its blackness seeped over the rim of my wheel and up to the ankle of the foot I put down upon my stopping.

Dragonflies in the great northlands of Canada are roughly the size of a blue heron, twice as blue, and more iridescent than a handful of diamonds. Had I been a child, I would have spent the day catching them in jars. Instead, I marveled at their flight, their ability to hang in the air, forward, reverse. Effortless. Amazing that God would give a senseless insect such a gift.

A distant rhythmic splash of Lake Ontario's waves and the buzzing of ever-present flies were the only sounds. While I was certain the marsh held its share of creepy things – leeches, snakes, millipedes, and spiders among them – it did *not* possess a moose. "Fiddy, fiddy," I mocked the codger's false warning triumphantly.

Then with a great whoosh of water, what I'd assumed to be a tangle of driftwood rose from the water not a stone's throw away. Antlers as wide as I am tall, draped in grass and algae, came up out of the water. The beast was every bit as ugly as the codger had alleged and its innate gruesomeness was compounded by willows and grasses hanging from its mouth.

Jesus may have walked on water, but the way Lester and I rode over the quagmire's mud was just as miraculous.

Chapter 27

Direction

Why is that taking you forever and a day? How many times in my childhood had Mother posed that question to me? My well-ordered way of thinking, even at a young age, thought it a ridiculous query. But as our backtrack around Lake Ontario that should have taken a day was now taking forever, I was coming to understand not only the saying, but my mother's frustration.

With me.

Once again, I had trusted my compass – you know – the one that would always instruct the right way to go. I was looking between it and another road that had disappeared into a barnyard, perplexed. Lester looked at the sun getting low in the sky, then at me.

"Maybe the road with the deepest ruts isn't always the one we should pick. Time and again it turns out to be just local traffic. Maybe the road less traveled is the one that goes to the Falls."

"Well, you would think that a road that actually goes someplace would be the one with…"

"A road only goes someplace if it's a place most people go. And most folks around here apparently only go about their day-to-day business."

"You would think most people would be traveling to see the Falls. It is a wonder of the world. We've got to be close."

"Well, hard to say how close we are with all the backtracking we've done."

Frustrated, I deposited my compass in my pocket, turned my bicycle and put foot to pedal.

Fifteen minutes later we were again at a crossroads considering compass and tracks while swatting in vain at a battalion of mosquitos Satan had released on us. Then, *thank the Lord*, a woman and two small children riding bareback on a swayback nag came around a bend and clomped up to us.

"I wonder," Lester asked at their unhurried arrival, "could you tell us which road goes to the Falls?"

Hair that was supposed to be tied up in the woman's bonnet was hanging about her face. She brushed it aside. "The falls?"

"Niagara Falls."

She apparently had to think on it a moment, so as she did, I considered the dirty children in her care, a girl in front and a boy behind with his arms wrapped around her. They most certainly had to be bowlegged little creatures. In addition, they were covered with red welts from Satan's hench-squitos and had apparently given up on trying to wave them away. As I considered them further, I began to believe the woman I'd thought to be their mother could likely be their sister – not either or – but as well, for they looked quite inbred.

"Oh." She pursed her lips. "Don't none a these go there." She extended her arm to point behind. "About three miles back you go west at the old shack."

I lifted my compass. "No. The Falls are *southeast* of here."

She laughed – a thing I imagined she did rarely. "It is, but the road winds west a bit first. Every once in a while you have to go around what was already here before people needed roads to get someplace else." She took to considering Lester and me, possibly wondering if I was Lester's brother or if he was my uncle – not either or – but as well. I was about to resent her insinuation when she pointed at my compass. "Why would you think that could tell you where to go if you don't first know where you are?"

Chapter 28

Majesty

"Unbelievable," I whispered to myself.

Lester said nothing. When I turned toward him he just raised his eyebrows in belated response. Enough said, I supposed, then turned back to behold in like silence and awe, the utter majesty of Niagara Falls.

We had felt its rumble in our gut before our ears could hear its thunder. We saw its mist creating rainbows in the waning sunlight before we had crested its gorge. Now we stood before the unbelievable cascade of its waters. It was by far the mightiest thing I'd ever seen and I imagined would ever see in my entire life.

I willed my mouth to form the words of the apology or more accurately, *apologies*, due Lester from the griping and complaints I'd subjected him to for the past twelve hours of misdirection and frustration, but my lips and tongue refused to address the pettiness of it all.

Sometimes you stand in the presence of God Himself. As the hymn advises: let all mortal flesh be silent – and maybe it was about time I was – you know – for a change. I'd griped about the day-long backtrack around Lake Ontario, then about mud-pits, trenches, and inexplicable disappearances of roads in the middle of nowhere. Let's not forget my grumbling about the senseless winding of roads, the five times we got lost by taking a wrong road, insects, heat, humidity, and really, wonder of the world or not, did we absolutely *need* to see a stupid waterfall if it cost us this much distress?

"Drops of water," Lester said reverently.

I turned toward Lester whose eyes had remained on the falls. Although he was standing at my side, he seemed distant.

He raised both arms to encompass all that we saw. "All that

comes from drops of water that fall from the sky, one-by-one, then flows from puddles into streams into rivers then from one lake to another to another to another and now..."

I raised my eyebrows and nodded. Lester was feeling the presence of the Holy as much as I was. We resumed watching in reverent silence, cascades of water suddenly set free from the river above, that hung weightless, silent, falling, falling, falling, then crashing and churning, lost and scattered in the torrents. I thought of time. I thought of stars in the heavens. I thought of all things infinite and all things eternal – drop by drop, moment by moment, inch by inch, speck by speck – for all things eternal are made of the temporal and all things infinite are comprised of the insignificant.

Sometimes you feel your place in eternity and the cosmos – small, human, mortal. I watched the waters that had fallen in such a hush and had hung seemingly suspended in freefall before entering the turmoil. They boiled in the caldron for only a while, then rejoined – seemingly no worse from the chaos that had threatened to destroy them. Then water being water, it began once again to flow in harmony, lapping happily at the river's bank as if nothing had ever happened. At peace. Still water. Still moving. Unaware that it had just given mortal eyes a glimpse of majesty, of eternity, of infinity, of perhaps even God Himself.

"Drops of water," I repeated to myself and in so doing, remembered not only my insignificance in time and the cosmos but the utter importance of my being and the incredible moment of life held in my hand.

Chapter 29

The Weathering of Storms

Surly: ill-tempered, uncivil.
Cantankerous: bad-tempered, quarrelsome.
Irritable: easily annoyed, oversensitive, apt to become impatient or exasperated.
Joe Wheeler Bruce: surly, cantankerous, irritable.

Allow me to explain. Until this point in our travels we hadn't realized how fortunate we'd been with good weather. We camped under the stars that night of our transcendence at Niagara Falls, still filled with awe and wonder. In Colorado, any arrival of rain is declared with an ample warning of thunder and lightning. This is apparently not how rain approaches in weather patterns around the Great Lakes. We were awakened in the night by a sudden, steady rain that came over us quite unannounced. Everything we owned was soaked by the time we got canvas stretched over our already soggy bedrolls. We then huddled together shivering wide awake until dawn.

The night's steady rain became relentless sheets of rain come daylight. We packed up in the unyielding drenching, then struck out on a virtually impassible road. Over the course of an entire day, we managed to traverse only twenty or so miles – not riding mind you – but by *pushing* our bicycles through ankle-deep muck. We eventually arrived in Buffalo, slogging to a halt as miserable and exhausted as we'd ever felt in our entire lives.

Times two.

Three horses that looked every bit as beleaguered as ourselves occupied a hitching rail in front of a dry goods and grocery. Without exchanging a word, we headed that way. Another horse that apparently lacked the will to wander off as it had no bridle and was therefore not tethered with the others had a quaint four-seater buggy it had in tow. A trim of tassels hung from its top. In the modern age of internal combustion, that kind of gentile antiquity wasn't something you saw much anymore. But then on a day like today when an automobile would be mired up to its axle in mud and essentially useless, a one horsepower conveyance had not so much to do with gentler times as it did with sheer practicality. We leaned our mounts against the rail then looked despairingly down at our mud-splattered, saturated, and otherwise sorry state of being.

"Now, don't just go in there and pick up one thing and go pay for it. Let's walk around until they threaten to kick us out and *then* make a purchase and loiter around again like we might make another."

"Got it." I looked at Lester with the same pessimistic expression he'd unfortunately had to look at all day. "You know we're never going to dry out no matter how long we're in there."

"I just want to hear nothing for a while. This constant pelt of rain is driving me nuts. We have to come up for a plan for the night and I can't think with all of this racket going on inside my head."

After a night of listening to the falls roar and a never-ending day of rain, my ears could use a rest as well. I looked at Lester's weary eyes as water trickled from the brim of his hat. God, how I wanted to be home sitting in front of the potbelly stove wrapped in one of Mom's knitted afghans sipping hot cocoa right about now.

A bell dinged upon our opening a creaky oak and glass door. From the way heads turned our direction, you'd have thought we were gunfighters entering a saloon. Curious eyes looked us up and down, then an aproned clerk stepped around a display of canning supplies. He exhaled loudly. "Wipe your feet." Then he added, "Please."

Not that it was going to do any good, but we stood on a woven hemp mat and brushed our shoes across it as dollops of mud fell off our pant legs. A tiny, sharp-featured lady roughly the age of time – if not a couple years its senior – donned in a black rubber slicker and prepared for such weather, belatedly poked her head around a shelf and looked us up and down as the clerk had. "Two drowned rats in the dry goods!" She laughed and slapped her leg.

Is there anything more annoying than a spry and happy elder who has not given up on life and dismissed the entire concept of hope as vain futility?

Oblivious to a snarl tugging at my nostril, she continued to speak to us, all the while craning her neck to look through the plate glass window at our bicycles. "You boys on the road?"

While I might have answered with a rather succinct, sarcastic, *duh*, Lester responded politely. "Yes Ma'am. On our way to New York City."

"Well, you certainly picked a fine day to start out."

"Oh no, Ma'am. We've been riding since Colorado."

"Colorado!" She stomped her foot and slapped her leg again. "Well, welcome to New York, boys!"

While this was our first official welcome back to the good old U.S.A. since our Canadian detour, I was clearly in the variety of mood brought on by sleeplessness, exhaustion, frustration and a generally mean and cantankerous spirit. Therefore, I feared that if I were to speak what was on my mind, we'd find ourselves booted from the store post haste. I took leave of Lester's naturally engaging manner, ignored the clerk's continued surveillance of my muddy wet tracks on his not especially clean wood plank floor, and set about perusing anything and everything, trying to buy us time in dryness and relative quiet.

I was doing my best to block out Lester and Mother Time's happy chatter by mulling over some merchandising ideas to take back to Dryhurst and Son when Lester approached me, bright eyed and smiling. "We have a place to stay tonight." Then to let me know where that might be, he slapped his leg and stomped his foot.

I looked past him. Mother Time was craning her neck to look back at me. When our eyes met, she raised her hand in a cheerful and far too animated wave. I forced a smile and spoke through my teeth as I raised a stationary hand in a more subdued return of her greeting. "I don't like the rain, but I don't know if I can take *that* much sunshine."

"Aw, we'll get you dried out and fed and you'll be fine."

A crease of doubt tugged at my cheek.

"Well, our alternative is stretching our canvas between a couple trees and listening to the happy pitter patter of raindrops as we shiver through another sleepless night."

Her name, if I got it correct, was *Missus I Never Stop Speaking*. However, given present circumstances, I managed to find in my heart a near instant fondness for her and her cheerful ways – you know – if it meant a dry, quiet place to sleep for the night.

When Lester brought me over to her for a proper introduction, he opened his mouth, but then never got to utter a single word. "Well, you must be Joe – oh sorry – Pike, intrepid explorer, surveyor of the wild, scout for the nation."

"Joe is fine, Ma'am." I was feeling a tug at my nostril and thinking a night shivering in the rain might be preferable to a night of Mother Time's wit and charm.

"Glad to make your acquaintance, Joe."

She thrust her hand out to shake mine. "You can call me Dorothy, but whatever you do, don't call me late for dinner." Then she laughed and slapped her leg.

I shifted my eyes toward Lester's annoying smile.

It turned out that the untethered horse and buggy belonged to her. We strapped our bicycles to the buggy's rear luggage rack and hopped inside. Lester and Mother Time prattled on seemingly in competition with the horse's splash and clomp. I blocked both out and looked numbly at rain-soaked, gray, bleak cityscape as it transitioned to rain-soaked, green, but equally bleak farmland.

"I lease my farmland out to the neighbor but am keeping the house. Can't bear that city living." Seeing as the horse knew the way and fortunately so, Dorothy jabbered on with both arms waving about as if she was conducting an orchestra. I closed my eyes and had nearly accomplished the bliss of dreamland when the rhythmic splash of hoof falls, gentle sway of the buggy, and rainfall's delightful pitter patter came to a stop. I opened my eyes to find the horse had walked itself into a barn whereupon it immediately commenced to grazing on the hay piled about.

Mother Time scrambled down from her seat, went immediately to the horse and looked directly into one of his big eyes. "Thank you my friend. Thank you." She caressed the horse's quite wet head and the mighty beast returned the gesture with a press of his head against her chest. I was thinking how odd it was for this tiny human to be not only the generous master of a mighty steed, but its friend. Mother Time gathered up her paltry purchases that quite frankly didn't seem worth a trip into town on such a day. "Now you two get Horace here unhitched while I go rustle you up some dry clothes – that's how you say it out west, right – rustle up?"

Being city boys who rode trolleys and not ranch hands who busted broncs as she apparently assumed of all westerners, we laughed and nodded politely at her wit. Proud that she'd brought us laughter, she turned and immediately headed out the barn door toward the house, all the while speaking over her shoulder – or to herself – one couldn't be sure – something about her late husband's coveralls possibly fitting us. I looked at Lester. Lester looked at me. We both looked at the horse and harness, shrugged and *commenced to figuring it out* – as they say out west.

Dry felt awfully damn good – even if her late husband was apparently more of a short, stocky John Adams type and we, by comparison, were more of a beanpole Abe Lincoln variety. I held the coveralls out at my waist. "I think there's room in here for another me."

Lester laughed and extended his leg to expose not only his hairy ankle, but calf halfway to his knee. "Well, look at it this way, if there's a flood, we'll be able to wade through it with dry pants."

We laughed – genuinely this time – which was refreshing in and of itself. I hated to affirm Lester's previous assertion, but just as he had predicted, my mood-o-meter had come up a good fifty percent just from being dry. This was enough to assuage some of the sullen, spiteful meanness that had overtaken my otherwise happy and carefree soul.

As instructed, we hung our wet clothes and bedrolls up to dry on a series of spider-webbed clothes lines strung about the barn in a way that old ladies tend to string things – over nails, through knotholes, around posts and as unevenly as possible. I couldn't help but notice white and black lines of bird shit directly beneath the lines as we draped our raggedy wardrobe over them. "You do realize what we might find tomorrow morning."

"I most certainly do, but consider smelling mildewed fabric for the remainder of our trip, not to mention pedaling over the Alleghanies with the extra weight of rain-soaked bedrolls."

Figuring I could scrape off a little bird poop, I looked up in the rafters, added bat poop to the mix of things we might have to scrape off the following morning, and shrugged.

Lester looked my mothball-scented apparel of generous lateral proportions up and down. "You ready to go inside?"

We approached the open barn door and looked with foreboding at her half-century-old farmhouse. "Who do you suppose her 'friends' are?"

"I don't know, but she hasn't stopped talking about introducing us to them since she abducted us from the dry goods."

"Let's hope they aren't the spirits of the dead."

"But we'll be prepared just in case they are. Right?"

"Maybe not so much prepared as not surprised."

Lester laughed and slapped his leg. I gave him a shove and we took off running through unceasing rain.

Even if not especially keen on more conversation, we had no sooner entered the house than we were coerced into the parlor. Mother Time began to rattle off her friends' names. She began with a bright green, red and yellow cageless parrot, then moved on through a gaggle of scroungy cats that leered at us and the parrot from every window, cushion and table in the room. They acknowledged our acquaintance with as much disinterest as I acknowledged theirs.

Upon completion of Dorothy's spirited introductions, I motioned between parrot and cats. "How does that work?"

The woman laughed and held out her boney hand. With a shower of feathers the parrot took flight from its perch and landed upon her hand. The really quite impressive parrot was then smothered with kisses that it returned with gyrations of its head and gentle openings and closings of its bill. "Oh, Agusto here is quite able to hold his own. Aren't you my amigo?"

She tisked her tongue against the roof of her mouth and her parrot returned her tisk as accurately as a 78 on a Victor Talking Machine. She laughed. "Go rout them, Agusto!" She gave her hand a jerk and Agusto took off with a screech and mad flapping of wings. It circled the room twice, enough to send every cat leaping for anything they could get under or behind.

Lester and I found ourselves laughing.

Agusto proudly returned to Dorothy's hand, where he was loved with kisses once again. "He weighs a third of any of them and has no fangs. His claws are quite ineffective for anything but hanging on, but my cats see his strange colors, hear his rush of wings and his screech and think they are about to die. Aside from a nick or two if one tried anything, he would never hurt any of them– isn't that right, Agusto?"

Then Dorothy gave her hand a jerk and Agusto returned to his perch. "Oh, little ones…" She spoke to frightened eyes that peered out at her from behind and underneath. She patted her legs as she lowered herself on the settee. In a minute she was covered with lithe furry bodies that rubbed, writhed, meowed and purred all around her. "Oh, my sweethearts, don't know that you would ever hurt my Agusto but I need to make sure you won't someday. Forgive me. *Forgive me?*"

I was still smiling when caught by Lester and so had to explain my change of mood. "Well, that's pretty sweet."

Then Dorothy asked a question of cats who could not understand her words. "Do you feel loved my friends?"

When I laughed again, her eyes sharply found their way up to mine. "Why is that funny?"

"Oh, sorry, it's just that I've never heard someone ask that before. People usually say, I love you."

She smiled gently, cats still writhing and purring all over her. "You think me a bit strange, don't you?"

I shrugged. Strange wasn't the half of it.

Her gentle smile remained, her fingers scratching and running along her felines – to their great pleasure. "What difference does it make if I *tell* them I love them if they don't *feel* that I love them?"

225

Then she spoke again to the cats. "Isn't that right?" She kissed one cat, then nuzzled another. "They're just like people you know."

Although the cats would have gladly swarmed over her for another hour, she set them aside. When she stood, she swatted a cloud of cat hair off her bathrobe, one she had donned upon entering the parlor. Since her robe already held so much cat hair that it looked more like a bearskin rug than a robe, it did no good. "You boys hungry?"

I imagined a plate of food garnished with cat hair. *"Ummm…"*

Then before I'd fully answered, she slipped out of her robe, hung it on a hook, batted a couple stray hairs from her hands, and looked expectantly at us. "I can rustle you up some vittles!" Then she slapped her leg and stomped her foot. After all, what could be more humorous than speaking genuine cowboy dialect?

Dorothy fed us everything she could cobble together. Now ordinarily, one might have expected a few moments of silence as our hostess ate with us. She did not. Dorothy observed our every bite with rapt attention and in our helpless states of defenseless mastication, continued to speak unchallenged. Our force feeding may have continued well into the night had we not both eventually raised our hands in surrender. If my ears had sought refuge from raindrops outside, they now sought refuge from Dorothy's incessant speaking.

As evening closed in, the cursed rain settled to a steady shower. Dorothy's downpour continued unabated. We retired to her parlor where she lit a kerosene lamp and commenced to regale Lester and me with what seemed to be every blessed detail of her entire life.

Turns out she had had a gaggle of kids who she'd summarily booted from home the day they reached adulthood. Then one-by-one, she told of their exploits and accomplishments in a plethora of far-away places they'd gone off to. Her sparkling eyes spiced her laughter and every story came with another slap on her thigh.

"I told them all, *go see the world, go be who you are meant to be, don't you worry about me, now scat!*" She laughed with fond recollection at their banishing as she rocked in her chair with a cat on her lap. I looked between her, the clock, Lester, the cat on my lap, the cat on his lap and again at the clock. This could very well go on all night.

226

I smiled numbly. "You know, after our past couple days' travel and that delicious dinner you fed us, I'm getting really quite tired. Would you mind terribly if we turned in?"

"Oh, listen to me going on. Of course you're tired." She lifted her cat, and despite its feeble complaint, set it on the floor. She popped up and did a cursory swat of hair from her robe of hair. "You mind sleeping in my boys' room? Bathroom's down here if you need to use it – oh the wonders of indoor plumbing – especially on a night like this. How I wish I'd had it back… oh never mind."

She took the lantern and led us through parlor and kitchen, to a narrow stair. Light and shadows danced crazily around us as she continued to speak the entire way up – not that I could understand a word since three sets of footfalls on creaky steps obliterated entirely what she was saying. I found it was best just to say, *"Uh huh,"* every now and then, lest she repeat herself and drive me another step closer to madness and possibly murder.

Rain in New York is not frigid like rain in Colorado. It is balmy and smothering with a dampness that permeates your very bones. The upstairs of her farmhouse had not seen an open window in oh, I'd say a decade or so. On this particular evening it smelled as musty as an old trunk, filled, I'd have to add, with used stockings. She opened a door to a tiny room. Its walls were the roof's planked underside. A single dormer window that held as many dead flies and perished moths as Carter has pills, let in a pittance of the day's all but extinguished light.

I looked at our accommodations. Twin beds were a plus. Cobwebs floating from their metal rail headboards were not.

Our hostess followed my eyes and took in the accompanying crease of my brow. "Oh, those will brush right away." She swept away a portion with her hand and redeposited it on her robe.

"That's fine. We can take care of that," Lester responded for us. I grimaced.

Between beds and beneath dormer, atop a rickety chest of drawers, was an ages old kerosene lamp. Dorothy set the one she carried beside it, then, using her cat hair robe, began to wipe dust and spider webs from its glass. It took a few minutes of fussing and a dozen or so matches, but she did eventually get it lit.

I'd like to say that silence enveloped us when Dorothy finally took her leave, but the roof seemed to amplify rather than muffle rain's delightful pitter patter. Smells of kerosene, singed dust, and burning cat hair launched me into a sneezing fit. I sat on what would be my bed to a resounding complaint of its springs and a puff of yet more dust.

Lester, ever the optimist, added commentary. "Well, it's better than a night in the rain."

I shrugged and bounced a couple times. This generated a cloud of lint and a symphony of squeaking springs loud enough to make us both laugh – and sneeze. Lester picked up a worn teddy bear from his bed that looked at least as scroungy as Dorothy's cats.

I added commentary. "I bet it felt loved."

"Apparently so." Lester set it down, then idly opened the chest's top drawer. He angled his head quizzically and reached inside.

I pulled the bedspread off my bed, sneezed six more times, then lifted both blanket and sheet – as spiderwebs generally indicate spiders in residence and I was not inclined to spend the night with one. I sniffed my bed and feather pillow – both of which made the room's stale air seem fresh by comparison. Tired enough to make do, I proceeded to remove my borrowed coveralls.

When I looked again at Lester, he was holding up a pair of children's knickers. "I think those are a little small for you." I laughed. "And a little out-of-style."

One corner of Lester's mouth raised in a smile of sadness. He folded the knickers, put them back in the drawer and slid it shut. Moments later we were both in bed, arms folded across our chests, lantern extinguished, listening to rain. "We sure have met some odd ladies on our trip."

"We have."

"Remember those two vagabonds back in One Horse?"

"One Horse?" Lester laughed. "You and the names you make up. Yeah, they were something." He shook his head. I smiled. "Then there was Red Stagecoach Lady in Julesburg."

"Oh yeah. Kind woman. Definitely a bit different."

Lester nodded. "Let's call her eccentric. And neither of us will ever forget Junebug."

"Nope. Can't forget Junebug – not even if we tried."

"Chicken Lady," I exclaimed.

"Chicken Lady," Lester exclaimed.

We both laughed, then fell silent, listening to rain.

"What's your name for this one?" Lester asked.

I smiled. "Mother Time."

Lester laughed. "Mother Time," he repeated to himself. I heard his bed squeak and covers rustle as he turned on his side.

Mother Time was up before the roosters, already clanging pots and pans as we roused from our slumber. Was that bacon I smelled? *Glory be!* The roof was silent above us. *Glory be!* If all went well, we'd be on the road under clear skies by sunrise. *Hallelujah!*

Lester was first to put his feet on the floor. I listened to him strike a match and watched the walls of the room come aglow as the wick took its flame. "Hey Pike, I'll go out and get our clothes."

Lester was already slipping into his roomy pair of coveralls by the time I rolled over, rubbing sleep from my eyes. "You sure?"

"Yeah, sure. You rest a minute longer."

'Nough said. As soon as Lester and lantern had taken their leave and darkness had returned I let my head fall back. Within moments, sleep took me back into its sweet embrace.

I was dreaming of a plate heaped with flapjacks when I felt my clothing land on top of me. I opened my eyes to find Lester already changing clothes. "Up and at 'em," he advised, then pushed on my bed to its great annoyance and very verbal protest of its springs.

Mother Time, as it turns out, is just as spry and talkative at dawn as she is any other time of day. While I may have dreamt of flapjacks, we filled ourselves with fried potatoes, sausage, bacon, eggs and coffee. Mother Time took full advantage of our busy mouths by filling any void of mutual conversation with monologue. She could not fully express, *not that she didn't try with all sincerity,* how her heart ached that she'd raised such wanderers and seekers.

"I can't tell you how I swell with pride that I have given my children that kind of freedom and instilled in them the kind of courage that allowed them to seek their own way."

I looked dully at the little woman sitting erectly across from us and nodded acknowledgement. Lester, this morning, seemed entranced by her tales.

"You did a good thing, setting them out in the world like you did. I admire your sacrifice and selflessness."

If the woman could have popped open and survived the occasion, she very well might have done just that. She oddly said nothing, sucked in her lips, sat even more erect, her tiny chest out, her chin firm, her eyes glistening.

Sunlight was about to crest the horizon when she rose. "You boys want thirds?" We again raised our hands in surrender. Lester stood lest our defeat not be taken as sincere.

"We better get going. Still need to get our stuff packed on our bicycles but we thank you so much for your hospitality and your kindness."

Then Lester did something I'd never seen him do to a virtual stranger. He stepped around the table, bent and hugged Dorothy with tender sincerity. Her boney, spotted hands clutched his back as if holding on for dear life.

When did they develop such a tight bond? I looked quizzically at him as he released her. I shook her hand and thanked her. We stepped outside as sounds of dishes clanking began to come from behind.

"What was all that about?"

"You'll see." Lester looked at me with eyes that held a mystery. An additional wink informed me he would be giving up his secret in his own sweet time.

I wasn't quite sure what to make of Lester this morning. Once in the barn, he and I rolled our still wet bedrolls and strapped them onto our bicycles in silence, then wheeled our bicycles into the open barn door. I watched through suspiciously narrowed eyes as he leaned his bicycle against the doorframe, then gestured for me to do the same. With an incline of his head, he beckoned me to follow him. I hated anticipation as much as he relished subjecting me to it. I trudged after him with a roll of my eyes and an impatient sigh.

"How many children did she say she had?" Lester shot me a look out of the corner of his eye as I came up to his side.

"I don't know. Six or seven. Six, I think."

I caught a glimpse of Lester's melancholy smile a moment before he stopped and held his arm outstretched. Before us lay a plot of trimmed grass delineated by a rusted fence of looped wire. I stepped closer and squinted in morning's yet dim light to read names and dates inscribed on mossy stones. Not only had none of Dorothy's six children survived childhood, they had all died within months of one another in the year of 1890.

"Eighteen ninety?" I questioned. "What happened in eighteen ninety?"

"Russian influenza, I think."

I nodded, recalling something about that from lessons at school, then pointed at a stone dated 1903. "Her late husband?"

Lester nodded. "I suppose."

I considered dates of birth and death of her children and the tender years of innocence between them. "Why did she tell us she booted them out at adulthood to go see the world?"

Lester tipped his hands out.

"Why did she make up all that about their adventures and grand accomplishments?"

Lester lifted his shoulders.

"How did she laugh and speak so happily and brag so about them?"

"The woman lived in pain – lives in pain. Maybe her pride and laughter are all that keep her devils of despair at bay."

"So, she's crazy?"

"Crazy is a strong word."

"Fine then; she's obviously not right in the head."

"Maybe not, but in her head, she's created a world that's right."

I nodded, understanding at least that much.

Lester wiped a crust of sleep from the corner of his eye.

We looked again at silent, mossy headstones, my eyes going from one to the next. I heard in their deafening silence – cries of injustice at a life cut short. I realized in an instant Dorothy's need to speak as she had and lowered my eyes, ashamed of my resentment. "I'm glad we stayed here."

"Me too." Lester put his hand on my shoulder and inclined his head back toward barn and bicycles.

The road's call insistent as always, I fell in at Lester's side.

Thirty-six hours ago, I'd stood before Niagara's falling waters, entranced, inspired, transported to a higher understanding of life and being.

But it was only a moment of transcendence – sandwiched between a day of not knowing where we were and the storm of the following day.

As I put my hands on my handlebar and lifted my leg over my mount, I had to wonder if I had only given meaning to that waterfall so that I could imagine a world that was right in a world that I was reluctantly coming to find – is not.

Chapter 30

The Risk and Peril of Felling Trees

After so much rain, our road was more one endless puddle with hints of road scattered here and there, than actual road. Lester and I rode apart from one another in order to navigate our own paths. I couldn't say how many miles passed that morning. I was lost to any concept of progress, absorbed in simply trying to find my way, *any* way, ahead. Lester occasionally appeared in my field of vision and then only for a second as we wove around each other. We did not speak nor did we stop – for to stop or give up momentum in mud was something we'd learned not to do if we ever wanted to get started again.

This was our road.

According to this morning's check of Lester's Cyclometer, we had now traveled over two thousand miles since leaving Colorado Springs. If all went according to plan, we would arrive in New York City by week's end.

Over those two thousand miles, everything I thought I'd known of this nation had changed. We'd ridden through choking dust and searing sun to a land flowing with water, green beyond imagination, where sunshine was forced to hide behind the haze of its own heat. We'd known only a town sprung up from windblown plains where all things were new. This world we had entered possessed a history that spanned centuries instead of decades. Sometimes I didn't know...

Whomph!

Lester skidded sideways to avoid a great oak that had suddenly landed in front of him, its limbs still bouncing. I came to a stop behind him thinking, *my God*, how close of a call was that? Do trees just randomly fall in New York?

A voice that was neither mine nor Lester's called out. "You all right?"

I looked up, half expecting the Almighty was checking in with us, but then turned to find two woodsmen, a saw with prodigious, sharp teeth held between them, walking toward us.

"We didn't get ya, did we? It spun 'round on us as it went down and..." the one speaking extended his arm to point out the eighty-foot oak that had nearly killed Lester – you know – in case we hadn't noticed its arrival.

"Yeah. I'm fine," Lester answered.

Personally, if the barrel-chested men hadn't possessed arms a dimension of which I'd never seen before in my life, I would have popped both of them in the mouth. But since I felt inclined toward leniency, I was willing to let their offense slide – you know – this time.

They came to stand with us, all of us looking at the once mighty oak that now lay sprawled and broken. "Well, I imagine we better get that cleared." The men began to step over limbs. "Don't imagine we need to hold you two up any. You can go on around."

I looked from chest-high grass and thick foliage to my left, to a muddy field of stumps and ankle-deep water at my right. I decided I was fine where I was and dismounted as Lester had already done. We leaned our bicycles against one another and began to help drag broken limbs off the road.

Now why is it that a motorcar's price correlates directly with its driver's impatience? A Reo came to a stop opposite us. Did its driver get out, roll up his sleeves and join in our efforts to clear the road? No. He did not. He honked his horn as if an oak should somehow part itself to allow his progress. And he honked in bursts every minute on the minute as the men took to sawing.

From the field of fallen trees right of us, all of which now lie mounded in great piles, appeared a few more men with saws and axes, bringing with them, *thank the Lord*, a team of oxen and a length of chain. At the rate we were dismembering the Oak and dragging its branches away, this mess would be cleared away in no time at all. This was in spite of a green oak being comparable in density and weight to cast iron.

Lester and I had worked up a pretty good sweat when upon completion of dragging a limb off the road, I happened to look up.

Indians! Well, more accurately, three actual Indians including one bonified savage. My breath caught. My eyes widened to such degree that I feared both might very well simply roll out of my head. He was no doubt a warrior. His face was painted red and as if that wasn't frightening enough, several lines of darker red ran from his partially shaved scalp, down his face, to his chin. He was shirtless, wearing a loincloth over leggings, and barefoot. A true savage. His squaw, papoose strapped to her chest was seated on a packed mule he led with a tether.

One-by-one saws and axes grew silent. The Rio's persistent honking remained the only sound. The savage stood motionless as a statue: shoulders back, head erect, chin set, eyes firm. He didn't move and neither did we. Tomahawk, knife and machete hung from his belt. He was inches from where we'd left our bicycles and we were mere strides away from him. Should he attack, we would be first to perish. I managed to close my gaping jaw. I swallowed hard.

Honking continued so that given any other circumstance I might have marched over, pulled the man from his car and given him a richly deserved routing – you know – as he was old, most likely feeble, and probably not very quick. Gradually the woodsmen's saws and axes resumed their work. The chain was at last hooked around the girth of denuded tree. Oxen strained and slowly the hulk began to be pulled from the road.

The Reo's beeping finally came to an end as it squeezed around the still-moving hulk and drove past with nary a turn of its driver's head, much less a tip of his hat or thank you from his lips. "Ass," I muttered, then glanced at the savage, still motionless, erect, stern. His squaw's breast hung exposed, her infant suckling at it.

Theoretically, we could have mounted up and ridden away, but since our bicycles lay beyond the savage, that would mean approaching him. Since I held a particular fondness for my head of hair, that was not going to happen on this fine day. Lester and I stood aside as the oak's trunk was pulled completely from the road. The squaw plopped her breast back inside her tunic. The Indian's resumed their journey. I, for one, breathed a sigh of purest relief after they had passed.

"Heathens," one lumberjack stated boldly once they were out of earshot. "He isn't supposed to get done up in paint like that. It's against the law. Damn heathens."

I had some familiarity of Navajo and Cherokee peoples, but these eastern Indians were both strange and fearsome to me. "What tribe was he?"

"Seneca, Iroquois, Onandowaga – take your pick – they all mean the same thing. Oh, and don't say tribe. *Nation* is what they call themselves," he scoffed. "Some nation. Their wise men couldn't even invent a wheel."

Another lumberjack spoke. "Did you see her flop her tit out with no modesty. Animals is what they are."

As people tend to get themselves worked up in matters such as these, I didn't like where this was headed. I gestured at the field of downed trees in hopes of changing subject. "So, what are you going to do with all these trees?" I imagined some fine mansion or hostelry soon to be erected.

Both lumberjacks looked at me as if I were stupid. "We're cutting them down. What does it look like we're doing?"

Lester attempted to clarify. "But what are you going to *do* with the wood? What are you cutting them down *for*?"

Huge shoulders rose in a shrug. "I don't know, let 'em rot. Burn 'em."

"Is this going to be farmland then?" I asked.

"Naw. Owner wanted them cut. Think it's just going to sit fallow. Why are you asking all these questions?"

"I don't know, I just..." I looked at mighty trees that had stood for centuries, heaped and mounded, never to be milled or used for shelter, never to be worked into a thing of beauty, brought low simply because they had stood. I squinted. "So just to create fallow ground?"

The lumberjack opened his mouth to respond – a flash in his eyes giving fair warning that his wrath was about to be incurred.

"I think we'll be on our way." Lester placed a hand on my

shoulder and quickly guided me back to our bicycles.

Our first encounter with the savage had been in the company of strong men wielding axes. Had we fully considered the dilemma now at hand, we would have chanced grabbing our bicycles while the Indian stood still and placid and then ridden safely away.

Now we had to pass him on a lonely road – the middle of which he had appropriated as his half. We hung back, waiting for a length of road not too saturated from days of rain and also wide enough for us to squeak past.

With that opportunity now at hand, Lester, hugging left on the road, stood on his pedals and took off. I watched his head turn sideways to peer at the Indian as he passed. When safely ahead, he slowed to our usual pace. I stood on my pedals in order to get my speed up. As I closed in on the savage, I returned butt to seat lest I appear in too big a hurry to pass, and in so doing, offend him.

How do mud puddles and bogs suddenly appear from nowhere? Well, one did just as I, head turned, attempted to pass the red man. My wheels sunk to their rims. I stood on my pedals and *clink*.

Clink, for your information, is the sound a chain makes when it comes clean off its sprocket. *Clink* is a sound immediately followed by a seizing of one's rear wheel and the subsequent and complete halt of progress. Both of my feet landed squarely in six inches of mud. Fortunately my ass was one ounce shy of producing enough inertia to propel me headfirst over my handlebars – not that it – being an ass – didn't try.

I do believe I was just as red as the Indian when I regained my balance and turned around to look at him. Need I mention that if I had extended my arm and he, his, we might well have shaken hands?

Time stopped.

Then he smiled. She laughed. He laughed, not in mockery, but with kindness. "That didn't go so well."

Mouth open and eyes wide, I shook my head.

He leaned forward, peering at my stuck rear wheel and quickly assessed my dilemma. "Chains will get you every time."

I nodded and pulled my mouth closed.

"You don't need to be afraid. I'm not going to hurt you." He gestured at his appearance. "You would not be able to comprehend the disrespect we get if I go into town looking like anyone else – like a civilized American."

"You speak very well."

"Yes, I know how to speak English."

My head pulled back in surprise.

He laughed again. "I've read Shakespeare and Thoreau, even your humorist Samuel Clemmons. I know the works of Socrates and Plato."

I didn't know what to say. This was a savage, a heathen, and then as if to discern my thoughts, he added, "And I'm a Presbyterian."

It was my turn to laugh.

"Let's get that chain back on."

As I wheeled my bicycle out of the muck, he pulled the ten-inch knife from his belt that I'd earlier observed. My breath caught, but then he knelt and began to pry my wedged chain from between cog and frame. I looked on, down at his red-painted head, shaved back to a point just above his ears. A few feathers were woven into a half-dozen braids mixed in the remaining tangle of shoulder-length hair.

This was the most fearsome man I'd ever seen. Proud. Exotic. Human. Presbyterian.

As he worked on my bicycle in order to help me along my way, I thought of teepees set amidst settler's wagons back in Julesburg, an unusual woman's odd tribute to those who had adventured across and inhabited this land before us – as if somehow this land ought to have made us one instead of rivals – set together as if our differences were something to treasure and our journeys more alike than not.

Then I thought of Queenie's son removing the chain from his Iver Johnson bicycle only to install it on mine. Two formidable men of color. One boy of white. They knew my world for it was in my world that they lived. I did not know theirs.

A moment later, my chain back on its cogs, the savage stood, returned the knife to his belt and faced me – exotic and bright of color. Dorothy's words of the previous day echoed in my mind, *"He*

238

weighs a third of any of them and has no fangs. His claws are quite ineffective for anything but hanging on, but my cats see his strange colors, hear his rush of wings and his screech and think they are about to die."

Then from behind, came a distant cracking of wood followed by the felling of a tree.

And shame washed over me.

Chapter 31

Empire

After our night in Buffalo, we paralleled the Erie Canal, crossed the Hudson River at Albany, turned south and began travel along the great river as it wound through the beautiful Hudson Valley. We no longer cared about towns and cities we passed through. We no longer counted miles. We were tired, fatigued of our journey. We only wanted to get to our destination. As such, our remaining days and nights came and went by rote. Finally, we made it to a city called Yonkers – a strange name – the sound of which made me giddy with excitement. We were close and getting closer with every turn of our cranks. I could feel New York City's heartbeat.

We rode south on a busy main road paralleled by a dozen equally busy railroads. Trains entering and leaving the city chugged past us as regular as clock chimes. We navigated busy intersections riding down New York's world-famous avenue of theaters and opera houses – Broadway – ever more amazed and entranced by all we saw. We pointed amazing sights to each other so often that my arms actually began to tire. I eventually concluded that everything I saw was a wonder, that Lester was seeing them as much as well as I was, and so gave it up altogether. We entered the boroughs. Lester, who always tended to look ahead more than I, and who had also tired of pointing out sights and had given it up for several miles, raised his arm and pointed one last time. "Pike."

I looked up. New York City's skyline had magically appeared in the haze of summer sky. Its pinnacles did not merely reach for the sky; they stood in absolute grandeur *in* the sky. Even if they were yet distant and not much more than a foggy outline, no photograph could ever have done it justice. This was real and we were at last seeing what we'd previously only been able to grasp in dots of black and white.

As we drew nearer to city center, we found boulevards teeming with people. Everything was in motion: elevated trains rumbled overhead. Taxis, motorcars, and limousines buzzed around us. Carriages, wagons, and heavy wooden carts of yesteryear clomped alongside modern electric and gasoline conveyances. Even buildings were in motion, rising up before our eyes under workers that swarmed on them like ants on an anthill.

I didn't even try to shut my mouth as I looked up and around more than I looked ahead. It was as if someone had turned a page and photos in shades of grey had not only turned to color but had begun to move. Everywhere I looked was the nation's wealth – and not just any nation – a nation on the edge of greatness – a nation of endless possibilities. This was *The Empire State*. I could have heard it a million times and never understood, but now I was seeing it. For two boys from Colorado's windswept plains overseen by lonely snowcapped peaks, this was magnificence and accomplishment of humanity on a scale beyond comprehension.

Our directions were simple: take Broadway south to 63rd Street, then go east a block and a half to the Y.M.C.A. We rode in near silence up to the front steps of a fourteen-story stone building that was as majestic as a cathedral and as superb as The Broadmoor Hotel that Penrose had erected back home at the base of Cheyenne Mountain. In New York, even a humble Y.M.C.A. was built on a scale that boggled my imagination. We dismounted and rolled our bicycles onto the sidewalk. It was August 16th. We'd been on the road or visiting relatives for 65 days.

My heart was racing. How was I ever going to be able to sleep tonight? *Calm yourself, Joe. Calm yourself. Breathe.* I took a few long breaths and decided I needed to take a moment to simply be where I was. I began to look closer at the building that would be our home for the next two weeks. Young men were hurrying up and down the walk, going in and out of its doors. Which ones would we come to know? What unknown friends would emerge from meaningless faces of strangers?

241

I turned to take in other buildings, tall around us. Just down the street I could see green trees and lush lawns. "Is that what I think it is?"

"Central Park," Lester confirmed.

"We are literally in the heart of this city."

"We are." Lester leaned to stretch crinks out of his back.

"I want to see it all today!"

Lester laughed at my unabashed giddiness. "I think first we better get a shower behind us, a meal inside us, and some clean clothes on us. We look like vagrants."

I laughed, full well acknowledging his statement's truth. I turned toward the building just as a group of young men bustled out speaking excitedly, balls, bats and gloves in their hands. None of them looked at us or our packed bicycles with anything much beyond slightest curiosity. I couldn't help but notice how many people hurrying around us spoke in thick accents. A few communicated in languages I recognized but didn't understand. As we'd ridden through New York City's boroughs, I'd heard tongues completely unknown to me. Here, in New York City, where the ingredients of America's melting pot are first thrown together, Lester and I, with our stuffed packs and road weary attire, were not anomalies. Here, I could already tell, was a mindset that however great our differences, we would find our similarities to be far greater.

Then Lester did what Lester needed to do upon this or any other milestone of our journey – he knelt and wiped dust from his cyclometer's dial. He looked up at me. "Two thousand, six hundred, ninety-nine miles." His eyes rolled up for a moment. "At twenty-six-and-a-half days of actual riding – not counting that disaster day between Niagara and Buffalo – that comes out better than one hundred miles a day." Lester smiled the biggest smile of his life.

My well-ordered way of thinking was set off-balance. For a moment I was inclined to ask Lester if we could ride around the block until that damn dial rolled to an even 2700 miles.

But I didn't. We'd done it. When he stood, beaming with joy, I triumphantly slapped his palm with mine.

I looked between our bicycles and doors that seemed never to actually stop moving or close. "Do we bring our bicycles in with us?"

"I don't know."

The answer to our dilemma came when a young man rolled a bicycle out and down the steps. "I guess we bring them in."

"I guess we do."

If we'd thought the entrance was busy, the front desk was darn near insane. Five men and a dozen boys scurried and twisted around one another: arms, hands, papers, mail, and keys in constant motion. They reached around and over one another as if choreographed. A wall behind them housed at least a thousand small wooden nooks. At the front counter were a couple cash drawers and people lined up three deep. We rolled our bicycles in barely noticed, leaned them against an opposite wall, and approached.

Even if every window was open, the building was warm from accumulated days of summer heat. It smelled of scores of young men and echoed with a game of basketball coming from an adjacent gymnasium. I hadn't played for now on two months. I leaned to Lester's ear. "I want to run in, steal their ball, dazzle them a little and score a basket or two."

Lester was by now quite focused on business at hand so his forehead wrinkled with annoyance. He waved me away. I had expected nothing less, so I continued to gaze all around at this athlete's heaven on earth. *"Next."* I looked ahead to see a man impatiently beckoning us to approach.

Lester stepped forward and tugged on my sleeve to join him – as I would have been content to stare at my surroundings and let him handle the business end of things – indefinitely. We both listened attentively to the desk clerk as he gave directions on how to get to our room, mealtimes, and general rules of decorum expected at the Y.M.C.A. Moments later we walked away with room keys in hand. It was that simple. We paid a fee and in exchange, room and board for our two weeks' stay in this grand city was ours. What a wonderous construction of organization we had in this United States of America.

"Tomorrow," I said as we waited with bicycles at our sides for elevator doors to open and take us to the twelfth floor, "we see the Green Lady."

A couple young men joined us, looked at our packed bicycles, then at us. "Are you talking about Lady Liberty?" one asked, having overheard us.

"Yes," I answered enthusiastically.

He grimaced. "I'm afraid the only way you're going to see her is from a distance."

My head pulled back.

"The monument is closed."

"What?" Lester and I both gasped.

The young man looked again at our bicycles. "Didn't you hear about the explosion?"

"On Black Tom Island?" Lester questioned.

"Yeah. That's the one. Closed."

"No, that was in New Jersey," Lester argued.

"New Jersey is a mile-and-a-half from Lady Liberty, just across the harbor. The explosion nearly blew her arm and torch off. She's riddled with pock marks from shrapnel. You can't even take the ferry out to see her. Divers are still dredging unexploded ordinance up from the harbor, and they don't want to..." He gestured an explosion. "You know, accidentally blow up a whole boat of sightseers." He looked again at our packs. "I hope you didn't travel far."

Chapter 32

Waiting for Anshel

"Pikes Peak has nothing on this," I marveled.

"Amazing," Lester confirmed.

Lester and I were looking straight down from the Woolworth Building's 57th floor observation deck. We'd been in New York City for a total of nine days. If a visit to Lady Liberty could not be our journey's crowning accomplishment, ascending the world's tallest building would be a close second.

Lester and I had spent most of our stay in New York City either looking skyward or going to building tops and looking downward. Not caring that we looked like bumkins fresh off a farm, we gazed down on dots of people and moving automobiles that looked like tiny rectangles. I never tired of them or of the virtual sea of rooftops that spread as far as one could see. This was a great metropolis. "I can't believe people built all of this."

Thumping the safety rail that held us, Lester added, "I can't believe that a chain of five-and-dime stores paid for this."

"Likewise. It is all so amazing." I shook my head. "Engineers, architects, steelworkers…"

"Window washers." Lester pointed out a couple men dangling off the side of another skyscraper.

"You couldn't pay me enough."

"Me neither. Those men have to be crazy."

We laughed. Then the dizzying view spread out before us began to get to me. "I think I'm ready to go back to earth."

Lester slapped my shoulder. "Next stop?"

"Food," we said together and laughed – for we were still always hungry.

Now we just needed to get back to terra firma – which meant

waiting for an elevator – you know – unless we wanted to walk down 57 flights of stairs.

"Too bad about Liberty being shut down," I consoled.

"Well, we made the best of it."

"We made this entire city our playground. It's been a good time."

"I guess we just won't be able to fulfill Guy or Bartholomew's quest to see the Green Lady."

Then a tall woman standing nearby leaned into our conversation. "Pardon my eavesdropping, but are you talking about Lady Liberty?"

We both nodded solemnly.

"We were there yesterday. It's open." Her husband who stood a half-head shorter than her, his face an emotionless, bronzed farmer's weathered hide, nodded at her side.

I blinked, then turned to find Lester looking back at me openmouthed. Elevator doors opened and a new group of bumpkins – I mean observation deck sightseers – began to gurgle out. As they dispersed onto the observation deck, excited oohs and ahs began to filter our way. We moved forward like so many head of cattle into the car for a ride back down.

With Lester in the lead, we wasted no time in catching subways to the docks. Yes, Liberty was open. Yes, we could get tickets. Yes, a ferry would be arriving shortly. Yes, we had time to eat before it got here – *glory be!*

Waterways in and around New York City blurred distinction between sea and river but as we waited, I was of a mind that the expanse of water rippling before us was no doubt quite deep and no doubt quite unforgiving. Lester was again chewing his fingernails and I was considering taking up the habit. Lady Liberty looked small, a fragment on the horizon, a mere piece of a much larger picture. Her back was toward the nation she stood before.

Some who struggled for rights claimed her back to be turned *on* the nation she stood for. How I wanted to gaze upon her face and now finally, with ticket in hand, I would. *We would.*

Even though we'd seen a number of rabbis around New York

City, it would have been hard not to notice this one. His garb was more traditional than most and judging by his years, likely clothing he'd acquired when it was still in style – that is – if rabbis possess any sense of fashion – which I doubted. He, like us, was waiting on the ferry steaming our way. I leaned to Lester and inclined my head toward the elderly rabbi. "Aren't there like a million steps we're going to have to climb inside Liberty?"

Lester looked at the old rabbi, then at me, shrugged and continued to chew his nails.

"I don't think he'll make it." I inclined my head toward the rabbi.

Lester smiled politely, if not sincerely. "Then we'll be sure to get ahead of him so we won't have to step over his body."

Then – and it seemed as always – the kindly old man noticed us looking his way, smiled and raised a hand in greeting.

I raised my hand in return – which he evidently took as an invitation to join us – and began walking our direction.

"Shalom," he greeted with an accent of some sort.

"Hello," I replied.

He looked us over. "You going to see Lady of Harbor?"

"We are."

"A fine thing, that lady."

We nodded. "We've come a long way to see her."

"So did I." His smile and wizened sparkle of his eyes hinted at a story he didn't seem inclined to reveal beyond those three words.

I nodded.

"I wait for Anshel."

"Anshel?" I questioned, not knowing if that was a Jewish rite, holiday, or possibly a kosher food.

"Anshel," he confirmed. "Anshel detained on island. Was approved today. We wait for Anshel." Then he preempted what was to be my next question. "Eldridge Street Synagogue."

I nodded. By now we could hear chugs from the ferry's powerful steam engine.

"Anshel unfortunate. Victim of pogrom. Looks…" The Rabbi's eyes rolled up as he searched for a word. "Criminal." His regret of

247

having to use that word was revealed by a slow shaking of his head. "Poor Anshel. I go everyday and beg for him – no – don't send him back. They kill him if he go back. His family I know. Some his family here. We take care of Anshel. We circle him with love. He be proud American. Work hard. Support himself. No burden."

I nodded, then glanced at Lester who was watching our ferry slide alongside the dock. The rabbi's eyes were now aimed that way as well. A great swell of peoples stood at the boat's rail, papers in hand. Their clothes were wrinkled, their hair greasy and uncombed. Their faces were gaunt. Oddly though, the sparkle in their eyes was as if they were gazing upon Heaven's very shore. They'd traveled for weeks to get here. For most, I suspected the pillowcase or satchel carried at their side was all they owned in this world. They were dressed with the particular flair of their given ethnicity. It was a flair I had observed often on New York City's streets and sidewalks. It was a flair that would soon be lost in America's homogenization.

"The sweepings of Europe," Lester commented under his breath, not in judgement, but ironically.

I smiled for I'd heard that before. "Your father might have stood at that very rail."

Lester raised his eyebrows and nodded. "Eighteen ninety. Not all that long ago."

I imagined the successful, confident, stern man Lester's father had become – once standing poor, ragged, greasy-haired, at that rail – and the courage it must have taken for him to cross an ocean to come live in and travel across an unknown land.

And then I saw him. No one had to tell me that was Anshel. Scars across his face told me the lost and alone looking lad standing off by himself was Anshel. The rabbi had moved on around us toward the gangplank of disembarking people, many of whom spoke little or no English. He wove around authorities who were attempting to direct America's newest citizens where they needed to go. I heard the rabbi calling in a language I didn't understand except for one now familiar word, *Anshel.*

I stood transfixed as a drama played out before me. The lad who I deemed not much older than Lester, saw his savior, his guarantor, and lit up. A smile spread across his otherwise disfigured face as he joined others coming to America.

This entire land was our playground, Lester and mine. But for these strange-looking people setting first foot upon this soil, it was their salvation. "What goes on over there?" I asked Lester.

"I don't know. I can't imagine leaving everything I know never to come back."

Anshel, with a small roll of belongings tucked beneath his arm squeezed free of the gangplank and ran to the rabbi. When they embraced, I could hear the young man's sobs of joy as if they were the only sound. The scars on his face were more than scars. They were gouges. I didn't know what could have caused such damage nor did I know how one could have survived such grievous wounds.

"What is pogrom?" I asked.

Lester shrugged.

We watched the rabbi present paperwork and converse briefly with officials. Then he and Anshel began to walk away, his arm wrapped tightly around the young man's shoulders.

The rabbi noticed us, smiled and raised a hand in farewell.

We raised our hands in return.

Anshel waved, then with a smile that spread nearly to his ears, boasted, *"American."* He said it with such pride and reverence that for me, the word would forever lose its commonality.

And then he thumped his chest.

Chapter 33

The Green Lady

"The date on her tablet is the date the world was begun over again."
Our guide's arms spread toward the colossus as our ferry rose and
fell on swells beneath us, for a moment stationary in its progress to
allow us this ocean view of Liberty and introduction to her by our
guide. *"We the people* threw down a gauntlet before the world's
powers. Our founding fathers had dared challenge not only the
world's order, but the thinking and hearts of their own countrymen.
*We hold these truths to be self-evident, that all men are created equal, that they
are endowed by their Creator with certain inalienable Rights, that among these are
Life, Liberty, and the pursuit of Happiness."*

I smiled cynically. A reordering of nations seemed a far easier
task than a reordering of either the minds or hearts of men.

As our guide continued with dates and names and such that I
cared not a whit to know, I became captivated by the shimmer of
Lady Liberty's patina. Liberty Enlightening the World was
magnificent beyond anything I'd imagined. I was entranced by her.

Lester turned to me. "You know we've traveled as far or maybe
even further than most anyone who has ever entered this harbor –
twenty-seven hundred miles." He smugly raised his eyebrows and
puckered his lips.

I nodded, amused by the divergence of our thoughts.

"We made it here one turn of a bicycle wheel at a time, under
our own power. How many people can say that?"

I fought an urge to roll my eyes, nodded again, and continued
counting the spikes of Liberty's crown. After Black Tom, some had
hung over her face. Others had been broken off. All were now
reaffixed and radiating her light to the seven continents and seven
seas, all the world. The ferry's engine that had fallen silent to allow us

these few moments of an immigrant's view, clunked back into gear. Water began to churn behind us. Ripples began to spread out from the ferry's side as we moved forward.

Even if Lester's thoughts had been of bicycles and miles traveled on our journey to get here, his eyes were now fixed on Lady Liberty. Amazingly, he hadn't chewed his nails much past leaving Battery Park. I observed him unnoticed, wondering all the while if maybe I was observing Guy instead. There was something different about Lester. I don't know that I'd ever seen it before. He always looked ahead. Today he was looking ahead but studying what he saw as if trying to understand it rather than overtake it.

"We were wrong," I offered. "It wasn't a close second."

Lester turned to me, perplexed.

"The Woolworth Tower. It wasn't a close second."

Lester nodded indecisively, unsure of my meaning.

"It isn't just about height or feat of engineering or beauty of architecture. This," I pointed, "is about the highest ideals of man. This says something beyond engineering or accomplishment, beyond modernity."

Lester squinted and continued to nod. He raised his eyebrows and turned again toward Lady Liberty. Always one to bring me back to what is at hand, he mused, "I've seen those eyes before."

I laughed for I'd been thinking it as well. We began to tap the drummer boy's clarion call on the vessel's rail. "I knew I'd seen that look of fierce determination before." We laughed and tapped it out again. It was a short riff, only enough to issue a call. We grew solemn as we neared the colossus, finding we could not take our eyes off her. I was transfixed by her Roman nose, thick forehead, and strong chin. "She isn't a pretty lady. Not frivolous or feminine in any way."

"She's no Mary Pickford," Lester agreed. "Nor a gentle lady, I'm sure."

"Defiant, I would say."

"Well," Lester shrugged, "she's standing against all the world has ever been. She's standing against tyranny. How could she be anything but strong, anything but defiant?"

I nodded. "She is the Lady of the Harbor."

By now we were looking nearly straight up at her. Words seemed inadequate, so we, along with others standing at the rail beside us, fell silent. We were in the presence of something more than art or hammered sheets of copper or work of man. All the hardships of our journey fell away as life's travails fall away for those about to meet their Maker.

But as with everything of this earth, upon docking, there were passengers to offload and passengers to board, business to be completed and we found ourselves herded along with everyone else. Security was tight today, reminding me of grim-faced soldiers guarding Canada's point of entry. It seemed we would experience Lady Liberty more as tourists at a monument – in and out – keep moving, not so much as sojourners there seeking some elusive truth for a reason we'd not yet discerned.

But in defense of Truth and the seeking of it, it finds a way.

As others entered Liberty's base to purchase trinkets and souvenirs, I stood before a plaque bearing words penned by Emma Lazarus. As I read them I felt pride, pride that this was my homeland.

Give me your tired, your poor, your huddled masses yearning to breathe free, the wretched refuse of your teeming shore. Send these, the homeless, tempest-tossed to me. I lift my lamp beside the golden door!

I'd seen, in these United States, inside this golden door, our own homeless, our own refuse, our own yearning to breathe free. I remembered Denver's slums but needn't have thought that far back. From what I had seen, New York City had its share of wretched, yearning to breathe free – some fresh from Ellis Island. Some had entered not a golden door, but a pit of further despair.

The date on Liberty's tablet – the date when the world was begun anew – had only been a world begun anew for some. Across this land we were not all equal, we were not all free, we did not all pursue happiness and some of us scarcely managed survival. Even *we the people* did not agree that we should be one people. There were divisions between us and whether we realized it or not, they affected our daily lives.

How, Liberty, do you hold aloft a flame of imprisoned lightening and yet keep it imprisoned, not let it pierce the skies? Had I viewed Liberty only from the ferry as it bobbed upon the ocean swells, I would have remained entranced by her beauty, but now after reading these words and having traversed the land she stands before, I found myself confronted with a dichotomy, her dichotomy.

I watched Lester as he finished reading the plaque. He turned to me. "Want to get started? There are many steps to climb and I have no intention of getting behind the old or infirm or worse, a dallier." Lester still had one speed, and *hell bent for leather* would be the haste with which he intended to assault Liberty's stairs.

There was no use in arguing. Discussion about the words before us, their sanctity and my ambivalence toward them, would have to wait, so I nodded.

My legs were tired before we'd yet cleared the pedestal. "Lester, let's take in the view for a few minutes." I hoped for a reprieve before starting the endless spiral staircase that loomed ahead. "I'd love to look out at the harbor for a few minutes."

Lester sighed, rolled his eyes, but acquiesced. I was milking the view from the base's fourth side when Lester's acute exhale and impatient tapping of his foot forced me to give up my ploy.

While Lester charged on ahead, I entered the Green Lady and stopped. It had never occurred to me how she stood, only that she stood. Mr. Eiffel had engineered her bones of steel and they were a serious business of diagonals, horizontals and verticals. Rivets held her together. Steel cable bound her to earth. She was after all, a structure, and without her beams and angles of iron she would crumple under her own weight.

Every footstep and word of those ascending and descending her stairs echoed off the red-brown copper walls of her graceful flowing skirt. Then Lester, who I was sure had not observed anything but more steps ahead of him stopped. Had I not been out of breath and grateful for a chance to catch up, I might have made fun of him. I came up behind him with burning legs and decided to say nothing lest he take off again. He was looking at Liberty's flowing sheets of copper with a deep crease in his brow.

"This whole side," he waved his arm, "is pockmarked."

I looked along with him. "Oh, yeah. I guess it is." Some of the dents were so deep they had pierced her skin and daylight shone through. "Black Tom," I surmised.

Lester nodded. "Black Tom." Then for a moment he peered all around, up as well as down. When he began his ascent anew, he did so not as an assault, but as one lost in Liberty's significance.

Several minutes and a hundred steps later we stood behind the face of Liberty looking out through the windows in her crown – in that moment – our faces the jewels in her crown. The sea that our forefathers had crossed to come to America stretched to an uncertain horizon of sky and water – both seemingly fluid as I could not tell where one started or the other ended. A few tourists had lingered at the windows from the group ahead of us. We were well ahead of anyone coming from behind and so we were able to take our time. Lester seemed to be thinking of something deeper than the view.

I had to assume his mind was on Guy. This long-awaited moment was in his mind, the closing hymn and final tribute of Guy's service begun graveside two years ago. In the silence I thought it my duty to remember the cripple I never knew. I wondered what his quest might have been had his fate in life been different than what it was. If he had possessed health and vitality, would he still have imagined Liberty? After a few minutes of reverence I asked, "Do you think they're here with us?"

Lester's eyes grew a little too moist. He looked down, smiled a little, then nodded. By now we were alone in the crown, the echoes of departing footsteps and distant whistles of ships the only sounds.

I waited.

"Guy had wanted to see this."

I nodded.

"I've wondered, was his quest for earth's horizons really what it was all about – his life – his always restless life?"

I didn't answer.

"Or was his quest something more ethereal, something Earth's horizons were never going to satisfy?"

"If it was, he's there now."

Lester's eyes grew wetter still. He shook his head. "I'm about the same age now as he was when he died." He scoffed and shook his head bitterly. *"God damn it."*

My eyes grew wide. Lester didn't often curse.

Then Lester quoted the filthy prophetess, "You is not alone."

I smiled to remember the Chicken Lady. "I can't imagine we are."

Lester wiped his eyes, looked out the window, over waters blended with sky and sniffed. "Wish you were here, my brother, live and in person. I wish you could be here."

I reached up, put my hand on Lester's shoulder and jostled him gently. I could feel muscle and bone. Maybe the adventurer's and cripple's quest hadn't been so much to see the Green Lady or even understand her. Maybe it had been to undertake the journey's sheer impossibility. Maybe their quest was just to get here.

Maybe a cautious and prudent boy is not so unlike a cripple confined by the walls of his own room. Maybe a hellion is not so unlike an adventurer, straining at the world's limits. Maybe in life's fates, what we imagined we did in their honor was instead what they pointed us toward – for *our* edification – for *our* understanding of *them*. Here we stood in Liberty's crown, imagined for so long as the end all of our effort, now real. I'd expected some divine revelation to be imparted or some decisive change to have overtaken us – but we were still just Lester and Joe. I guess reaching a horizon isn't nearly as significant as the pursuit of it.

"Pike," Lester began, his eyes still on blended sea and sky, "it's coming. I can feel it."

He didn't have to explain what he was talking about. I knew what he was talking about. "I can feel it too."

We listened a moment to the yet unheard horrible rumble of war. "Do you think this lady will still be standing when it's all over?"

"I think she has to stand. If she doesn't, the world begun anew will have failed."

Then a voice feminine, aged, and sure spoke. "She will stand."

I looked at Lester with wide eyes.

Lester looked at me open-mouthed.

"Down here."

We both looked down the descending helical steel staircase where Mother Time's only slightly younger sister had deposited herself. Her hair was grey. Her dress was black. It puddled around her on a landing of metal grating. She reclined against a gate installed to block access to Liberty's badly damaged raised arm and torch.

"I have to believe that America will stand," she repeated.

"I hope so," Lester replied.

"Did you see her broken chains?" she asked.

"Huh?"

"Look straight down at her feet."

We contorted to peer down from the crown. "Oh, yeah."

"Without those broken chains, her torch would be meaningless. Her tablet would be a lie."

This woman was obviously a sojourner of some sort, a woman who sees beneath that which clamors for attention. I felt drawn to her. I'd seen enough of horizons and had tired of great heights. I began to descend. Lester followed. The sojourner was wrinkled, tanned, and seasoned in a way that life flavors the survivors of its tumults. She smiled graciously. "I passed under this lady when her copper was red-brown, shiny and new. I always said one day I wanted to come back and see her again, understand her, and today, here I am."

I nodded.

"I'm making a day of it. Taking a few steps at a time. Listening to others as they pass me by. Examining this colossus. Taking my time." She examined us. Her eyes were draped under soft, wrinkled lids. Wise. Insightful. "I've been listening to you speak." She looked directly at me. "You're a thinker."

I lifted my shoulders. "I guess you could say that."

The woman smiled ever so slightly, then extended her hand to me. "I found this. A boy such as yourself might be interested to see it."

In her hand was a shard of amber glass.

"From her torch," the sojourner explained.

She jiggled her hand, offering me to take it. I took a bit of extinguished flame that had held Liberty's imprisoned lightening.

"The flame of her torch was blown to bits in the explosion."

In my hand was a symbol of sanctuary, not for light to land upon from outside but for light to radiate from. It was broken, a fragment that would cut you if you were not careful. Inside the colossus, away from light, it was dead, only dull glass. I handed it back.

"You boys be good."

I smiled, nodded, and stepped around her. Lester followed. We'd gone down a dozen or more steps when I stopped, turned and looked up. "Can I ask you something?"

The woman's eyes peered down at us through the maze of steps between us. "Certainly."

Did you read the pedestal plaque, the poem?"

"I did."

"It sounded beautiful, but that isn't what I've seen as we've crossed this nation to get here. We've seen and heard things that weren't right. I feel caught between the ideals of our fathers and their sins. Is Liberty all just words? Are we pretending a world that's right while we defend a world that isn't?"

"Ahhh." She nodded. "Let me tell you a story you may not know. This Lady was originally intended to stand sentinel at the Suez Canal – to be a sight along with Egypt's other antiquities – pyramids and the Sphinx. She was originally designed to be a simple peasant woman holding a lantern. A mere lighthouse to guide ships.

"But that didn't work out so her sculptor came to America – a land where new things can happen. He looked coast-to-coast for a place she would fit, for perfect surroundings that would complement her, still just envisioning her as a sculptured lighthouse, a thing of wonder, beauty, and utility." The sojourner paused.

"Do you think it's just a coincidence that she ended up in America, this world's only nation audacious enough to proclaim all men equal, all men free? Do you think it's just a coincidence that she ended up here, in this harbor, the world's only harbor that justified a raised torch rather than a hanging lantern? Young man, she came here not because of what this country would one day be – but in many ways because of what it already was."

I began to hear distorted echoes of conversation and footfalls of tourists beginning their ascent on Liberty's metal steps.

"No one imagined she would ever be green. It was the ocean's salt air that made her green. She transformed from mere art, a masterpiece of sculpture to a statement of mankind's ideals when she came to stand here. She found her meaning standing here.

"A world begun over again doesn't happen overnight. Maybe it doesn't even happen over a span of centuries, but one day those words written below will be in reality what they proclaim in ideals. You have to have faith, my son. You have to have faith. I figure if a spark can set this world at war, then a lifted torch can lift this world out of darkness. As long as there is liberty, it can happen. As long as there is liberty, it *will* happen. By and by, it will happen."

I nodded, thinking that brand of patient hope and ultimate confidence sounded familiar. The clamor of those approaching was becoming louder. Soon we would not be able to hear one another. I was tempted to raise my hand in farewell and continue on my way, but I'd yet to understand Lady Liberty as maybe this younger sister of Mother Time understood her. "I get the meaning of her torch, her tablet, her crown, her broken chains, but we've come so far and I still don't understand her, the Lady that holds and bears them all. What exactly is Liberty?"

The woman smiled ever so slightly – as if she expected my question. "I've wondered myself. I suppose that's why I'm here. I think she has to be justice," the sojourner said in a voice clear and pure. "I don't think equality is possible without justice. I don't think freedom can happen without justice. Justice broke her chains. Justice is the only force that can make the tablet she holds, reality. I think this lady has to be justice."

Lester had once told me that freedom is won, something that you take and don't give back. As I stand here inside Lady Liberty it occurs to me that maybe this is how liberty is kept: you stand for it and you don't back down.

I nodded.

She nodded.

We continued on our way. Lester stopped one more time. I turned at his delay. He reached over the handrail, grasped an upright, and began to study Liberty's bones of steel, the serious business of diagonals, horizontals and verticals that supported her weight of ideal and kept aright her promise – not against the travails of man – but against the calm of apathy and pleasant sunshine of complacence.

I was reminded of Teddy's words: *The dreams of golden glory in the future will not come true unless, high of heart and strong of hand, by our own mighty deeds we make them come true.*

Ever one to figure out how something works, Lester was by now leaning so far over the handrail to look up and down Mr. Eifel's structure and Mr. Bartholdi's sculpture that I took hold of his shirt lest he lose his footing and fall. He examined her bones a little longer, righted himself, patted the upright he'd held onto, then looked at me. "There's got to be a million rivets in this thing."

My laugh echoed throughout Liberty's structure. "At least."

Lester didn't say much after that and neither did I. I guess we both had far more to think about than we'd considered. I wasn't certain if I had completed someone else's quest or begun one of my own. We'd not seen this Green Lady as we'd envisioned her. We'd encountered this Green Lady and found her damaged by the duplicity of the very nation whose integrity and ideals she proclaimed to the world.

Black Tom Island's railyard explosion would be blamed on German saboteurs and I guess that would be accurate. But just as in assessing blame for the Lusitania's sinking, a villain's guilt would be used to divert accusations away from those truly culpable – investors who speculated on victories and losses – manufacturers of steel and makers of munitions – suppliers of both sides hiding safely behind America's flag of neutrality – using civilians as shields. It was another blow to truth, a pock mark on justice – an irony this Lady would have to bear until justice can be examined under truth's stark light, not colored by our ideas of what it is.

I suppose I have to have faith that justice will someday be as this Lady has come to be – in the right time – in the right place – by and by – eventually. Oh, the weight of this lady's skin.

We then stood in line with tourists, waiting to board our ferry home. I amused myself, thinking that we looked like everyone else today. No one could look at us and know we were travelers. After boarding, our ship swung over to Ellis Island. America's most recent wave of immigrants waited on the dock – all wearing their best clothes – even if their best was wrinkled, dirty and tattered. They looked weary. I could feel their hunger. I sensed their unease as well as their excitement. Lester and I observed them board their journey's last leg.

And then we all headed home.

I watched Lady Liberty growing distant behind us, her torch not giving light as it ought, but broken, twisted, exposed. "All the ruins of history were once the ideals of men," I mused.

"What?"

"Just thinking out loud. I hope they fix her. I hope they take care of her."

Lester nodded distractedly. He was deep in his own thoughts. His intense blue eyes were focused not straight ahead, but behind. It occurred to me that Lester no longer chewed his nails. He was no longer wary of our ferry's gentle rocking. Maybe now that he'd fulfilled Guy's quest he no longer needed fear Guy's fate.

"Lester."

He turned to me.

"Tomorrow could we just play basketball in the gym and maybe go to Central Park, sit under a tree, listen to birds singing? I don't need to see anything more."

"I don't think I need to either. That sounds good to me."

We watched our boat's wake lose itself in ripples and swells, mingled waters of sea and river. "I'm ready to go home," I admitted.

"Me too."

We watched gulls swoop low across the water.

"Remember that night in Julesburg?" Lester asked.

We'd been through so many towns and burgs it took me a moment. "Red stagecoach lady, Erstine. Yeah. I remember it well."

Lester nodded his head slowly. "I danced my ass off that night." One corner of his mouth pulled into a smile that was half pain, half joy – all remembrance. "Best dance I ever danced."

What a night beneath the stars that had been. A concert of frogs and crickets had melded with the music of an impromptu band. We had been strangers of the road who had stumbled upon the kind hospitality of strangers of the land. Music brought us together that night and made us one. The week of toil had ended. The Lord's Day of rest was coming. We laughed and sang and danced together – the simple joy of mortals simply alive in the night between the two.

My smile was half pain, half joy – all remembrance. "Me too. Best dance I ever danced."

My name was Joe Wheeler Bruce. Over the summer of 1916, my good friend Lester Edward Atkinson and I rode our bicycles from Colorado Springs, Colorado to New York City.

And back.

Four thousand, two hundred, eighty-four miles.

Thank you Lester.
Thank you Joe.

What you did that summer of 1916
was absolutely remarkable.

I hope this story has honored you.
I didn't want what you had done to be lost to time.

This article appeared on the Local History, 'A look back' page of the Colorado Springs Gazette on August 18, 2016.

In 1916: Word has been received here that Bruce and Lester Atkinson, the two Colorado Springs boys who have been making a cross-country bicycle tour, have arrived in New York city. They traversed the entire distance of 2,699 miles in the actual riding time of 26 ½ days. The boys will return in time for the opening of the high school, the fifth of next month.

I was wrinkling up my mother's recycle newspapers to start a fire in my wood stove when this article caught my eye. I found it so remarkable that I set it aside and began telling friends about it. Everyone was so intrigued that I started researching the boys. Due to an errors regarding *Joe* Bruce's identity in the article, I'd originally believed the boys were brothers, but quickly found out they weren't. The more I learned of the boys and their families, I realized I needed to tell their story.

I hope you came to know and love these boys as much as I did. Thank you for reading this. It was a privilege to write it in honor and remembrance of Lester and Joe.

If you would like more information on the boys and their families, futures, and whatever else I was able to find, you can go to **RogerLGreene.com** and click on **4,284 miles** cover image.

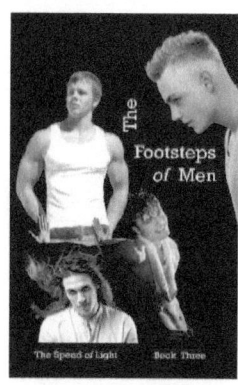

Audiobook on
Audible and iTunes

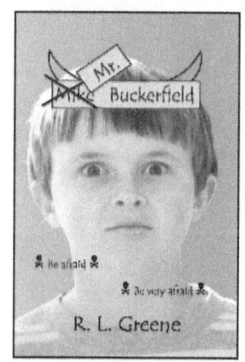